The Poet's Stern Critic

One Night in Blackhaven
Book 5

MARY LANCASTER

Dragonblade Publishing, Inc.

ARE YOU SIGNED UP FOR DRAGONBLADE'S BLOG?

You'll get the latest news and information on exclusive giveaways, exclusive excerpts, coming releases, sales, free books, cover reveals and more.

Check out our complete list of authors, too!

No spam, no junk. That's a promise!

Sign Up Here

www.dragonbladepublishing.com

Dearest Reader;

Thank you for your support of a small press. At Dragonblade Publishing, we strive to bring you the highest quality Historical Romance from some of the best authors in the business. Without your support, there is no 'us', so we sincerely hope you adore these stories and find some new favorite authors along the way.

Happy Reading!

CEO, Dragonblade Publishing

Additional Dragonblade books by Author Mary Lancaster

One Night in Blackhaven Series
The Captain's Old Love (Book 1)
The Earl's Promised Bride (Book 2)
The Soldier's Impossible Love (Book 3)
The Gambler's Last Chance (Book 4)
The Poet's Stern Critic (Book 5)

The Duel Series
Entangled (Book 1)
Captured (Book 2)
Deserted (Book 3)
Beloved (Book 4)

Last Flame of Alba Series
Rebellion's Fire (Book 1)
A Constant Blaze (Book 2)
Burning Embers (Book 3)

Gentlemen of Pleasure Series
The Devil and the Viscount (Book 1)
Temptation and the Artist (Book 2)
Sin and the Soldier (Book 3)
Debauchery and the Earl (Book 4)
Blue Skies (Novella)

Pleasure Garden Series
Unmasking the Hero (Book 1)
Unmasking Deception (Book 2)
Unmasking Sin (Book 3)
Unmasking the Duke (Book 4)

Unmasking the Thief (Book 5)

Crime & Passion Series
Mysterious Lover (Book 1)
Letters to a Lover (Book 2)
Dangerous Lover (Book 3)
Lost Lover (Book 4)
Merry Lover (Novella)
Ghostly Lover (Novella)

The Husband Dilemma Series
How to Fool a Duke (Book 1)

Season of Scandal Series
Pursued by the Rake (Book 1)
Abandoned to the Prodigal (Book 2)
Married to the Rogue (Book 3)
Unmasked by her Lover (Book 4)
Her Star from the East (Novella)

Imperial Season Series
Vienna Waltz (Book 1)
Vienna Woods (Book 2)
Vienna Dawn (Book 3)

Blackhaven Brides Series
The Wicked Baron (Book 1)
The Wicked Lady (Book 2)
The Wicked Rebel (Book 3)
The Wicked Husband (Book 4)
The Wicked Marquis (Book 5)
The Wicked Governess (Book 6)
The Wicked Spy (Book 7)
The Wicked Gypsy (Book 8)
The Wicked Wife (Book 9)
Wicked Christmas (Book 10)
The Wicked Waif (Book 11)
The Wicked Heir (Book 12)
The Wicked Captain (Book 13)

The Wicked Sister (Book 14)

Unmarriageable Series
The Deserted Heart (Book 1)
The Sinister Heart (Book 2)
The Vulgar Heart (Book 3)
The Broken Heart (Book 4)
The Weary Heart (Book 5)
The Secret Heart (Book 6)
Christmas Heart (Novella)

The Lyon's Den Series
Fed to the Lyon

De Wolfe Pack: The Series
The Wicked Wolfe
Vienna Wolfe

Also from Mary Lancaster
Madeleine (Novella)
The Others of Ochil (Novella)

Prologue

T HE VALE TWINS, still rather pleased with themselves over the success of their first family meeting, were reluctant to go to bed.

At the age of fifteen, they were the youngest of the siblings and yet sensed the troubled spirits of their elders, rippling only just beneath the surface. In their opinions—they usually matched—this stemmed from secret loneliness. Since returning to Black Hill House, the Vales had all found a certain purpose and security, even contentment, in being together. But the twins understood that this could only be temporary, that for true happiness, their brothers and sisters needed to spread their wings and seize more from life. The upcoming ball at the Blackhaven assembly rooms was the perfect beginning for this quest, and the twins had just persuaded all their siblings to attend, even providing extra reasons for the reluctant among them.

As they retreated at last toward their own bedchambers, Leona murmured, "Let's see who is still awake and worrying," and darted left at the top of the landing.

All was in darkness, apart from her own flickering candle. Satisfied, she was about to turn back to Lawrence when, for the sake of thoroughness, she decided to just glance around the corner to Cornelius's chamber.

Cornelius was the hardest working of them all. Having

trained since boyhood to be a land steward, he had now taken on the whole neglected estate of Black Hill, on behalf of their eldest brother, Sir Julius Vale, and worked from dawn until dusk. Cornelius rose early and retired early, and Leona fully expected him to be sound asleep.

However, a distinct light showed beneath the door of the half-hidden little chamber Cornelius had chosen. Leona hesitated, then hurried back to her twin.

"There's a light in Cornel's room," she whispered.

Lawrence frowned. "Perhaps he's fallen asleep and left the candles burning. We should make sure."

"He won't like being wakened," Leona warned.

"He won't like setting fire to his bed, either." Lawrence brushed past her, strode along the passage, and scratched at Cornelius's door.

Greeted by silence, he raised his hand to knock more peremptorily, while Leona reached for the latch.

"Yes?" said a surprised voice from within.

The twins exchanged glances. Leona lifted the latch, and Lawrence pushed open the door.

Cornelius, in his shirt sleeves with his waving brown hair rumpled, sat at his desk in the lamplight, surrounded by papers and notebooks. He looked both tired and distracted.

"What is it?" he asked.

"Nothing," Leona said. "We just saw your light and were worried you'd fallen asleep. Are you still busy?"

Cornelius stood up, just a little too quickly, and bent to retrieve a fallen piece of paper from the floor. Throwing it on the desk, he came toward them. Like all the Vale males, he was tall and somewhat imposing. On top of which, his scowl was ferocious.

"Just finishing up," he snapped. "It's you two who should be in bed. You are on garden duty tomorrow."

"So we are," Lawrence said peaceably. "At least we know now you do stay up later than ten of the clock, so you *will* go the ball, won't you?"

"I have said I will." He took hold of the door above Lawrence's head and shooed them out. "Bed. Goodnight."

"Goodnight," they chorused, and walked back along the passage until they stood outside their own rooms.

"He is hiding something," Leona said.

"Undoubtedly."

"Perhaps we need to find out what… or is that rude?"

"Rude," Lawrence said. "Everyone needs *some* privacy, and God knows he works harder than any of us. He deserves to be happy. On the other hand"—he frowned—"Cornel has *depths*. And he is too serious. We should keep an eye on him."

"Agreed."

Chapter One

"YOU ARE NOT dancing."

In the face of his younger sister's irrefutable accusation, Cornelius Vale turned from his idle perusal of the glittering ballroom and played his trump card. "I am not acquainted with any ladies here. Apart from you, Delilah, and Felicia, and who wants to dance with their brother?"

"Have no fear." Lucy rose to bestow her hand upon the eager young man who had invited her—with Delilah's gracious permission. "Felicia knows everyone and will introduce you to lots of ladies."

Since Felicia was, in fact, bearing down upon them with a purposeful expression, Cornelius hastily excused himself to Lucy and her swain and strode off in the direction of the card room, attempting to lose himself in the well-dressed and bejeweled crowd.

Cornelius had no desire to waste his time on the frivolity of a ball. Nor was he as convinced as his siblings that dancing was the best way to cure his brother Julius of whatever malaise had dulled his spirits. In fact, he was sure Julius would slope off at the first opportunity. He had already made one attempt, thwarted by means unknown to Cornelius, who had a certain amount of sympathy for his eldest brother's plight.

The ball was much better attended than he had expected of a

small town assembly. But the local gentry, and even the aristocracy, appeared to be out in force, along with the many visitors to the town. He recognized several gentlemen he had met in the course of his role as Julius's steward of Black Hill. There was the squire, Winslow, shaking hands with the Earl of Braithwaite, who had recently returned from London to his ancestral castle on the cliff. Cornelius had met the earl only yesterday when he had ridden over to confer with the Braithwaite steward, and found him refreshingly knowledgeable as well as friendly.

However, he knew from experience with his former employers that he was as likely to be snubbed in public as greeted in private, so he veered aside and almost walked into *her*.

That Girl.

Fortunately, she was so deep in conversation with another young lady—no doubt pointing out all her flaws—that she did not glance in his direction. Cornelius congratulated himself on his luckiest escape of the evening. The last thing he needed was another lecture on poetry from a rich, ignorant girl.

What on earth had brought her to Blackhaven? The town had many visitors, of course. Its fresh spring water, pumped down from the hills, was supposed to cure every ailment known to man, and a few more besides. Which was one of the reasons he and his siblings had chosen to come home to Black Hill, to let Aubrey, who had been sickly from birth, discover if the waters could do more for him than the doctors. Judging by the swath Aubrey was cutting through the female population of Cumberland, it might have been working.

On the other hand, there was nothing remotely frail or delicate about *that* fashionably dressed, forceful, and horribly opinionated creature who had bent his ear and stretched his courtesy to breaking point in Gold's bookshop in London last month.

Passing the entrance to the ballroom, Cornelius swiped up a glass of wine from the table, took a sizeable gulp, and strolled on until he found a quiet corner where he could sit down alone and observe his sister Lucy and his brother Julius, as he had promised. Lucy was dancing quite decorously, though her whole being sparkled with vitality and enjoyment, which made Cornelius smile.

At the other end of the room, Julius was stepping out onto the balcony. *Still here, then,* Cornelius thought wryly, and took note that the balcony might well be another good place to hide from Felicia. His widowed sister had the best of intentions, of course, to help her siblings make friends and be happy. Cornelius was all in favor of that, but he himself was not a sociable man. He observed people, but he did not, as a rule, like them much. He had learned the hard way not to. And besides, he infinitely preferred work.

His mind drifted off to the morrow's tasks, prioritizing them according to urgency. The whole estate had been badly neglected, and to that was combined the constant rain of the summer so far to severely threaten the harvest and the prosperity of everyone at Black Hill. The rain also emphasized the poor state of repair of most of the tenants' cottages. How they had survived the winter, with wind and water howling through roofs and cracks in walls and windows, he had no idea. It made him angry.

In mid-glower at nothing in particular, he felt a prickle of awareness that he was being watched. Alarmed that it might be That Girl, he hastily refocused on the stretch of ballroom in front of him, and beheld, as though straight from his dreams, Cecily Armstrong. The only woman he had ever loved.

He leapt to his feet, appalled and yet delirious.

As though relieved—he had probably been staring directly at her without seeing her for some time—she moved toward him with the incomparable grace he remembered only too well. Shining gold ringlets framed her extraordinarily pretty face with its short nose, rosebud mouth, and flawless white skin.

She halted two feet away from him and curtseyed. "Mr. Vale," she said huskily.

"How do you do?" He bowed, unable to say her name, no

longer Miss Armstrong, but Lady Morgan. "An unexpected pleasure to find you here."

"I accompanied Lady Morgan, my mother-in-law," she blurted. "She wished to try the waters."

"And Sir John?" he replied, asking after his former employer.

"He will join us later." Her eyes seemed to devour him. He wondered if she regretted choosing Morgan over him, and doubted it.

"Another pleasure to look forward to," he said, with little effort at sincerity. He set his glass down on the nearest table, and, as though to stop him leaving her so quickly, she stepped closer.

"How are you, Cornelius?" she asked quickly, and flushed. "I mean, Mr. Vale."

"Well, as you see," he said, desperate to escape. "And as I trust I find your ladyship?"

She tried to smile. "So formal, Mr. Vale."

"So formal," he agreed bleakly. "You will excuse me? I have my sisters to attend." He bowed and walked away from her, almost laughing because suddenly Felicia and her alarming introductions to prospective dancing partners were more welcome than the only woman he had ever loved.

It was some time before he realized someone else was staring at him.

Damnation. That Girl, who had so set his back up in Gold's, was gazing directly at him. *Oh no…*

She walked quickly, directly from the dance floor, to intercept him, and there was no way out. Why had he not stayed with the wretched Cecily? She could not be more annoying than this…

He walked on, sure that such blatant rudeness would discourage her.

It didn't.

Her hated voice, light and amused, drawled at his elbow. "Bolting, Mr. Sacheverill?"

LADY ALICE CONWAY, second-youngest sister of the Earl of Braithwaite, could hardly believe her eyes. The great poet Simon Sacheverill was here already at the Blackhaven assembly room ball! She had been granted a second chance.

She did not miss his appalled expression as he kept walking away from her. It mortified her, but she had to apologize to him, whether or not he ever spoke to her again. Hurrying toward him, weaving among the couples leaving the dance floor, the memory of their previous encounter made her cringe.

She had been in Gold's bookshop near St. Paul's, having managed to escape the vigilance of all chaperones, including her mother, her sister-in-law, her younger sister Helen, and their old governess. Overwhelmed by her first London Season and astonished by her unexpected "success," she had needed the peace and the reminder of life beyond parties and gowns and trivial conversation.

The shop had been quiet, just as Alice liked it, and she sat on a stool among the shelves, inhaling the delightful smells of paper and leather and browsing in various biographies, travel books, and works of fiction and poetry. In fact, she had been there so long that Mr. Gold had probably forgotten about her.

At first the other customer's voice had not registered with her, until the name "Sacheverill" attracted her attention. The work of poet Simon Sacheverill was her discovery of the year, all that had made the beginning of the Season bearable. In her head, sometimes, she set his beautiful verses to music and listened to that rather than the inane chatter among her fellow debutantes.

And now Mr. Gold seemed to be persuading Mr. Sacheverill himself to sign copies of his leather-bound volume of poetry. Alice already owned one.

"It may make no difference," the bookseller said, "but what have we to lose if the books then fly off the shelves? It makes my shop stand out, and your book, too. You could always sign them personally for each customer, if you could spare even a day to be here—"

"I cannot," Sacheverill interrupted. "I am leaving town today, but if you wish it, I will sign a few books now. Let me know if it affects your sales."

Considering the beauty of the words that touched Alice's heart, the poet's voice was surprisingly blunt and down to earth, though he spoke with the accent of a gentleman. Curiosity brought her to her feet, heart thumping, before she meant to move. Seizing two books from her pile at random, she shoved the others back on shelves anyhow and emerged from hiding.

Mr. Gold, standing by the counter with a tall man, raised his eyebrows in surprise to see her, but came at once to take the books from her.

"Thank you, miss. May I have these delivered for you?"

"No, I shall take them with me, thank you."

While Mr. Gold bustled behind the counter, wrapping her books—whatever they were—into a parcel, Alice glanced sideways at Simon Sacheverill. Her heart almost stopped. Windswept dark brown hair with a mere hint of chestnut shining in a blink of sunshine, a surprisingly young if weather-beaten face—so handsome, with its high, broad bones, tapering chin, and sensitive, expressive mouth, that her knees began to melt. As for his eyes, when he raised them suddenly to hers, they were deep blue and distant, as if he looked constantly to the horizon for something he never found.

Attraction hit her all over, almost like a blow. It did not hurt, precisely, but her whole body tingled and trembled.

Worse, the shock seemed to turn her brain to mush. Instead of greeting him like the intelligent young woman she was, she stammered, "M-Mr. S-Sacheverill, f-forgive the interruption of a stranger, but I-I have to tell you, I have read *all* your poems." She blushed at her own foolishness. "Th-that is, all that are published. I'm sure you have others, better—" She broke off, appalled by her clumsiness and the insult he might read into it. "I mean—I don't mean… After all, how could they be better?"

To her relief, a twinge of humor gleamed in his eyes. Crow's-feet crinkled at the corners, only adding to his devastating attraction.

"How indeed," he said, "when composed by such a dolt?"

Was he offended or teasing? She suspected the latter, but fearing the former, she immediately tried to show her genuine appreciation of his work by seizing one of the volumes he had just signed and turning immediately to her favorite poem.

"This—this," she gibbered. "Exquisite language. I only wish it were longer."

"You do?"

"Oh yes, it is much too short," she said fervently, and proceeded to explain why, only the words came out wrong, and when she tried to explain again, it sounded as though she were justifying a poor opinion she didn't even hold in the first place.

And suddenly she had not been able to stop talking herself into the ever-widening pit, kindly explaining to him the forms and purpose of poetry, and in trying to show how he had so brilliantly thrown off convention, her muddled words seemed to criticize him for it.

When he tried to argue, she ploughed on through him, desperate to rectify her mistakes before he annihilated her, and succeeded only in making them worse. Appalled, she heard herself hector and lecture and could not seem to make herself stop.

Eventually, when she paused for breath, he had turned immediately to the open-mouthed bookseller.

"My thanks, Mr. Gold. Good afternoon." He had then flicked one short, contemptuous glance at Alice, merely snapping, "Ma'am," as though getting the short, cold word in quickly before she resumed haranguing him.

He had then walked out of the shop leaving her vilely embarrassed, humiliated, and ashamed.

Even now, several weeks later, catching up with him at the assembly ball to apologize, she had no idea what had happened to her on that awful afternoon. And so she tried to make this encounter light, even witty, to prove she was not normally so direly inarticulate and gauche.

"Bolting, Mr. Sacheverill?"

He glanced down his nose at her, and her false confidence wilted. His eyes did not lighten, though a breath of sudden laughter did issue from between those expressive lips.

"Yes. I seem to have been doing little else all evening."

He was still heart-thumpingly handsome, even more imposing in austere black evening dress and pure white neckcloth. He offered no greeting, no help, and she could not blame him.

She took a deep breath. "Mr. Sach—"

"*Will* you stop hurling that name around?" he hissed, and quite suddenly caught her gloved hand and dragged it into the crook of his arm so that they could walk more closely together. "Since you are here, we had better talk."

Fortunately, her normally quick brain popped up from the sea of awe and shame trying to drown it. "Ah, you are incognito."

Another quick, rueful glance. "Sort of. Where can we go? Unless you are allowed to waltz?"

"Of course," she said in surprise. Even in London, she had been granted immediate permission to waltz by the patronesses of Almack's, right at the beginning of her Season.

Without further invitation, Mr. Sacheverill whisked her onto the dance floor among the waiting couples, bowed perfunctorily, and took her in his arms. Alice's knees threatened to give way again. Overcome by his closeness, she struggled to recall how she had got here. And why.

"Incognito," she murmured, frowning. "Why?"

"I have another life that is nothing to do with poetry," he muttered. "I have responsibilities, family, people who depend upon me."

She gazed up at him in wonder. To her surprise, his eyes slid away. Was he embarrassed by this other life? He certainly looked well enough on it, though it was true he wore no jewels, no fobs or frills. Even the pin in his cravat was plain.

"I have to beg the favor, the kindness of your discretion," he said awkwardly. "With regard to the name and the profession—"

She caught her breath. "No one else knows you are—?"

"No," he interrupted her. "And I ask you to keep it that way."

"But why?"

"Because it does not fit with my real profession," he said, glowering.

"Which is what?" she asked, intrigued.

"I am a land steward."

She blinked. "I thought you were going to say undertaker, or strict Calvinist minister, where there might be conflict with entertainment or beauty! Where is the shame in being a land steward?"

"There is none," he snapped.

She opened her mouth, then closed it again as the revelation hit her. "You are ashamed of the po..." Under his warning glare, she bit back the word and swallowed. "But that is ridiculous!"

"It does not fit with the rest of my life," he said quickly. "I am not ashamed."

"Good, because you have no reason to be."

An ironic gleam entered his eyes. "I am astonished to hear you say so."

Heat burned up into her cheeks. "Everything came out wrongly at the bookshop, and I could not stop talking."

"I noticed."

She swallowed, wishing some kind floor or monster looming out of the nearby sea would swallow *her*. "I came to apologize to you. I daren't try to explain in case my stupid tongue twists everything around again, but it was never my intention to criticize, hector, or harangue. In fact, without your p—*work*, I would have found the last few months unbearable. Thank you."

His brow twitched. Those beautiful, distant eyes focused

more intensely on hers as though reading her soul. She should have been terrified.

"That," he said slowly, "must be the handsomest apology I have ever received. And in the circumstances, it is not even necessary. After too many gushing reviews and compliments, our encounter was a timely reminder to me that opinions must vary."

"Is that why you are incognito?" she asked guiltily.

"In a roundabout way, perhaps. But I have always been incognito. Do I have your word that you will keep my secret?"

"Of course, if it is worth it for the next few days. Though since we are dancing, you had better tell me your other name."

"Vale," he said. "Cornelius Vale."

"I am Al—Wait." She blinked. "Vale is the name of the family who have just come home to Black Hill. Are you one of those Vales?"

"I am. Sir Julius is my brother. I act as steward for his land."

Alice frowned. "Then *Vale* is your real name! Does your brother not like you to be distracted by…your other work?"

"He doesn't know anything about it."

Her foot faltered, and she hopped to catch up. "Even your family does not know?"

"No one knows but my publisher. And you."

She shook her head. "That is silly. You cannot hide such a great thing from your family."

"I can and I do."

"But why? It is bound to come out, especially—" Only when his eyes hardened again did she realize they had softened somehow during their conversation.

"That is not your concern," he interrupted her.

"No, but it is yours," she retorted. "It is so much a part of your life. Your family should know."

"As you tell *your* family everything? Such as spending hours unchaperoned in the city?"

"That is different," she said impatiently. "A trivial moment of freedom, not something that consumes my whole life as music does for me, and poetry for you."

"You make a false equivalence between our situations."

"Why do you think so? Because your work is great and I merely tinkle at the pianoforte to impress potential suitors with my accomplishment?"

"Yes," he said baldly. "My work is serious."

"And *you* are so full of your own importance you make me sick. If you do not wish to appear ridiculous when I abandon you mid-dance, kindly escort me from the floor."

Only when his arms fell away did she miss their strength and warmth. She laid only the very tips of her fingers on his sleeve as they slipped between waltzing couples. She was far too angry even to look at him.

As soon as they were free of the dancers, she dropped a minute curtsey and stalked off in the middle of his bow.

Chapter Two

DAMN IT, NOW I *am in the wrong.* Cornelius was not quite sure how or why, but he grasped that he had both offended and hurt her. Hardly kind—or wise—when she had promised to keep his secret.

But seriously, he thought as he strode back to the table in search of Aubrey's abandoned flask of brandy, there could be no comparison between her life and his. He worked hard every day for his family's livelihood. His escape into poetry was a necessity, like a lifeline for his survival, even without the small amounts of money it made for him.

While she, whoever she was—how could he not even know her name?—led a life of idleness, having learned only how to attract a husband. The responsibility would never be hers. And what the devil did she know about the sweat and suffering of writing?

What do you know about her life? Her music? Oh, damnation. In his own way, he had done exactly the same to her as he'd imagined she had done to him in the bookshop. Only it had hurt her more because she had done nothing but listen to him and agree to his request without even understanding why he asked. From her kindness.

Cornelius had not been kind. He had, as she so rightly pointed out, been full of his own importance. What did he know of a young lady's life? Only what he observed of his sisters—who

15

might not spend hours a day improving or even working on the land, but they certainly made the house comfortable and homely. They were also wrestling with the gardens in order to grow vegetables and herbs and fruit next year, as well as to make them look pretty. They did not know about his necessary release of poetry. He knew nothing of their private moments either.

Had he really become so self-obsessed and, even worse, self-pitying?

Appalled, he realized it was his pleasure to perform his part for his family, to use his training and knowledge for the benefit of all. And he had always written poetry, even before he left home to take up his first position. If music was That Girl's joy or escape, who was he to belittle it? He had just recalled excruciating evenings at Cecily's house, forced to listen and applaud her and other young ladies as they murdered pieces of pleasant music his brother Roderick had made shine as a boy.

Throwing himself into a chair at the empty Vale table, he reached for Aubrey's flask, unstopped it, and found it empty. He scowled at it and set it down, just as Aubrey, strolling past with an extraordinarily beautiful young lady on his arm, took another flask from his pocket and threw it to him.

Cornelius caught it just as casually. How many of the damned things had Aubrey brought with him? *The boy drinks too much.* His older brothers did not seem perturbed by the habit, labeling it as a slightly belated phase of growing up. No doubt Cornelius only worried more because, subjected to early mornings since his training began at the age of seventeen, he had missed that crucial part of a young gentleman's development.

Besides, as this evening had proven beyond a doubt, he really was not cut out for parties. He was socially awkward and had no small talk.

He took a sip from the flask, enjoying the jolt of heat on his tongue, and trickling down his throat. *"Ode to a Brandy Flask,"* he thought, and amused himself by composing some funny lines in his head. He wished he was home alone in his small bedchamber, with paper, pen, and ink.

He was on to a second verse—knowing quite well that he was merely putting off the task of apologizing to That Girl—when someone eased into the chair next to his and a glass of brandy appeared in front of him.

Expecting a brother, Cornelius turned with a grin and a suitably disparaging word of thanks—only to see a complete stranger. The man was probably in his fifties and looked as if he had been squeezed into his straining evening coat. But his eyes were bright, friendly, and, fortunately, amused.

"I beg your pardon," Cornelius said. "I assumed you were my brother!"

"All brothers under the skin," the gentleman said cheerfully. "I brought you a glass of brandy so we can get to know each other. My name's Daubin. Cloverfield, my land, marches with Black Hill."

"Ah, of course. Cornelius Vale." They shook hands.

"You're the one who manages the land?" Daubin said, picking up his glass.

"I am."

"I believe you called in on my man, Norrie, with some concerns last week. Sorry I missed you. So when Lord Braithwaite told me who you were, I thought we could just sort the matter out as friends should."

"Indeed, I should much prefer it," Cornelius said. He did not want to quarrel with his neighbors, and Daubin, who may not have spoken like a gentleman, seemed to be behaving like one. In contrast with his rude and unhelpful steward. He raised his glass to Daubin.

"To friendship." Daubin beamed and clinked glasses before downing half his brandy. "So what exactly was your problem? What did my fool misunderstand?"

"Border incursions," Cornelius said with a quick smile. "There was a gap in the hedge, and three of our cattle wandered into your land. Mr. Norrie was reluctant to give them back."

"I'll speak to him," Daubin promised comfortably.

"Also, there is the matter of the top east meadow—where the stream flows down."

"I know the place."

"I'm afraid your sheep are all over it, and I plan to graze ours there over the winter."

Daubin blinked. "I'm no farmer, but seems to me there'll be none left for your sheep by winter."

"Seems so to me, too," Cornelius said. "So I would take it as a favor if Norrie would move your sheep onto your land."

"Bless you, lad, they *are* on my land."

"You've moved them since this morning? My thanks."

"Well, I'm not precisely sure what Norrie gets up to. But that meadow is mine."

"With respect, sir, that meadow has always been part of Black Hill."

"Until Sir George signed it over to me."

Cornelius set down his brandy. "The devil he did! When?"

"Oh, must be three or four years ago. Norrie will tell you."

"But my father was not even in England three or four years ago."

"Oh, people do business from abroad all the time," Daubin said indulgently. "You just have to keep your eye on things. Sir George let the place go a bit, didn't he?"

"Yes," Cornelius admitted, trying not to hiss the word between his teeth. "And trusted the wrong man to steward it for him. I'll speak to Barton again and get to the bottom of it."

Daubin patted his shoulder. "You do that, lad, and we shan't fall out over a bit of grass!" He beamed again. "And are these beautiful ladies, your sisters?"

HAVING EXTRICATED HIMSELF from Daubin, only to fall foul of

Felicia and the shy young lady he felt obliged to dance with, it was some time before he again spotted That Girl. She was with another young lady who could only be a sister—a gentler, lighter version of her dramatic beauty.

Cornelius shocked himself with this thought. She had been so annoying that he had never acknowledged her beauty. But it was definitely there.

The sisters had been intercepted by a confident, fashionable young gentleman, whose smile was quickly wiped from his face by some sharp set-down from That Girl. The sister, who seemed to be smoothing the waters, nevertheless took her sibling's arm, and they walked away together.

Cornelius sighed and walked purposefully after them. At the last moment, just as they sat down beside another young lady, Cornelius was halted again, this time by none other than the Earl of Braithwaite, who said, "Ah, Vale," and thrust out his hand. "I just met your brother Sir Julius and two charming sisters. Good to see the Vales out in such force."

"That's not what people usually say."

Braithwaite laughed. "Nonsense. Have you met my wife?"

"No, I have not had that honor."

"Then let me rectify that. Eleanor." He turned toward the nearest table, and the woman beside That Girl glanced up, smiling. "This is Mr. Cornelius Vale, Sir Julius's brother. Vale, my wife, Lady Braithwaite."

Cornelius bowed, and the countess murmured, "How do you do, Mr. Vale?" before the earl moved on to That Girl. "My sister, Lady Alice Conway, and our youngest sister, Lady Helen."

Oh, the devil! thought Cornelius, with no idea why he should be so angry when That Girl turned out to be so aristocratic. There was nothing he could do except bow to both the young ladies and, as Lady Helen went off to dance with some army officer, take the proffered chair next to Lady Alice.

As soon as the countess became involved in conversation with an apparently old friend, Cornelius got the matter over with.

"I'm sorry to have been so ill-natured and presumptuous. I should not have disparaged your music, particularly not from my position of ignorance. I beg your pardon."

Although he half expected Lady Alice to stick her nose in the air and pretend she had not heard him, she cast him a quick, crooked smile. "Not at all, sir. You have actually given me a new and worthy ambition."

"I have? What?"

"To hold a conversation with you that does not require one of us to apologize to the other."

Cornelius grinned and was oddly gratified to see the relieved smile lighten her rather lovely dark hazel eyes. "With that in mind, tell me about your music. *Do* you play the pianoforte?"

"Yes, and the harp and the guitar and the violin a little."

"And you are good?"

He was curious to see if she would be modest or proud in her reply, but in fact she said nothing for so long that he thought he had offended her again.

"My sister—Helen, whom you just met—paints," she said, without obvious connection to his question. "Everyone tells her she is good. But then, she has had lessons from Lord Tamar, our brother-in-law, who is now a successful and fashionable artist. Many people attribute her skill to Tamar rather than to her own genius, her own relentless practice. Women—certainly women of our rank—must be accomplished but never great. Helen gives her beautiful paintings away to family and friends when they should be seen and admired by the whole world. Her talent is *confined*."

"Because she is a lady," he said slowly. "And your talent, is that also confined?"

"Yes. As you imagine, I display my accomplishments beside that of other debutantes. I am better than them without trying, and yet if I do try, I am accused of showing off, of blighting the chances of lesser mortals who do not have the benefit of my rank, my dowry, my brother's influence. Unless I break with my family, I will never share my music in great concert halls, never even publish my compositions under my own name."

"Ah. No wonder you are angry with me. I *could* publish under my own name and choose not to."

"I am not angry with you," Lady Alice said ruefully. "I am angry with the world. You just represented it for a moment. It is I who should apologize. Again."

"I would like to hear you play," Cornelius said, almost surprised to find that it was true. She was a most unusual young lady. Even her anger intrigued him. He wondered if he were merely flattered because her awe of him had caused her incoherent and distinctly *unflattering* babble in the bookshop.

"Oh, you're bound to. I know you will be at our garden party, where I am permitted—nay, encouraged!—to play. We have also managed to secure Frederick Baird, the wonderful Scottish pianist. Do you care for music, Mr. Vale?"

"I rarely have the leisure to listen these days, but yes, I used to. When I was a boy, my father took us to several of the great concert halls of Europe—when war permitted. I heard Beethoven play in Vienna. He was… soaring." He gave a quick, embarrassed smile. "If you see what I mean."

Lady Alice's smile was much more open. "I do. And how I envy you. Did you really travel about Europe during the war?"

"Yes, up to a point. My father was a diplomat, and he took us all with him when we were young, wherever he was sent."

A hint of envy crossed her face, a spark of excitement. "Helen and I dream of traveling the world, soaking up art and music, learning, playing, and painting."

"We took it for granted as children, but yes, we were lucky in many ways. When is your garden party?"

"Next Wednesday."

"I have to wait so long to hear you? Wait." He frowned, recalling his quick search for Julius earlier in the evening. "Is there not a pianoforte in one of the smaller rooms here?"

Her eyes widened, and a whole array of expressions chased each other across her face, among them impatience, suspicion, longing, and then a breathtaking sparkle of mischief. Suddenly he could imagine her as a child, a precocious handful of daring and devilry and, probably, talent. A little like his sister Lucy, only more obviously forceful in character.

She rose from her chair, obliging him to stand with her. "Very well, let us stroll a little," she said as though in answer to his invitation. She made a silent gesture to her sister-in-law the countess, who nodded by way of acknowledgement.

When there was space, he offered his arm, and she took it quite decorously.

"Did I mention," Cornelius murmured, "that the room with the pianoforte was empty and in darkness?"

"Then what were you doing there?"

"Looking for Julius. We thought he'd legged it as soon as we arrived but discovered him later ensconced in the ballroom."

"Why would he—er… leg it?" Lady Alice asked in amusement.

"He didn't want to come in the first place. The twins, my youngest siblings, manipulated him. All of us, in fact."

"Then none of you truly wants to be here?"

"Oh, most of us do. Julius and I—and possibly Roderick—are the sticks-in-the-mud. Although I admit I am having more fun than I expected."

"Well retrieved, Mr. Vale," she said sardonically.

As they approached the ballroom doors, Cornelius slowed. "This is not wise for your reputation."

Lady Alice did not slow. "I am the Earl of Braithwaite's sister, outspoken and original. As I discovered during my ghastly Season, I can do almost anything with impunity."

"Including approaching strange men in bookshops?"

"Especially that."

"But not playing in concert halls."

"Especially *not* that."

"It makes you rebellious."

"Only up to a point, sir," she said with a hint of bitterness.

"Our childish plans were fantasy. The reality is, we have family we care for and cannot hurt."

"And yet you are hurt by staying."

She cast him a quick look of surprise. "I did not expect you to understand."

He was not sure he did. Nor, as they crossed the empty foyer and she pushed open the door of the chamber with the pianoforte, was he sure he really wanted to hear her play. She was an earl's sister. For that alone, people must have over-praised her all her life, and he more than half suspected that her opinion far outstripped her talent. Somehow, it would pain him to know that, and to tell her. She would think it revenge for her rant about his poetry.

The room was darker now than before, since the summer night had finally fallen. But, using the taper by the door, he took a light from the nearest wall sconce in the foyer and lit the candelabrum in the room until the pianoforte stood in the midst of a halo-like glow.

She watched him from the open door, which she did not close before finally walking toward the instrument. So she retained some sense of self-preservation.

He drew out the stool and placed it for her while she stripped off her fine white gloves. Her hands were not small, but they were slender and curiously elegant as she swept them over the keys in a ripple of sound. Her brow twitched as though she heard a note not quite in tune, and then smoothed again as she settled her fingers over the keys and began to play.

He did not recognize the music, and she played very softly, but from the first bar, he was captured. He drew nearer her, hoping to banish the competing dance music drifting from the ballroom and determined not to lose a note of hers. The melody was haunting, intensified and complicated by fragments of others that all blended into a sweeping whole. Her fingers flew and glided, far beyond the skill of merely hitting the correct keys at the right time. Lady Alice *felt* the music. She breathed it, lived it.

Her whole body moved with it, her face alive with expression that transformed it beyond mere beauty.

Dear God, and he had been trying to think how to advise her tactfully to concentrate on improving for family and friends. How utterly condescending and just plain wrong. It was as if every emotion he tried to portray in verse was expressed here in the music conjured so exquisitely by her fingers.

Cornelius was lost.

And then a man walked into the room.

"Lady Alice," he drawled, bowing, and the beautiful music cut off like a tap.

Her hands still resting on the keyboard, she stared at the newcomer, showing neither pleasure nor displeasure, neither welcome nor fear. Yet suddenly she looked as lost as Cornelius, bewildered, almost rootless, as though the music had been taken away from her.

Perhaps it was the effect of the music stopping so suddenly, but the newcomer seemed to be a powerful presence. Perhaps in his early thirties, only a few years older than Cornelius, he was tall, handsome, fair, and fashionable, holding himself with a natural pride and self-confidence.

"Braithwaite sent me to find you," said this vision in elegant black satin.

Lady Alice stood abruptly. "Nonsense. He said, *She is here somewhere,* and you took it upon yourself to look."

"Perhaps it is as well I did." His gaze moved unhurriedly around the room before landing expressionlessly on Cornelius and returning to Alice. "Not everyone is as understanding as I of your innocent liveliness."

"Not everyone presumes to judge," Alice snapped. "Courtesy compels me to present our neighbor, Mr. Cornelius Vale. Mr. Vale, His Grace the Duke of Atherstone."

His Grace did not offer his hand, returning only the slightest of bows to Cornelius's. Cornelius, who might have been merely his brother's steward but who had in his boyhood mingled with kings, princes, and ministers of state, was hardly overwhelmed by the ducal presence.

As he turned back to Lady Alice, she said, "Your arm, Mr. Vale, if you please."

Cornelius obliged, and they left the duke standing alone. However, any triumph Cornelius might have felt was lost in the realization that the fearless Lady Alice was shaking.

Chapter Three

ALICE HAD BEEN completely focused on the music, and yet there was also awareness of *him*. His awe elated her—her music moved the great poet! And then all her emotion, all her passion, had crashed at the first sound of Atherstone's voice.

Somehow, she had held her own, greeting him with bare civility that verged on contempt. How dare he contaminate this moment? How dare he contaminate her *home*?

"What is it?" Cornelius said, his voice urgent and yet so gentle that she wanted to weep. And throw things. "My lady, what is wrong?"

Of course he could feel her trembling. And that made her angry too. "Nothing," she snapped. "I just imagined I had left all that stupidity back in London, but it has *followed* me!"

He had swept her back into the ballroom, where she was once more enveloped in the warmth of the crowd, the chatter, and the music. It infuriated her because she had so enjoyed the peace of being alone with him. But Atherstone had spoiled that too, and now she was back with the ever-familiar. And yet she felt safe here, and that made her ashamed.

To her relief, Mr. Vale did not return her to her family. Instead, he conducted her to a miraculously quiet corner, and a glass of wine appeared on the table before her. She picked it up with both hands to avoid spilling it.

He watched her, his eyes steady, still curiously gentle, though there was something implacable about the set of his long, firm mouth. "Atherstone has followed you? What did he do to you?"

The wine slopped over the edge of her glass, dripping on her fingers. "Nothing!" she said in fright. "He merely represents the ghastliness of the Season for me."

He presented her with a large handkerchief to wipe her fingers. "Why ghastly? I thought young ladies loved the Season. My sister Felicia did, and Lucy, as I recall, was furious she could not have one when my brother-in-law had the temerity to die."

"My sisters enjoyed them too," Alice said. "Or at least the oldest two did. Frances and Serena were wild and daring, of course, as well as beautiful and charming. Fortunately, Frances caught a Scottish earl—who is incredibly kind and sweet—before she could ruin herself, and Serena was sent home for dancing three times with Lord Daxton and jilting her perfectly respectable betrothed, after which she met Tamar and now lives happily ever after." She ran out of breath, inhaled, and began again. "Maria is more shy and anxious, of course, so no one minded that she married beneath her."

She took another gulp of wine. "I'm babbling again. You have an ill effect upon me, sir."

"Were *you* shy and anxious?" he asked curiously, almost as if her contradictions interested him.

"No," she sighed. "Worse. I am bookish and opinionated."

He smiled. "You are."

"I suppose we younger three were left more to our own devices when Frances and Serena came out, and then Gervaise— my brother, Braithwaite—went into politics. We all went our own ways, following our own inclinations, which has given us too much independence of spirit. On top of which, I am too blunt to be conciliatory. No one, least of all me, expected me to have a successful Season."

"Did you?"

"Gervaise received twelve offers of marriage on my behalf."

He blinked. "That sounds successful."

"Well, three were from gazetted fortune hunters and one from a schoolboy, but even so, Mama was impressed."

"Were you?"

"Lord no, not one of them had any interest in me, only in my dowry, my birth, and my family's influence—in various orders of importance depending on the suitor."

"Which was the Duke of Atherstone's chief interest?"

She glanced at him, not sure whether his perception pleased or annoyed her. He was watching her, twisting the stem of his glass in his large, yet elegant, fingers. "Birth, probably. Certainly, he thinks I cannot refuse him because he is a duke."

"And yet you did."

"How do you know I did?" she challenged.

"You were hardly glad of his presence."

"I'm not. And I did. Refuse him, I mean." She took another sip, glad that she could hold the glass now in one steady hand.

"Why? Most girls would give their eye teeth to be a duchess."

She curled her lip. "I didn't like his manners." She sipped again. "I can't imagine he likes mine."

Mr. Vale—dear God, Simon Sacheverill!—raised his own glass, clinking the base off hers. "I could have throttled him for interrupting. You play divinely."

Heat seeped into her face. "I hope you are not saying that merely to cheer me up."

"No." He gave a quick, self-deprecating smile. "I thought I would have to find a tactful way to explain your limitations to you. If you have any, I am not knowledgeable enough to discern them. I understand your frustrations better now. What was it you played? It was exquisite."

She could hardly breathe for happiness. "Thank you," she gasped. "I…I composed it myself."

His eyebrows flew up, perhaps in disbelief, though she hoped it was merely surprise. "What do you call it?"

She set the glass down on the table before she gulped it dry and blurted everything. "It does not have a name yet. Perhaps I shall explain my dilemma to you one day, and you can help me decide."

"I would be honored." His gaze flickered toward the entrance and then back to her face. "Are you promised for the supper dance?"

"Do I need to be?" she asked, and he understood immediately.

"The duke has seen you but is moving toward Lady Braithwaite. I can offer you protection if you wish it."

"I don't," she said at once. "I have any number of old friends who will dance with me without my having to hint."

"And if I ask because I want the pleasure of your company?"

"That is different."

IN THE SHORT carriage ride home to Braithwaite Castle, only Gervaise and Eleanor made desultory conversation. Helen, who was Alice's closest sister yet sometimes now seemed miles away, seemed lost in her own dreamy, rather pleasant thoughts. So Alice thought of Cornelius Vale, who was also Simon Sacheverill.

He had surprised her so many times and yet seemed to have no idea how rare he truly was. He had been rude, haughty, forgiving, apologetic, delighted by her music, kind, and interested in *her*. On top of that, during the supper dance and then supper itself, he had revealed an unexpected sense of humor. That should not have surprised her, of course, for Sacheverill's poetry was littered with sly witticisms and subtle jests. But thinking on one's feet was different from composing. He had made her laugh. And he was certainly well educated, for they had conversed on many intriguing topics that proved his knowledge and his depth of thought. And he was observant. She was sure he guessed the nature of Atherstone's offense against her.

And yet none of these were the reasons she thought of him now. She had been too anxious and angry during their first dance to properly appreciate him, but now she found herself remembering the strength of his arms, the breadth of his shoulders, the grace of his every movement. And as she felt it again now, she remembered the odd, tingling heat his nearness had brought her.

In London, she had waltzed with many men, of all ages and character. Some had been handsome. Many she had liked. Many had amused her, both consciously and unconsciously. But this physical reaction, which she had felt in the bookshop too before she ruined everything, was new to her, and peculiarly precious.

She found herself smiling as she gazed out of the carriage window at the dark fields and tall, silhouetted trees lining the castle road and the curved, sweeping drive.

"Alice?" Gervaise said when they were inside the castle and she would have run upstairs after Helen to talk over their secret plans.

"Yes?" Alice paused her foot on the steps. Eleanor had swept toward the nursery wing to see her children.

"You danced twice with Cornelius Vale and sat out a dance with him."

"Did I? Well, no one counts such things in Blackhaven." They might when his true identity was revealed, although she was more likely to be lost in the storm of adulation.

"I suspect His Grace of Atherstone does," Gervaise said. "Though fortunately he did not see your earlier dance with Vale."

"I'm surprised you did."

"I didn't," he confessed. "Eleanor is more aware, as she tries to take her chaperone duties seriously. You would not take advantage of her, would you?"

"Of course not." Alice smiled crookedly. "Are you afraid Mr. Vale takes advantage of me?"

"No. I am more concerned with your spoiling your chances with Atherstone."

"I have no chances with him. I refused him."

"And yet here he is in Blackhaven. I believe you have made a conquest. If you knew how many caps had been set at him…"

"I can guess. I'm sure that is half of his own attraction to me, because I never did."

"What do you think is the other half of his attraction to you?" Gervaise said, smiling.

"You," Alice replied. "Gervaise, he is not for me, and I am certainly not for him. I wish he had not come." She could not quite hide her shudder of revulsion, and then she thought again of dancing with Cornelius Vale, who was also Simon Sacheverill.

Why had he not yet even warned his family of his alter ego, when he had only a week before the castle garden party revealed all?

CORNELIUS COULD NOT wait to get home. Julius had, inevitably, vanished halfway through the evening, but the rest of his siblings chattering away about dances and acquaintances was a mere annoyance to him. His head was full of music and beauty and words he was desperate to spill onto paper.

Once in the house, he yelled a general goodnight loudly enough to reach the twins—who were doubtless skulking somewhere in the house to hear all about it—and ran straight up to his bedchamber.

"He has an early start, poor fellow," Delilah said in the hall below.

"Can't he have *one* day off?" Aubrey returned. "I certainly intend to."

There came the sound of a slap on the head. "No you won't—you'll drink your waters like a man. And Cornelius, refreshed by sleep…" Roderick's voice faded into the drawing room.

If only they knew his rush was not to sleep, but to get the

words down on paper while everything was still in his head. After kicking his bedroom door shut behind him, he lit the lamp on his desk, tore off his coat, cravat, and waistcoat, and threw himself into the chair.

In shirt sleeves and his black satin breeches, he wrote feverishly, then scored out with fury where the language proved unequal to the task and replaced the words with others. His vision seemed to tumble onto the page, more like music than mere words.

Dawn was breaking before he set his pen back in the stand. He was far too tired to know if it was any good, but he felt a certain satisfaction as he stood up, dropped the rest of his clothes on the floor, and fell naked into bed. Two hours of sleep and he would get up to oversee the drainage ditch in the lower field and fix the gutter on the Battys' cottage, then, hopefully, get the cows back from Daubin and get some truth out of the lazy Barton, who had been his father's steward.

To his relief, Lady Alice's lovely face with its myriad expressions no longer haunted his vision, but as he closed his eyes and drifted off to sleep at last, her music still played in his head.

"I WISH HE had not come."

Alice's shudder when she spoke of the Duke of Atherstone did not go unnoticed by her brother. On the other hand, the next instant she had looked so untroubled, even happy, that he could easily have mistaken the cause of that shiver. She was probably merely tired and cold.

However, when the duke called the following morning, not long before midday, Braithwaite was wary.

An alliance with the duke would be most advantageous for the whole family. Alice would be a duchess, with all the wealth and position of her husband's family behind her. The political and social connections were second to none. And the marriage settlements would be generous.

Braithwaite was not an avaricious man, but there was no denying there had been many demands on his purse in the last few years. As well as alterations and repairs to the castle, he had loaned a fortune to his brother-in-law Tamar for the repair of his ruined house and lands. He had bought a house in London for his sister Maria and her husband. He grudged none of it, and he was hardly facing ruin. However, his coffers were not inexhaustible and a few more bad years could certainly make things difficult. A marriage alliance with a wealthy man would stabilize his finances nicely.

And so he received the Duke of Atherstone in his library with great affability, and gave him a glass of wine.

"I shan't beat about the bush, Braithwaite," Atherton said in his cool, oddly expressionless voice. "My offer for Lady Alice stands."

"Sadly, so does her refusal," Braithwaite replied. "I spoke to her on the subject last night. It may not be the answer either you or I wish for, but there it is."

Atherton blinked slowly, sipping his wine. "Do you have no say in your family affairs, Braithwaite?"

To his annoyance, Braithwaite felt heat seep into his face. "I do," he said, "and I have always let my sisters choose."

"You'll forgive me for pointing out the mistake. Females—especially young females—do not have the gumption to make wise choices. To be blunt, your own sisters are living proof of that. Torridon may be very well, but Tamar? The Gaunts are a ramshackle bunch—bad blood and profligate to a fault. I would not allow *my* sister to marry there, even for the honor of being a marchioness."

"Well, it is hardly an option," Braithwaite said as pleasantly as he could, "since Serena is the marchioness."

"Costly," Atherstone remarked. "As for Lady Maria's disastrous marriage, the least said, the better."

"There I agree with you," Braithwaite said icily.

"A little advice for you, Braithwaite. You are the head of a noble family. Act like it. If you wish Lady Alice to marry me, tell her so. Neither of you will regret it." With another sip of wine, the duke set his half-full glass on the table and rose. "I am going up to Scotland for a few days. I shall hope for a different answer upon my return to Blackhaven, for it will be my final offer." He smiled without warmth. "I would appreciate a personal interview with Lady Alice at that time. I would not like to think you stand against me."

Atherstone held out one languid hand, and they shook with outward cordiality. "Indeed, I hope you would not," Braithwaite said.

And yet, as the duke departed, Braithwaite found he liked him less. He did not care to feel threatened.

Chapter Four

WHEN LORD BRAITHWAITE appeared at Black Hill the following day, Cornelius was up to his knees in a ditch and felt a sudden twist of his stomach, like a schoolboy caught in some misdemeanor who knows the game is up and he is about to be punished.

"Good day, Vale!" Braithwaite greeted him. "Sorry to disturb you, but I hear you are looking for good men. This is Rob Smith, son of one of my own respected tenants, former soldier. Would you happen to have a place for him?"

Cornelius almost laughed. He was not embarrassed to be caught covered in mud, laboring beside his workers. Instead, he had expected to be harangued for overfamiliarity with the earl's sister, which was untrue, unfair, and ridiculous in reality, whatever flights of fancy his imagination indulged.

"I can give you a few days' work," Cornelius said to Smith. "But I can't guarantee you anything beyond that."

"I'll take it," muttered Smith. Nudged by Braithwaite, he remembered to tug at his cap. "Thank you, sir."

"Well, you can start by taking my place here," Cornelius said, suddenly cheerful. "I have to see a man about some cows."

"Thanks, Vale, I appreciate it," Braithwaite said, though he seemed in a hurry to be off, almost shame-faced. Which was a curiosity for another day.

After his talk with Mr. Daubin at the ball, Cornelius had hoped to have the Black Hill cows already returned from neighboring Cloverfield, and Daubin's sheep off the top meadow. Since nothing had changed, he collected his horse and rode over to again confront Norrie, the Cloverfield steward.

Reluctantly, almost as though they were his own property, Norrie eventually allowed the removal of the cows, but Daubin's sheep still ate their heads off on the Black Hill meadow.

"It's not your field!" Norrie almost shouted at Cornelius when he remonstrated with him.

"Oh, nonsense." Cornelius glared at him. "It is clearly marked on every local map for hundreds of years."

"But it won't be on the next one. Sir George, your father, sold the meadow to Mr. Daubin. Look." For the first time, Norrie thrust a document under Cornelius's nose. The signature at the bottom certainly looked like his father's.

Infuriated, he rode back to Black Hill and went to see Barton, his father's old steward.

Although paid faithfully during all the years of the family's absence, Barton had neglected the estate quite shockingly for at least ten years. Which hardly endeared him to Cornelius, who could not abide the wasting of good land.

Barton was getting on in years, of course, and after forcibly retiring him, Julius was inclined to overlook the negligence—no doubt from guilt that neither their father nor he had paid any attention to Black Hill for fifteen years. Their father had pursued his diplomatic career, largely abroad, while Julius had been almost constantly at sea with the Royal Navy.

Barton had never invited Cornelius into his cottage. All their business had been conducted in the office at the big house. But on this occasion, Cornelius stepped deliberately over the threshold, and Barton was obliged to show him into the tiny parlor. Considering the state into which the land had fallen, Barton's cottage was very neat and tidy and pleasant. No leaky roof or cracked windows here.

Throwing himself into one of the upholstered chairs, Cornelius said abruptly, "I need your help, Barton. Did my father really sell the top east meadow to Daubin?"

"Believe he did, sir."

Cornelius scowled. "Why?"

Barton shrugged. "Couldn't say. I just did what he told me."

"Really?" Cornelius said sardonically.

"Really," Barton said.

"And how exactly did he instruct you to sell the meadow?"

"By letter, of course."

"Do you have the letter?"

Barton scratched his head. "Don't know that I do. But the documents of sale are in the office."

"I have found no such things. Nor is it in the account ledgers."

"You must be looking in the wrong place. I'll come up in a day or so and find them for you."

"No," Cornelius said, jumping to his feet. "Come now."

For a moment he thought Barton would defy him. After all, he might have been granted a pension, but he was no longer employed at Black Hill. But after a tense moment, Barton inclined his head and led the way to the front door, where he collected his hat and coat.

It was not a long walk up to the house, although Barton made heavy weather of it. Cornelius walked beside him, leading his horse rather than riding him, and asked more questions about Daubin.

"When exactly did Daubin buy Cloverfield?"

"Oh, must be four or five years ago."

"He has some good land there," Cornelius allowed. "Makes it work for him."

"That he does. Takes no nonsense from his tenants, either. Evicts them if they don't pay. Only a matter of time before ne'er-do-wells like Fred Gaffney are gone for good."

Cornelius frowned. "Wastrel he might be, but I like Gaffney.

He has a big family, does he not? In fact, his daughter is our new parlor maid."

"Must be how he came up with the rent money last minute. Norrie was already on his way to evict the lot of them when Gaffney waved the money under his nose."

It struck Cornelius that Barton seemed to know more detail about goings-on at Cloverfield than about the land he had been paid to manage for almost two decades. Also, a parlor maid's salary would hardly cover her father's rent. At best, she had staved off eviction for another few weeks.

"You've changed everything," Barton said twenty minutes later, in an accusing kind of voice, as he surveyed the rows of ledgers in the bookcase, and the cabinet full of documents. "How am I supposed to find anything in this?"

"Imagine how I felt," Cornelius said wryly, remembering the chaos he had found here only a few months ago.

Barton did not appear to hear. Instead, he went to the cabinet, raking through the first drawer. Cornelius already knew it wasn't there because he had searched it from top to bottom. Impatiently, having a mountain of other things to do, he wondered if he should leave Barton to the search, but he knew the man would merely leave again and they would be no further forward.

At long last, Barton scratched his head. "Where's the outside correspondence gone?"

"What do you mean?"

"Anything to do with land that's not Black Hill. I usually shoved it in here." Barton tugged open a small drawer in the small desk next to the large cabinet. Cornelius had glanced through the contents of the drawer some time ago, but it consisted merely of old correspondence about other people's farming methods, most of it from the last century. He sighed in frustration as Barton pulled the handful out and rifled through it.

Then Barton pulled something out of the pile with an air of triumph and spun about to present it to Cornelius with a somewhat sarcastic bow.

Frowning, Cornelius snatched it from him.

It was indeed a copy of the same document Norrie had shown him, an agreement, transferring the top east field from Sir George Vale's ownership to Daubin's. It was signed by both parties and witnessed by Barton and Norrie.

Flabbergasted, Cornelius leaned back against the large desk. "Why on earth did my father do that?"

Barton shrugged. "Needed the money, I reckon, and we can get by without that field."

"Actually, it would have been damned useful," Cornelius snapped. "How did my father sign this?"

"I posted it to him as he asked, when the solicitors had drawn it up. He sent it back, and Mr. Daubin signed too."

Cornelius shook his head in irritation. "The amount he was paid for it is wildly below its value. What was he thinking of?"

Barton scratched his head. "Don't reckon he cared much for the old place. Never came home." *None of you did.* The words hung in the air, an unspoken rebuke.

"Thank you," Cornelius said with difficulty. "At least I know where we stand now."

It was only later, when he showed the document to Julius, that he wondered what the devil it had been doing among papers about implementing new agricultural methods.

THE ANNOYANCE WAS lost for a few days in trying to solve the mystery of the apparently wild horses careering over Black Hill at night and threatening the already shaky harvests. The twins had seen them two nights in a row. On the third, Julius took the matter in hand, and, having discovered the horses were in fact being driven by men, he injured his bad leg trying to capture one, who promptly escaped. Aubrey did manage to capture one of the horses, which wasn't wild at all, although neither was it well cared for. However, since that was the last incursion of the horses, Cornelius quickly lost interest again.

On Sunday, he went to church with the rest of the family except Julius. Cornelius did not always attend, but on this occasion he admitted to himself he wanted to see Lady Alice again. His poem about her remained in his chamber, untitled. He was uncertain about it, and he told himself that was why he wanted to see her again, to avoid any excessive sentimentality in his work.

He wondered what she would say if she read it. Would she laugh? Criticize his choice of words and form? Dismiss it as overly romantic drivel? Would she be flattered to be asked her opinion? Would she blush and look shy? Or storm at him about something trivial he had not noticed?

Smiling to himself as he entered the packed little church in Blackhaven, he saw her at once in the front pew reserved for the Earl of Braithwaite and his family. She was bending over a small child seated between herself and her sister, playing some finger game with him. It was yet another facet of her character, and she looked so unexpectedly sweet that his stomach seemed to turn over with more longing than lust…

No. It *was* lust. He had felt it at the ball too, when he held her in his arms for the waltz. And later, it had certainly been among the wild surge of emotions when she played the pianoforte.

Fortunately, she did not see him as he followed his siblings into a pew on the other side of the aisle. He sat on the end and, feeling the tingle of being observed, glanced across the aisle. Cecily Armstrong—Lady Morgan—smiled uncertainly and inclined her head in greeting. Cornelius nodded curtly and, with some relief, faced the front as the vicar emerged from the vestry.

Tristram Grant was a very decent man, unexpectedly young and dashing for his role, but there was no denying he brought in the congregation and generally entertained them too. His sermons always had a point, but it was made with a light touch and enough humor to make at least some of his flock think and act for the better rather than merely sink into shame beneath the burden of their sins.

Or, at least, that was how Cornelius usually felt. On this occasion he was too aware of Cecily a mere yard away from him. And of Lady Alice, happily oblivious with her beautiful, noble family.

It was a theme of much of his poetry—the huge gulfs that exist between people. He had never felt it so much as now, when the girl who would not marry a lowly steward sat so close to him, and the noble lady who deigned to argue so very far away…

He was glad to emerge from the church into fresh air, passing the Countess of Braithwaite and Mr. Winslow, the magistrate, who seemed to be discussing Julius's wretched horses.

Broodingly, Cornelius toed a stone in the path while he waited for his siblings to stop gossiping, though he was in no hurry to return to the carriage. Glancing up, he saw Lady Alice parting from another young lady, and on impulse he moved toward her. He wanted to speak to her again, although he had nothing to say.

"Cornelius."

He paused, blinking at the lady suddenly in his path, blocking his view of Alice Conway.

"Lady Morgan," he said, bowing. "Excuse me."

"Oh, Cornelius, wait," she pleaded. "I have so much to say to you."

Painful memory tugged at his heart. "I cannot imagine what," he said coldly.

"What is done is done. I cannot change that."

His lips twisted. "There is no need to state the obvious. I cannot imagine you mean me to understand that you would if you could."

A flush stained her cheeks. "There is no point. I merely wish to ask how you are."

"I am well, thank you. How are you?"

Instead of answering, she returned, "I hear you are stewarding your family's lands now."

"My brother's."

"Are you happy?"

"Deliriously," he said with savage flippancy. "Are you?"

As soon as the words were out, he saw that she was not. Beyond his own remembered pain, he finally saw hers. He did not want to get involved again. He did not want to revisit the ache of her marriage to another man. He wanted to draw around him the shield of his new life, the peace he had found at Black Hill without her.

And yet he could no more walk away from her pain than that of an injured animal.

"What is it?" he asked more gently. "Has something happened?"

Unshed tears filled her eyes. "Jack does not love me."

I could have told you that before you threw me over to marry him. Keeping the bitterness at bay, he said, "I'm sorry. I'm sure he does in his own way. How could he not love you?"

"Oh, Cornelius, I am so unhappy," she whispered.

A year ago—only a few months ago—this would have made him fiercely, angrily glad, so great was his hurt and sense of loss. He would have done anything for her, given up everything and run away with her. Now he was aware mostly of pity.

He took her elbow, turning her away from any watchers in the churchyard.

"Jack is not faithful and his mother despises me," Cecily blurted. Her eyes lifted to his in total misery. "I know now that I married the wrong man."

ALICE MIGHT NOT have seen Cornelius enter the church, occupied as she was with her small nephew, but she certainly noticed him taking his seat beside his family. Goodness, there were a lot of them, even without the imposing, one-eyed sea captain, Sir Julius. Alice's gaze ran over the stern-looking major who had danced with Helen, and then a slight, even more handsome, if somehow decadent, young man.

There were also three extremely beautiful ladies, including the widowed Mrs. Maitland, whom Alice vaguely remembered from an encounter in Hyde Park several years ago, and a ridiculously identical boy and girl of around fourteen or fifteen who could only be twins.

The family spilled over one row and onto the end of the next, where Cornelius sat. Across the aisle, a lady had fixed her gaze on his face.

Something sharp and sour clawed at Alice's stomach. Dear God, why had it never entered her head before that he was married? From his poems, he was clearly no stranger to the joys and pains of love…

Singing was one of her joys in the Sunday service, but today, she did so rather mechanically, and for once paid little attention to Mr. Grant's sermon. Had she lost Cornelius Vale before she had even won him?

The thought shocked her. He was not some prize in the town fair! And Alice had already decided she would never marry. Why was she even thinking of Cornelius Vale in that way? Just because he was also Simon Sacheverill.

I want to win his friendship, she told herself firmly, and that was certainly more comfortable, although again, as on the night of the ball, she remembered waltzing in his arms and how it had made her feel. How looking at him made her feel. Well, looking, the decorous touching of gloved hands, and the loose embrace of the waltz were all miles away from the intimacies of marriage.

She shuddered. She had no reason to care whether he was married or not. *She* never would be. In fact, only yesterday, she and Helen had taken a huge step toward the independence they had always dreamed of by secretly hiring the theatre in Whalen, the nearest town, in order to show Helen's paintings and hold an evening recital of Alice's music. *That* was where her future lay. If they could only go abroad, then they could be incognito, like Sacheverill, never upsetting their family as they made their own way in the world…

Still, as she followed her family down the aisle after the service, she refused to look in Cornelius's direction, though she could not resist casting a quick glance at the woman opposite him. She was fiddling with her prayer book and her gloves and didn't notice. But she was young, surely no more than two or three and twenty, and pretty, with smooth, perfect white skin and tragic, sad eyes.

Just the sort of woman to inspire love in a poet…

During her few words with the vicar, his wife, and his small, lively daughter, Alice was aware of the Vales emerging en masse and diverging to speak to different groups of people. And Cornelius was again speaking to the beautiful lady.

"Is that lady married to one of the Vales?" Alice asked Kate, the vicar's wife, who always knew everyone in Blackhaven.

"Oh, none of the Vale men are married. She is Lady Morgan, merely visiting so that her mother-in-law may take the waters. Her husband is Sir John Morgan—he has land in Yorkshire. Charming man, so far as I can recall." Kate, a former toast of the *ton* and darling of the scandal sheets, also knew everyone everywhere. "They do seem to be having a terribly intense conversation," she added.

Just then, Lady Morgan dropped a minute curtsey and hurried after an older lady stalking to the gate. Cornelius gazed at them for a moment, his face unreadable.

Suddenly, he turned his head, and Alice refused to look away. She nodded civilly, and he touched the brim of his hat. And then one of his sisters—Mrs. Maitland—took his arm, and Alice's attention was seized by an old friend glad to see her back in Blackhaven.

"I KNOW NOW that I married the wrong man. What can I do, Cornelius? I should not ask it of you, but I am desperate. Please help me."

His thoughts were in turmoil. Was Cecily asking him to run away with her? Or to fix her marriage? Whichever, he was fiercely glad she had asked. It felt like justification for his pain over the last two years. And yet he knew in his heart he could never play second fiddle, which was surely all he could ever be to Cecily.

No, she wanted his help with Sir John, that was all. After all, if you loved someone enough to marry them, surely that love did not truly vanish? His own aching heart testified to that.

The following day, Cecily's problems vanished to the back of his mind when he found a letter waiting for him at his solitary breakfast. It was crumpled and dirty, the scrawled direction almost illegible. It looked as if it had come from a battlefield rather than from his publisher in London.

The reason for that became more obvious when he broke the seal and read the date at the head of the letter. It had been written three months ago—round about the time, probably, that he had first met That Girl, the Lady Alice. His rueful smile froze.

He jumped to his feet roaring, *"What?"*

A maid and a manservant bolted into the room to see what the problem was. Ignoring them, Cornelius scrunched the letter in his hand and stormed off to the estate office at the back of the house, leaving his breakfast untouched.

"What the devil do I do now?" Throwing himself into the chair by his desk, he smoothed the letter out and read it again.

Galsworth, his publisher, wrote that Simon Sacheverill had been invited, by no less a personage than the Countess of Braithwaite, to read his poetry at a gathering at Braithwaite Castle in June. In fact, on Saturday! Since this event was bound to be one of the best attended outside the capital, it was, apparently, a wonderful opportunity for Sacheverill's career and his financial situation. His publisher had had no hesitation in accepting on his behalf.

No wonder Alice had seemed so bewildered by his determination to remain incognito. She must have known about this, that his true identity was about to be revealed to his family, his neighbors, the world in general.

Well, it won't be.

Pulling a sheet of paper toward him, he dipped his pen in ink and began to write.

Mr. Sacheverill presents his compliments and deepest respects to the Countess of Braithwaite.

While honored by her ladyship's flattering invitation to read at her party, which has only this day been made known to him, he must sadly decline on the grounds of prior commitments. Mr. Sacheverill therefore begs her ladyship's forgiveness and apologizes most profusely on behalf of himself and Mr. Galsworth for the misunderstanding.

He remains her most humble servant,
S. Sacheverill.

Satisfied, he replaced the pen in its stand, sanded the letter, folded it, and sealed it with a plain splash of wax. After inscribing the countess's direction on the front, he seized his hat, stuffed the letter in his pocket, and set off for the stables.

Chapter Five

"OH, DRAT THE man!" Eleanor, Countess of Braithwaite, exclaimed at luncheon, hurling a short note onto the table.

Alice exchanged glances with Helen, for this was an unusual show of temper.

"Which man in particular?" inquired their mother, reaching for her soup spoon.

"Simon wretched Sacheverill. He has just cried off in the curtest way with the feeblest of excuses, and now I shall have to eat humble pie before all those superior town hostesses who claimed he would never come to such a provincial, out-of-the-way event as our garden party, when he never chose to grace one drawing room in London. It seems they were right."

Incensed, Alice reached across the table, ignoring her mother's tuts of disapproval, and picked up the offending letter.

"How dare he?" Alice exclaimed. "Prior commitment indeed! I shall give him a piece of my mind that he shan't forget in a hurry."

"How?" asked Eleanor with a rueful smile. "There is no address to write to."

"I shall send it via his publisher, as you did."

"What is the point if it takes three months for Mr. Galsworth to send it on? Perhaps Mr. Sacheverill lives abroad."

He lives half an hour's ride from here! Alice fumed to herself. How could he let Eleanor down like this? She was so angry she had to bite her tongue to prevent herself blurting out the truth about him. No wonder he had never reacted to her remarks about revealing his identity soon enough—he had never had any intentions of coming. Why the devil could he not have simply said so in the first place?

Somehow, she got through the meal without any further outbursts, although she caught Helen looking at her curiously. Well, Helen had clearly been harboring her own secrets of late, too. The closeness of childhood had gone, which was another sadness in Alice's heart, though at least they had their event in Whalen together, and after that, who knew? She had no time to worry about Helen right now, when every instinct was driving her to Black Hill to tear the contemptible Cornelius Vale to shreds.

Accordingly, as soon as luncheon was over, she excused her-self, sent words to the stables to saddle her horse, and changed into her riding habit. She had three of those now, one old and comfortable, two charming and fashionable, which had been purchased for her Season. She had merely grabbed the first one she saw. Then, catching sight of herself in the glass as she stormed past to the door, she saw how becoming it was and raged all over again in case the popinjay imagined she had dressed for him.

Well, she would waste no more time changing. Her clothing hardly mattered. She could shout at the selfish, shiftless beast in any costume she chose.

She rode hard most of the way to Black Hill, and inevitably the exercise cooled her temper to some degree. Since no one came forward to take her horse, she rode around the side of the rather beautiful house in search of the stables.

"Where might I find Mr. Cornelius Vale at this hour?" she asked the one-armed groom who emerged from the stable building, a brush in his hand.

"Believe he was going to the hill cottages," the groom said, waving his hand vaguely toward the hill behind the house. "If he's done with them, he's probably at the lower meadow." He peered at her. "I'll find him for you, and you can wait at the house. One of the ladies is always at home."

"Thank you, that won't be necessary," she replied, and kicked her horse back into motion.

She rode toward the hill, wondering with a resurgence of ire if she would have to waste the entire afternoon looking for him.

In fact, she found him at the first of the row of cottages—crouched on the roof, hatless and coatless, and shouting down to someone below.

"Ha!" he announced with clear satisfaction, and seemed at last to become aware of her approach, for he turned his head toward her and immediately slid down the short, sloping roof. As if he had planned it, he grasped the ladder and slid most of the way down that too, arriving in front of her horse breathless and smeared with dirt. Yet the air seemed to vanish from her lungs. And when his distant yet intense eyes began to smile…

Infuriated all over again by her inexplicable reaction to this man, she snarled, "A word, if you please, Mr. Vale."

"Will you come down?" he asked. "Or shall I come up?"

She slid from the saddle before he could move to help her and, grasping the reins, stalked off the way she had come. The horse allowed himself to be led.

"Say on," Cornelius invited her, materializing on her other side, "before you burst."

She halted in fresh fury at his flippancy and glared up at him. "Oh, I *will*! How dare you break your word to my sister-in-law? How *dare* you write her such a curt, cruel, lying letter to save yourself a mere moment of effort and discomfort? You are entirely despicable!"

He blinked. His eyes had become blank. The man was too used to hiding. "Clearly," he drawled, although color had begun to seep along the blade of his cheekbone. "Though I fail to see how it concerns you."

"Because Eleanor is a sweet and rather wonderful person who does not deserve to be treated with such contempt!" Alice raged. "She was not brought up to this position, you know—she had to learn it from nothing and suffer the condescension of lesser people who imagine their gentle upbringing entitles them to look down on hers. And she has been *wonderful* to all of us, a true, kind sister to Maria and Helen and me, dealing with our difficult mother, and working so hard to be the countess she feels Gervaise needs. All under the scrutiny of the people who want her to fail. And *you* could not allow her one tiny social triumph! They will laugh behind their hands at the poor, deluded creature, just because *you* lack the courage your rotten poems rant about!"

At some point, the rain had come on, soft and drizzly. As though it had washed all the color out of Cornelius's face, his skin looked white, even his lips.

"Is anyone brave all the time?" he said. "Are you?"

Her stomach tightened unbearably. "We are not talking about me!"

"*We* are not talking about anyone. *You* are criticizing me, loudly and at length. But if you wish to make this more of a discussion, allow me to ask if it is only your birth that makes it acceptable for you to slight *my* sisters?"

"Slight your sisters?" she repeated, pulled back from her own righteous anger.

"Is it not more courteous to call at the house, even if only to leave your card, than to pursue me over hill and dell just to vent your spleen?"

"Vent my—"

"You might well have hurt their feelings," he went on relentlessly. "But then, they are not countesses nor related to you, so perhaps they do not matter."

She stared at him, trying not to let her jaw drop. "Of course they matter! I did not mean—"

"Or perhaps you were afraid?"

"Afraid of your sisters? Why on earth…?"

"Of me, then?"

Her breath vanished. She could not even speak, but something must have changed in her eyes, for his own suddenly blazed, and he stepped so close she could smell him. Soap and sweat and rain. Indescribably masculine. She was suffocating—not with fear, as usually happened when a man came too close, but with the sudden desire to know, to feel, what it would be like with *his* mouth crushing hers. A shocking fantasy that took her completely by surprise.

It wasn't the same situation at all. Yet just as that vile first time a man had invaded her boundaries, she had no protection, no words, no strength. So she laughed in his face, turned, and leapt for the stirrup. She half expected him to seize her, but when she wheeled the snorting horse around, he had not moved.

"Goodbye, Mr. Sacheverill," she mocked him, and rode back down the hill.

She didn't know whether to scream, shout, or sing away the tension in her, for amidst her anger and the jolt of fear had come that insidious glow, that surge of imagination and hunger, just because he had been so close and because she had seen *that* in his eyes.

Damn him…

If she had not been holding the reins, she would have hugged herself. Distraction came as she rode past the house and paused.

He was right—the least she could do was call on his sisters. She did not wish to slight any of them. Turning the horse's head, she rode past a stretch of formal garden to the drive.

Dismounting, she tied the reins to a small tree and marched up to the front door. A manservant without livery opened it almost at once.

Alice dragged a somewhat tattered visiting card from the pocket of her habit, but before she could speak, a female voice from inside called, "Who is it, Dan?"

Dan stood aside, and a lady in the entrance hall, her eyes

widening with surprise, hurried forward.

"I'm Alice Conway," Alice said hastily. "I was just about to leave my card—"

"Won't you stay for tea? My sisters are out, and I would enjoy the company."

Alice wrinkled her nose. "I have been out riding, as you see, and I smell horribly of horse."

"I like horses," the lady said, smiling.

Alice liked that she made no apology for her own workaday dress. Visitors had to accept her on her own terms. She had one of those strong-featured faces that don't immediately seem pretty, until you looked more closely. Helen would want to paint her like this, in an old, darned gown, busy about the house.

"Do come in. I'm Delilah Vale. I suspect you met some of my siblings at the assembly ball last week."

"I did." Alice followed her across the hall to a light, pleasant drawing room with, she was glad to see, a pianoforte. "In fact, I danced with your brother. And we met Mrs. Maitland in London some years ago. My sister and I were feeding the ducks, and she was very kind to us and our poor governess."

Delilah waved her to a choice of chairs grouped for the best view out of the window, and then sat herself. Despite what Cornelius had told Alice, her hostess did not appear to lack confidence or expect to be slighted.

"So, which of my brothers did you dance with?" Delilah asked before any awkward silence could begin.

"Mr. Cornelius Vale." Alice willed the rising blush away.

"Ah, you must be the one Lucy noted. She was afraid he would go on about crop rotation."

"He never mentioned the subject," Alice said. "I found him a delightful waltz partner."

To her surprise, Delilah's eyes softened. "Oh good," she murmured, and changed the subject. "What a pity Felicia has gone into Blackhaven with Lucy. I'm not sure where the others are. Cornelius is out on the land somewhere, of course."

"I met him when I was riding," Alice said casually. "He seemed to be repairing a cottage roof."

"I'm not surprised. He turns his hand to most things. To be frank, there is so much to do on the estate that if the matter is urgent, he often refuses to wait for carpenters or builders or other. He works from dawn until pretty near dusk most days. Roderick and Lawrence help where they can, but he is the one who knows the land. He whisks through it like a whirlwind, issuing orders as he shovels, digs, and hammers. Ah, here is tea."

The manservant appeared carrying a heavy tray. Helped by a pretty maid, he set out the tea things, with delicious-smelling scones and cakes.

Delilah presented a cup of tea to Alice. "To be honest, we would be lost without Cornel. His experience and training have been a godsend to us. When Julius decided to come home, he had no idea how neglected the place had been. I was shocked. The steward my father appointed had apparently grown too infirm and muddled, though Julius says he should have come home years before to look the place over."

"I believe you lived abroad with your father for much of your life," Alice said. "That must have been exciting."

"Too exciting sometimes! But we are glad to be home at last, and all together for the very first time. Julius had already gone to sea by the time the twins were born." She paused. "You have not met the twins?"

"Not yet. Though I believe you are all coming to the garden party on Saturday."

"We're looking forward to it."

Even Cornelius? She did not ask it aloud, and in any case, she already knew the answer.

WHEN ALICE RODE away, Cornelius stared after her, awash with anger and irritation—That Girl was back with a vengeance—but also with shame and regret. And he could not help the triumphant drumming of his heart, because behind whatever fear he had touched, she was not indifferent to him. He had seen it in her desperate eyes, in the twitch of her lovely mouth and the pulse that beat at the base of her slender throat, when he had stood so close to her he could smell the perfume of her hair, her skin. Close enough to kiss her.

Was that what she feared? Did she feel it, too, this damnable tug of attraction that neither of them wanted?

Hell, it was more than a tug. He wanted her so badly she filled his waking thoughts as even Cecily never had. Sometimes, she stormed into his dreams…

There is nothing remotely sweet or gentle about this feeling, he told himself savagely as he strode back to the cottage. It was all instinctive and raw and furious, like her… Such passion, such strength of feeling. He longed to distill it into words and rhythms, but mostly he yearned to taste it.

Obsession. I can write my way out of it.

He would have to, because living with it would be damnably hard.

He threw himself into work for the rest of the afternoon, until, mindful of the dinner party Lucy and Felicia were arranging in order to bring Antonia Macy, Julius's one-time betrothed, once more into his life. Cornelius, who suspected more from his brother's manner than anything else that she was already back in his life, had promised to be present at the dinner, to which one Lord Linfield and his sister Miss Talbot had also been invited.

Having returned his tired horse to the stable, Cornelius strode toward the house and came upon Smith—the laborer foisted on to him by Braithwaite—standing too close to Betsy, the pretty parlor maid who was smiling up at him and smacking his hand at the same time. Catching sight of Cornelius, they sprang apart, but a chord had already struck.

He stopped beside them, frowning at Betsy. Smith seemed

about to say something, perhaps to insist he was the one distracting her, so Cornelius charged in quickly.

"You're Fred Gaffney's daughter, aren't you, Betsy?"

"I am, sir," she said, both surprise and suspicion clear in her eyes. Perhaps she feared being dismissed for the sins of her family.

"He's Mr. Daubin's tenant over at Cloverfield?"

"That's right. I hope Mr. Daubin's not complaining again, 'cause Dad's paid his rent all right and tight."

"Good," Cornelius said. He shifted to the other foot. "Is your father happy in his tenancy? Are the other Cloverfield tenants?"

Smith's eyes were fixed to Cornelius's face. Betsy looked frightened like a trapped deer.

Cornelius smiled. "Don't look so panicked. I'm asking you in confidence because—between ourselves—I'm afraid something isn't right at Cloverfield. Is Mr. Daubin a good landlord?"

Betsy's gaze flew to Smith's.

"No," Smith said bluntly. "He doesn't understand the people or the land. He treats them like his mill machines and tries to throw them out when they're not working. Only he doesn't have the knowledge to repair them."

Damning. But Cornelius, who had perceived when he first surveyed all the land in the area that Cloverfield could be better farmed, moved on. "Do you remember when he bought the top field from my father?"

"Must be five years ago now," Betsy said. "That's when he moved the sheep there. I thought Mr. Barton would raise a fuss, but he just said the field was Mr. Daubin's now. So my dad says, though he had it from his cronies in the tavern. Excuse me, sir, I got to get back to my work, and so does W—Smith!"

Thoughtful but not much wiser, Cornelius went on into the house through the back door, and encountered Delilah coming out of the kitchen.

"They're here," his sister told him without enthusiasm. "Mrs. Macy and the Linfields. Felicia and the twins are with them. I'm just going to change. You had better do the same!"

As they climbed the back staircase, Delilah said, "I had a morning caller—Lady Alice Conway, no less."

"Did you?" He could not help staring at her in surprise. "What did she want?"

"She was just out riding, apparently, and after encountering you at the Hill cottages, she remembered meeting Fliss and Lucy at the ball. And you, apparently."

Suspicion almost choked him. He had kept his secret so long that if he ever revealed it, he wanted it to be in his own way, on his own terms. Not like this, a vengeful revelation caused by his own mistakes.

"What did she say about me?" he demanded with too much aggression.

Delilah looked amused. "That you danced delightfully. And did you often do the tenants' roof repairs yourself?"

Laughter shook him.

"I told her you did," Delilah went on, "because there was so much needed doing to everything. I like her," she added, floating off to her chamber and leaving Cornelius to stumble into his.

He was wrong. Who had he been trying to fool? Only himself. God help him, Alice *was* sweet. Quick to anger, perhaps, and sharp-tongued, but also quick to forgive, to rectify her mistakes, and generous enough to apologize, as she had to him at the ball. Free of his own anger, he could recognize her gentleness as well as the fierceness of her protection of her family. And her kindness. Delilah, always aware of her illegitimate birth, was both lonely and insecure, but she liked Alice.

I like Alice.

Chapter Six

MOST OF ALICE'S time was spent practicing for her recitals at the Whalen theatre and the castle garden party. In fact, the latter provided her cover for the former, and if she occasionally felt guilty about scolding Cornelius Vale for his dishonesty when her own was rife, she kept it to herself.

Helen was also busy, sorting her paintings and sketches and deciding which to show. She had completed three particularly beautiful pictures of the nearby ruined abbey, two of which were new—one under glowering skies with a mysterious figure poised in front of it, the other by moonlight. Deliberately, Alice did not ask about the painted figure or when she had seen the abbey by moonlight. It hurt that Helen was keeping such secrets from her, but then, she did not want to reveal her own secrets either. For Helen's safety, though, Alice must keep a closer eye on her...

Only after their sister Maria had arrived, and her husband Michael escorted them to Miss Talbot's "at home" at the Blackhaven Hotel, did Alice begin to guess Helen's secret. It had something to do with Cornelius's older brother, the dashing Major Vale. Helen followed him with her eyes, and whenever her attention was distracted, the major gazed at her. Could Helen be having secret moonlight assignations with him?

Or was Alice merely obsessed with the Vales herself? Her heart had lurched with excitement when Sir Julius entered the room, closely followed by the major and the ridiculously handsome Aubrey, who looked like a slightly sulky, very naughty fallen angel. But Cornelius was not with them.

Alice had wanted to apologize to him. Again. She still thought he should have honored his commitment to Eleanor, and that he should be honest with his family. But she had been unnecessarily strident. He always brought out the worst in her for some reason. She also felt guilty because at Black Hill House, Delilah had told her, "Cornelius is not a great man for Society. He is too shy."

Shyness was not something Alice suffered from. But she could see the difference between writing poetry that bared the soul and reading it aloud to a crowd. For a man as private as Cornelius, that would be excruciating. Only... Why had he agreed in the first place?

Her older sisters, Frances and Serena, arrived before the garden party, complete with husbands and small children, and as always when they were all together, excitement levels in the castle soared. Mama even forgot her displeasure with Alice for rejecting the Duke of Atherstone.

"So the Vales are back at Black Hill?" Frances said in the drawing room on the first evening of her return.

"Captain Sir Julius Vale has inherited, and brought all his siblings with him," Gervaise said.

"All?" Serena said, amused. "How many are there?"

"Nine," said Helen.

Mama pursed her lips. "They are not all legitimate. But they are all foisted on Society as though they were equals."

"Well, it is hardly their fault," Frances said.

"Is Cornelius illegitimate?" Alice blurted, and everyone turned to gaze at her in surprise or, in Mama's case, disapproval. Heat crept into her face. "I only ask because he seems to be the steward at Black Hill."

"He is," Gervaise said. "It was the profession he trained for—very knowledgeable fellow, too. Which is fortunate, because he has his work cut out for him at Black Hill. The man Sir George left in charge seemed to do nothing. But no, his birth is perfectly respectable. I believe it is the eldest daughter and the youngest two who were born, as they say, on the wrong side of the blanket."

"Miss Delilah Vale," Alice remarked. "I like her."

"Mrs. Maitland is a good woman," Mama pronounced.

"They are a charming family," Eleanor said. "I spoke to the twins at church, and they are most amusing. They will all be at the garden party." She scowled. "Although Simon Sacheverill will not."

However, the following morning, a small parcel was delivered to the castle, addressed to the Countess of Braithwaite. She opened it at breakfast to discover a leather-bound volume of Sacheverill's poetry. The poet had respectfully inscribed it to her on the flyleaf, and a note fluttered out onto the table.

Alice had to stop herself reaching for it, but then Eleanor read it aloud to them and Alice felt a lump rise into her throat. This was a much more personal letter than the original refusal—written in the first person, to begin with—and expressed his deep regrets for the miscommunication between himself and his publisher. Accepting the blame, he apologized for letting her ladyship down and wished her a happy and successful party, which he was most saddened to miss.

"Well, that is a little more gracious," Helen allowed.

It was, and for Eleanor it made a huge difference that she was not despised. Alice, touched and gratified that her words had influenced Cornelius, wanted to rush over to Black Hill and thank him, but she knew instinctively he did not want that. She must put him from her mind, for he was unlikely to come to the garden party with the rest of his family, and concentrate on her recitals and all the arrangements for the secret concert and exhibition at Whalen.

She was also looking forward to hearing again the Scottish pianist, Frederick Baird, who, already famous in Edinburgh, had so impressed Alice in London. Travelling north to Blackhaven, she had been delighted to discover him staying at the same inn one night, and had induced Gervaise and Eleanor to invite him to play at the garden party.

Although she felt rather like a juggler with too many balls in the air to catch, she remembered to be more observant of Helen, even lying awake too long at night to listen for any sound of her creeping out on secret assignations. Who would hurt gentle Helen? The very thought made her shudder. Alice was only comforted by the knowledge that her kind and outwardly biddable sister possessed an inner steel as well as a sound brain.

Guests also began to arrive at the castle to stay, mostly old friends of the family like the Daxtons, although with a scattering of new. Alice, reminded of the London Season, hid her unease, although she did once ask Maria, "Do you know if the Duke of Atherstone is coming?"

She dared not ask Eleanor or Mama in case they assumed she wanted him there.

"I believe he is coming to the ball," Maria said, searching her face. "I don't know if he will stay at the castle, though, since his plans are always uncertain. You don't like him, do you?"

"No," Alice said flatly.

What with guests at the castle and local morning callers, the day before the garden party, it was almost impossible to find time to practice or arrange the things they had to before the Whalen theatre adventure, which was to be the day after.

Fortunately, Mama was not present when Mr. Daubin and his son called.

Mr. Daubin, the "new" owner of Cloverfield, had made his fortune in cotton mills, so he was not a gentleman by birth. Mama might condescend to invite him to parties she considered public, but she certainly would not have welcomed him to her drawing room. Eleanor, kinder and less haughty, would not send him away.

He was announced along with his son, Mr. Darcy Daubin. The latter turned out to be quite stunning. With his tall, willowy frame, blond good looks, and graceful speech and manners, he appeared to be of an entirely different family—nay, a different species!—to his father.

"Oh my," sighed Willa, Lady Daxton, with such drole faintness that, beside her, Alice giggled.

Whether it was Willa's sigh or Alice's laughter, they immediately drew the beautiful creature's attention. His smile was amiable, his eyes unexpectedly predatory for a man so apparently effete. His bow to the room in general was a model of elegance compared with his stocky father's perfunctory jerk.

Welcoming them, Eleanor gave her hand to each gentleman. Mr. Daubin looked gratified. Darcy bowed so low over her fingers that Alice thought he would kiss them.

"Who…?" Willa murmured to Alice. Sharing a sense of humor and an appreciation of the ridiculous, they had become friends during the Season when the Daxtons had made a brief visit to London.

"Neighbor," Alice replied, low. "He's in trade—cotton mills, I think. I've never met the son before." His looks alone would have the entire town buzzing around him like bees to a honey pot.

Eleanor, aware of the elder Mr. Daubin's lack of grace, sat beside them and poured them tea. But five minutes later, Alice was surprised to be called over to join them.

"Do you know Mr. Daubin, Alice? And this is his son, Mr. Darcy Daubin. Gentlemen, my sister-in-law, Lady Alice Conway, who is also a poetry lover. Mr. Darcy Daubin is a poet."

He looked like one, Alice thought, with his too-long flyaway hair and his pale coat and lace cuffs. There was even lace trimming on his carelessly knotted necktie. A little too studiedly careless, in Alice's cynical opinion, though she made impressed noises.

"I heard the great Sacheverill has let you down," Darcy said. "And I wondered if I might help as a poor substitute for the famous man."

"*In*famous man, if he can't keep his promises," Mr. Daubin

interjected.

"One does not know the circumstances," Darcy said with more generosity.

"He wrote a very kind letter with a gift," Alice said. "We have decided that my sister, Helen, will read some of his poems instead. And we should be very glad to have you read some of your own work afterward, if that is agreeable to you?"

"I am honored," Darcy said humbly. "May I hope that you will hear them?"

"Yes, and I shall hope so also," Alice said. The man unnerved her slightly, so good-looking and playing his role so well, almost like a child, except for those strange, avid eyes. He could only have been two or three and twenty.

Fortunately, he knew the rules of morning calls and ushered his father away after only a few more minutes.

"What an extraordinarily beautiful young man," Willa remarked.

"Do you think so?" Eleanor sounded surprised. "But then, you have not met Aubrey Vale yet!"

Alice could not see that either. On looks alone, she preferred Cornelius to either of them.

"WELL, THAT WENT very well," James Daubin said smugly to his son as their carriage set off in the direction of Cloverfield. "I don't mind telling you, I expected the old witch to deny us."

"You did tell me," Darcy pointed out. "Several times. Fortunately, the old witch was not in evidence. And the young countess is quite ravishing, is she not?"

His father looked alarmed, which amused Darcy. "You'll not touch that particular potato—you'd ruin us all."

Darcy smirked. "I could have her eating out of my hand if I chose. And her favor will assuredly be useful, but I have quite another potato in mind."

"What potato?" his father demanded. "I thought we went to get you invited to the damned party."

"And I have been. Which provides access to my—er…tuber of choice."

"Don't get above yourself," his father growled. "You'll end up with egg on your face. And mine."

"Don't be an old woman," Darcy said. "Didn't you see the way they looked at me?"

"I don't deny you're a pretty picture, but so's the earl, and if you imagine—"

"I want only approval from the countess. It's Lady Alice I shall have."

His father whitened. "Dear God, you cannot deflower a noble girl!"

Darcy laughed. "Oh, straighten your breeches, Papa, I mean to marry the girl." *Eventually.*

How does a woman retain—or recover—the love of her straying husband?

Cecily Morgan's problems did not trouble Cornelius's mind as often as they should, considering he had promised to do his best to help her. Finally, guiltily, he forced himself to consider the matter and realized he needed help.

At the last moment, he stopped himself from asking Felicia, whose own husband, apparently, had been far from faithful. Cornelius, busy with his own life far from London and any of his other siblings, had been unaware of this fact until after Maitland died, when the scoundrel could no longer be beaten, coerced, or even reviled.

The day before the garden party at the castle, it struck Cornelius that Cecily might well be present. Only a few months ago, this would have loomed so large in his life that he would have been able to think of little else. Now, he realized only that, despite his assurances to her, he had no solution to offer and would inevitably let down her hopes.

Of course, he was the last person who should be advising Cecily on the subject of marriage—he had not even been able to hold her love—and he had no idea how to keep his rash promise.

After dinner that night, as his family wandered out of the dining room, he finally broached the subject in a roundabout way with Delilah, his eldest sister, who was both observant and wise. But Delilah merely said, "Sounds as if she shouldn't have married him in the first place."

Which was so much Cornelius's own view that he failed to press further. Instead, approaching from a different angle, he spoke to Julius later in the evening.

In fact, he was worried about Julius, who, after the ball, had begun to liven into the old Julius that Cornelius remembered from childhood. However, he now seemed positively aloof with tension. So Cornelius spoke vaguely of Cecily's problem without naming her.

"Would *you* be a faithful husband, Jules?" he asked.

"No point in being married otherwise," Julius retorted so sharply that Cornelius backed away again.

Matters did not proceed well for Julius, he guessed, with Antonia Macy, the lady from his past who had come to dinner one night and sheltered from a sudden, raging storm. He was happy to listen if Julius wanted to talk, but he would have died rather than pry. He wished quite intensely for Julius's happiness, and he rather liked Antonia. Importantly, she had also been approved by Lucy, who had the uncanny knack of accurately reading everyone's character. On the other hand, Delilah seemed to *dis*like her, and she was aware of more about the couple's past.

Cornelius knew better than to get involved. In truth, he had no desire to touch Cecily's marriage either. More than two years ago, Cecily had rejected him for his employer, and, unable to live so close to that, he had moved to a different position.

But he had not parted from Sir John Morgan on bad terms. On the contrary, Morgan had given him glowing testimonials to take to his new employer. Cornelius's best bet was to wait for him to arrive in Blackhaven and speak to him, man to man, explaining how he was hurting Cecily by his behavior. That way, Cornelius would have discharged his duty to Cecily and, once they left, never have to speak to either of them again.

Which conveniently left Cornelius free for now to brood over his own obsession with Alice. *Lady* Alice, whom he would definitely see tomorrow, if only from a distance. In response to what she had told him about the young countess, he'd sent the gift of his book and a much kinder letter, which he hoped would make up for Sacheverill's absence. If only the poor lady knew how much less awkward it would be than his presence!

On his way upstairs to bed, he encountered the twins sitting on their favorite step. "I thought you went to bed half an hour ago."

"We're going," Lawrence assured him. "Are you truly going to the garden party at the castle tomorrow?"

"If nothing prevents me."

"I can't wait to see the castle," Leona enthused. "And I'm so glad you will be there."

Cornelius regarded her with suspicion. "Why?"

"Because you don't normally have any fun."

"I do. Sadly, I just don't enjoy parties."

"Then why are you going to this one?" Lawrence asked.

Cornelius closed his mouth, blinked, and then laughed. "Damned if I know," he said, and climbed over the twins to the landing.

Chapter Seven

THE VALES WERE among the first to arrive at the garden party. Alice almost fainted, for among them, strolling across the lawn toward her, flanked by the twins, was Cornelius.

He wore smart morning dress—buff pantaloons and a blue coat. It must have been the unexpectedness of his presence that made her tremble. There could be no other reason. Somehow, she forced herself to keep walking.

"Mr. Vale," she said, pausing to drop a slight curtsey. "What a pleasant surprise."

"Why?" the girl twin asked.

"You two are the surprise," Cornelius said. "To most of the world. Lady Alice, allow me to present my brother and sister, Lawrence and Leona Vale. Twins, Lady Alice Conway, the earl's sister."

The twins, who each had eyes as intense as Cornelius's but considerably more friendly, beamed at her while they bowed and curtseyed with unexpected grace.

"Will you excuse us?" Lawrence asked. "The countess is waving to us."

Eleanor was indeed waving from the pall mall lawn, where she was surrounded by other children.

"Of course," Alice agreed, and the twins dashed off.

"They're very excited," Cornelius said. "They don't really

know anyone of their own age in Blackhaven."

"They will after today," Alice said. She swallowed. "I am glad you came. Does it mean you will read after all?"

"No, it means I shall listen."

"Still incognito," she said ruefully. "Which is your right. I'm sorry I lost my temper. I had no right to say what I did."

"Nor did I."

Remembering only too clearly what he had said—and how close he had been when he said it—heat seeped into her cheeks. But honesty conquered embarrassment.

"No, you were right. I should have called at the house. I have got into the habit of doing just what I like under the mask of being 'original.' I did not think of duty, or your sisters' feelings, only my own determination to tell you off. Again."

"Well, you were right about that, too."

"Thank you for sending the book to Eleanor. It means a lot to her."

He shook his head. "That is what I cannot understand. That she would care so much never entered my mind."

She regarded him curiously. Although he would defend his rights—particularly to privacy—and he was not remotely overawed by rank, there was no arrogance about the man.

"Pride is not one of your sins, is it?"

He shrugged. "I have done nothing to be particularly proud of."

"Your poetry, for one."

His smile was crooked. "That is something I cannot help. It's only words, and if people like them, I am glad. They make no difference."

She gazed at him in consternation. He truly believed what he said. "You are wrong."

"My dear, your brother is likely to be a government minister soon, possibly even prime minister one day. *My* brother is a hero of Trafalgar and Lord knows how many other victories since. My other brother has been mentioned in military dispatches several times and honored for his bravery at Waterloo. In the grand scheme of things, scrawling a few lines of verse and telling a few farmers what to do really does not compare."

They had walked straight past the door into the great hall, where people were gathering around a table of refreshments. Alice did not mind, leading him onward toward the formal gardens.

"Actually," she said, "your scrawled verses make a big difference to the lives of individuals. There may not be mass glory, but it is the small things that make the difference to most people. As for managing the land, you do rather more than order about a few farmers. Improving the yield of the land benefits all of us. It is a battle in its own right. To say nothing of the battle against hunger and poverty."

His startled gaze met hers. "You have a grandiose view of what I do."

"No, you merely suffer from overachieving brothers. We cannot all be famous heroes or leaders of entire countries, but I don't believe it is they who make the real difference. It is the things you call insignificant, like words and art and music, that bring about important changes, that nurture the people and make men and nations great."

His eyes widened and he slowly began to smile. "You have thought about this a good deal."

"Of course," she said airily. "I have to justify my own ambitions. But there is truth there all the same."

"Perhaps there is. Even if there is not, thank you for saying it."

Warmth seeped around her heart as they walked on. She wished he would offer his arm. She wanted the physical intimacy of touching him, of feeling the muscle and sinew rippling beneath his coat sleeve. What was the matter with her?

SHE NEVER FAILED to surprise Cornelius. He had not expected so passionate a defense, nor to find his view of himself adjusting accordingly. It was certainly true that turning Black Hill back into profitable land would save his family from ruin, and that he was the only one who could do it without a fat salary. That his poetry was good enough to change the world, he regarded with rather more skepticism. But if she liked it enough to say so, well, that sparked his soul with pleasure.

"Oh, goodness," she exclaimed suddenly. "It is almost time to begin the poetry. Come and see if it makes a difference to hear Helen reciting. She has a beautiful voice and reads with feeling."

Cornelius tried not to cringe. He didn't want to hear his words spoken, let alone with overt sentimentality. However, since he wished to remain with Alice, he accompanied her back to the great hall, where he was given a choice of wine or punch and greeted by Lady Helen.

By then, a shower of rain had driven most of the adults inside. Many were examining the paintings in the gallery above or milling in conversation while a trio of musicians played near the shining pianoforte.

"Will you play?" he asked Alice.

"She had better," Helen said severely. She cast a quick glance around the hall as though looking for someone in particular. "I'm going to the poetry room to prepare."

Cornelius followed the sisters into a passage, off which were several smaller salons. Entering the first, Lady Helen went straight to the lectern, where a familiar leather-bound book had been left open, several bookmarks sticking out.

"Simon Sacheverill sent it as a gift to our sister-in-law," Helen said, "because he could not come to read himself. I thought that was a kind touch. Do you like his poetry, Mr. Vale?"

"I enjoy poetry," Cornelius said awkwardly.

Alice snorted and picked up a book from the nearby table beside a list of readings and readers. "What is this?"

Helen giggled. "Look."

"A collection of poetry by Darcy D'Aubin," Alice read incredulously. "D'Aubin?"

"What is the joke?" asked Cornelius, who had never heard of the man. "Is he not good?"

"He's the son of Jimmy Daubin, the mill owner," Alice said drily. "I didn't know he had been published, but I would think a lot more of him if he didn't try to gentrify his name."

"Many writers have pen names," Cornelius said mildly.

"Perhaps, but this one does not seek privacy." She flipped through the pages.

"This is the same Daubin of Cloverfield?" Cornelius said.

"His only son, I believe," Helen said.

"I did not even know he had a son."

"And what a son he is," Alice said mischievously. "Prepare to be dazzled."

Since other people were drifting into the room, eager to speak to Alice and Helen, Cornelius moved to the far corner, where the light was gloomiest, and leaned his shoulder against the wall. Secretly, he hoped Alice would come and sit in the chair beside him, but she stayed near Helen as the room filled and the countess could be heard announcing that the poetry readings were about to begin.

He could see that Helen was nervous about reading, and Alice's support soothed her. He liked her kindness, brusque though it often was. What was it about her that so fascinated him? Surely he was old enough and certainly wise enough to know better. But he liked her dark, subtle beauty, her feminine curves beneath the flowing Grecian dress she wore. He remembered the scent of her as if she pressed against him…

A lady inclined her head to him, breaking the spell of his daydream. In fact, he came back to earth with a bump, for the lady was Cecily Morgan and with her was old Lady Morgan, the spiteful old besom. If she saw Cornelius, she gave no sign of it, so he bowed only to Cecily. He could not see Sir John, who was no doubt still in London or elsewhere dallying with his mistress.

For a moment, the bitterness returned. Why had Cecily not married Cornelius, as he had begged her? He would have been faithful to her…

But would he have been *happy* with her?

He almost felt guilty for wondering. He had carried her so long in his heart as a mere idea, he had never realized before that, whilst he had often been lonely, he didn't actually miss *her*.

Stupidly, he missed Alice, though they were nothing to each other and never would be.

Lady Helen's voice intruded into his thoughts, introducing the poem by Simon Sacheverill. Anxiety clawed at his stomach. He had never been forced before to watch other people's reactions to his work, and he was ready to hide himself in shame.

By ill chance, she read the lament he had written for Cecily when he realized he had lost her forever. He wanted to stick his fingers in his ears, and yet he found himself listening intently, for the poem still struck a chord in him. He pitied the poor man who suffered such torments.

Everyone did. With amazement, he watched the emotions glide over anguished faces, saw a few surreptitious handkerchiefs dabbing at watering eyes. And then he saw that Helen understood too. She read with feeling, but not a whit of sentimentality. Her voice changed subtly between the humor and the tragedy, grew soft and husky as if her throat had closed up.

So had Cornelius's. He was no longer gazing at Helen but at Alice, who sat with her face turned away from him, but he could still see her profile, the fluttering of her lashes as she blinked rapidly, fighting emotion, confusion…

As was he.

Everything he had ever written, everything he had ever felt, was about *her*.

Suddenly she turned her head, looking directly at him, her eyes full and yet blazing with laughter as she shot a glance toward the doorway. He followed her gaze to a fair, willowy man in an ivory coat, with flowing lace at his cuffs and his throat.

Darcy D'Aubin, I presume. Dazzling, indeed.

He caught Alice's eye once more and grinned.

"THIS IS GETTING complicated," Lawrence murmured to Leona, realizing how many of his siblings' lives they were now interfering with.

"Do you think we should stop?"

Lawrence grinned. "No."

Although they were having a whale of a time and had already made several new friends—including Rosa Benedict, who was the daughter of a colonel turned botanist, a small German prince, and a whole gaggle of Gaunts and Winslows—they slipped away without regret. Family came first, and someone had to look after their clueless siblings.

Descending an old stone staircase, they found themselves just outside the great hall. As they wandered in, Leona grasped her twin's arm.

He saw immediately. Cornelius's friend Lady Alice was edging away from a male vision in white lace.

"Goodness, he's pretty as a girl," Lawrence scoffed.

"No, he isn't pretty at all," Leona said, in rare disagreement with her twin. "She wants away from him, and see how he gazes after her?" She shivered. There was something both cold and predatory about the man—and that was over a distance. God knew how awful he was close up.

"You're right," Lawrence said, frowning. "He'd hurt her if he could. Why? She's the earl's sister. Untouchable."

"Power," said Leona. "As you say, she's the earl's sister."

"And she needs rescuing," Lawrence said with the flicker of a smile. "We have just the brother for that."

Leona plucked at her lower lip. "Should we, though?"

"We'll have to time it well… But yes, we should."

As one, they made their way toward the dazzling gentleman, who was now surrounded by other ladies.

"Who is *he*?" Leona asked a complete stranger in an awed voice.

"Mr. Darcy D'Aubin," came the lady's dreamy reply. "He's a poet."

"Of course he is," Lawrence murmured.

"Is he good?" Leona asked.

"Who cares, when he looks like that?"

Lawrence snorted, and Leona swallowed a giggle in order to thank the lady before they edged closer to their quarry.

Mr. D'Aubin took the adulation in his stride, and in time drifted in the wake of others to listen to the music at the other end of the hall. With the ease of practice, the twins surrounded him, one on either side.

"Mr. D'Aubin, your coat is beautiful," Leona told him.

He glanced down at her with a complaisant smile, then blinked to find himself addressing a girl with her hair loose and her hems still above her ankles. The smile faded.

"Love the lace," Lawrence said on his other side, taking a cuff gingerly between his finger and thumb. "So intricate."

"Isn't it," D'Aubin said discouragingly, brushing the boy's hand away as though it were an annoying wasp. "What do you want? And where is your mother?"

"Buried in a rather fine tomb in Bavaria. Sadly, she died when we were very young."

"I'm not surprised," muttered D'Aubin.

"That's not a very nice thing to say," Leona scolded. "Especially when we came to offer our services."

His lip curled as he spared her another assessing glance. "Come back in a year or two. Ouch!" he added, glaring at Lawrence.

"Sorry, I'm so clumsy," Lawrence said. "Comes from walking so close to you."

"Then don't. Shab off."

"We *could*," Leona said. "But then we wouldn't be able to deliver our message."

He paused in the midst of an intended hail to Lady Launceton, and dropped back instead, frowning at Leona. Someone was playing the pianoforte. Leona glimpsed Lady Alice at the front of the audience, her face rapt and eager.

"What message?" D'Aubin asked with exaggerated patience.

"In the interval between this musician and the next," Leona said, improvising, "she would like to talk to you privately about a book."

A gleam entered D'Aubin's cold eyes. "Who would?"

"A gentleman does not bandy about a lady's name," Lawrence said pompously. "But… it's the one you were staring at like the cat with the cream."

D'Aubin's nostrils flared. He opened his mouth to annihilate the impudent boy, but Leona spoke first.

"In the poetry room," she said, and she and Lawrence slipped away.

The next bit would be more difficult—and more dangerous.

ALICE HAD RECOGNIZED Lady Morgan the moment she entered the room before the poetry readings began. She had seen the silent yet meaningful greeting between her and Cornelius and suffered a foolish pang of jealousy that at least she could laugh at.

And then, as always, she had got lost in the beauty, the sheer *feeling* of the poem, which Helen read only too well. She had been afraid to look at him and kept her gaze averted—until Darcy Daubin had entered the room in all his splendor.

Only then had she glanced behind her, to share the joke with Cornelius. She saw the glistening of emotion on his eyelashes, a terrible look of raw pain and passion and loss. And suddenly she knew who the poem was about.

Lady Morgan was his lost love.

The pain of that took her breath away. Whipping back to gaze blindly at Helen, she wondered why the knowledge should hurt so much at this moment. She had always known the poem was a lament for his lost love, yet somehow the sight of her here in Blackhaven, apparently not so lost after all, threw her completely.

She still loves him. That is why she is here.

And he still loves her.

The rest is inevitable.

She found she was rubbing her hand against her gown, over the place her heart must be, trying to ease the pain. She forced herself to stop, to listen to the next poem, which spoke of the beauty of the land in a way that both touched and amused. She had always liked it, and Helen entered into the spirit of it perfectly. Alice could not.

She only pretended to listen to the subsequent poets, Mr. Fanshawe and Darcy Daubin, who both read their own works. She was desperate to escape, to run until she collapsed and could do no more than howl.

Why do I feel like this? It's not as if I want to marry the man. Any man!

Somehow, she forced herself to stay for the rest of the readings. And then it was almost time for the Scottish pianist Frederick Baird to be introduced. After his recital, there would be a short break, and then Alice would play before tea, followed by informal dancing.

In fact, the children were dancing now, in the marquee on the lawn to protect them from the rain. Perhaps she had time to go and watch or join in. It was bound to be a fun distraction.

However, she had only just reached the great hall when she walked straight into Darcy Daubin. Steeling herself, she praised his work—having heard barely any of it—and received a complaisant smile.

He moved closer, not enough to offend, but enough to make

her uncomfortable. "I find the ladies love such poor morsels. But until now, I did not fully realize the truth within. I might have written them with you in mind. Would you do me the greatest of honors?"

"What?" she asked warily. She recognized predatory lust in a man's face. She had seen it often enough, but never with the strange sort of flat coldness in Daubin's eyes.

He bent his head, and she only just stopped herself jumping backward. "Accept the gift of my poor book of verse."

She could smell the wine on his hot breath, felt the rise of panic.

She moved away just a little too quickly. "How very kind. Of course, I would love to accept," she babbled. "Thank you! Will you excuse me? My sister needs me to introduce our wonderful musician. You must listen to him..."

And at last she was away from him, breathing normally.

Frederick Baird was a breath of fresh air—shy, down to earth, and wildly talented. And when he began to play, she lost herself in the music, even while she admired his techniques and tried to learn from him.

He received tumultuous applause and the eloquent gratitude of her whole family. He even said he would like to stay to hear Alice play. She fetched him a glass of wine, and then, on her second effort to escape outside, was waylaid by one of the Vale twins.

"Come," said Leona mysteriously. "A gentleman wishes to talk to you about a book."

Cornelius! Did he want to talk about his own book, or the one Daubin was presenting to her? Had Daubin made some indiscreet inscription to her?

She was not sure she could face Cornelius until her feelings were clearer in her mind. But, it seemed, nor could she stay away. She was already following Leona across the hall to the passage and back into the poetry salon she had been so desperate to leave.

A man stood by the window with his back to her. But it was

not Cornelius. He was golden blond and he wore a pale ivory coat over exquisite lace cuffs.

The door closed with an ominous click, and Leona's footsteps sped along the passage beyond.

Chapter Eight

DARCY DAUBIN TURNED slowly from the window, a faint yet avid smile on his lips. Insolently, his gaze traveled all the way down her body and all the way back up. Perhaps he imagined it was flattering. Despite the heat of anger burning in her veins, she shivered.

His smile broadened. "Lady Alice," he purred. "It *is* you. I thought those repellant brats might have been gulling me."

"Mr. Daubin," she said, pronouncing his name the plain English way, with no French frills. "They have certainly gulled me. Shall we talk somewhere more public?"

It was not really a question, and she was already reaching for the closed door when he slid against it, right in front of her, and she snatched back her hand to avoid touching him.

"Absolutely not. Now that I have you alone, I have a much better use for your time."

Since he lunged as he spoke, she had little doubt as to his meaning.

Leaping out of his reach, she said coldly, "Mr. Daubin, you forget yourself!"

"Truly, I don't." He advanced purposefully, and she backed away until her hip struck the table.

She sprang to the side to elude him, but the obstacle had given him all the time he needed, and he seized her, ramming her hard between the table and his body.

"Let go of me!" she cried in panic, and then, in desperate hope rather than certainty, "Someone is coming!"

"Oh, I hope so," he said fervently, and slapped his mouth against hers.

She gave his head a hefty buffet, but he only laughed into her mouth. With one hand he grabbed her right arm, and squeezed her breast with the other. She couldn't breathe. It was happening again, and a scream of revulsion, rage, shame, and helpless fear began to rise up from her toes.

"WHAT THE DEVIL'S your hurry?" Cornelius demanded as Lawrence towed him back inside the castle, all but galloping him from the side door along the passage. All his siblings seemed to have gone mad. Delilah was following Antonia Macy around, Julius and Roderick were both scowling like thunder, and Lucy seemed to be flirting with every man she could find. Now Lawrence was dragging him about like a sack of flour, muttering something unlikely about Lady Alice needing his help.

Cornelius shook him off. "For God's sake, Lawrie, where is she?"

Leona came into view, beckoning wildly from the end of the passage. Her distress was clear, and suddenly Cornelius shot toward her. She didn't wait for him but threw herself into the salon.

"Leave her! Leave her alone!" she cried just before Cornelius burst through the doorway.

Leona was sobbing, but it was the scene beyond her that froze Cornelius's blood.

Alice was clutched in Darcy Daubin's insolent arms, his mouth devouring hers, his hand clamped over her breast. Her whole body was heaving helplessly against his strength, and she was so clearly terrified that Cornelius never doubted that Daubin's attentions were unwelcome.

He didn't remember moving, but suddenly he gripped Daubin by the elegant cream collar and plucked him off her. In utter fury, he crashed his fist into the brute's face, then hurled him at the door.

Lawrence had already shut the door for the sake of discretion, so Daubin slammed into it and staggered forward again, his stunned eyes beginning to roll up into his head. Cornelius grasped him by the collar once more. Without being told, Lawrence wrenched open the door, and Cornelius threw him across the passage.

"Keep him out of here," he snarled at Lawrence. "By any means." He swung on Leona, who was about to run to help her twin. "Oh no—you close the door and stay here."

Only then did he have time to look at Alice.

She had collapsed to the floor, her shoulders still heaving as though she could not breathe, her face buried in her hands. Tears squeezed between her fingers.

"Oh, my dear," he whispered, going to her and crouching beside her. His every instinct was to take her in his arms, and yet he knew she would not allow it. He had already guessed her fear, and part of him was already following Daubin and beating him to a pulp.

He stretched out one hand, touching her hair. "You're safe," he said achingly. "He's gone, and he will never hurt you again, I swear."

She gasped and, to his surprise, seized his hand and held it painfully hard between her own.

"I'm so sorry," she whispered. "I thought he would be you, and he wasn't, and then… Oh God, why do I have to make such a fuss? He has not hurt more than my dignity."

"I'm afraid I've hurt rather more than his," Cornelius said shakily.

"He'll have a black eye and an egg the size of an ostrich's on his forehead," Leona said in a surprisingly small voice. "I'm so sorry, Lady Alice."

Cornelius caught his breath, turning slowly to face her. "You did this."

"You went outside at the last minute and upset the timing," Leona said despairingly. "You were meant to rescue her *before* he touched her."

Leona almost cringed before his anger. She had never done that before. But then, he could not recall ever being so angry.

"*Why*, for God's sake?" he demanded.

"Because you need a push," she said miserably. "You all need a push in the right direction."

He swallowed, his anger dying, at least against her and Lawrence. "Not like this, Leona."

"No, not like this," she agreed.

Alice straightened her shoulders, wiping her arm against her eyes like a child. She still held on to his hand.

"Don't worry. Your timing was almost perfect," she said, clearly aiming for lightness. "He only grabbed me for a moment, and I'm afraid I froze. I cannot abide being mauled."

"You shouldn't have to," Cornelius said between his teeth.

"He didn't let her go even when I barged into the room," Leona said.

"No, I think it was rather the point to be seen," Alice said. "He wanted me compromised. I am quite a catch, you know, to an ambitious young man not of gentle birth. It's the only way he imagined he could marry me. Truly, there is no harm done."

She struggled to rise, then realized she was still clutching Cornelius's hand. She gave a shaky laugh, while he straightened and raised her to her feet.

"I'm sorry to make such a fuss. I shall just go and wash my face. I'm meant to play in..." She glanced at the clock on the mantelpiece. "Oh dear, in five minutes."

"One moment," Cornelius said, striding to the door.

Lawrence lounged there, his guilty eyes flying to Cornelius's.

"I gave him to two very large footmen. No one else saw. They threw him out. I don't imagine he will find anyone in the castle at home to him again." A quick smile lit his eyes. "He was gibbering with rage because there was blood on his coat. I told him he was lucky there wasn't more. Sorry, Cornel. Will you tell Lady Alice?"

"Yes. As it turns out, there is no real harm done. But Lawrence?"

"Yes?"

"No more tricks like that again. *Ever*. Not to anyone."

Lawrence swallowed. "I promise."

Cornelius stepped back into the room and met Alice's gaze. She was still trembling, and dried tears streaked her face, but she had herself in hand once more.

"Will Leona go with you?" he asked. "Or shall I send for Lady Helen or your mother?"

Alarm sprang back into her eyes. "Oh, no! I am better alone. Thank you, Cornelius."

She murmured something to the twins on the way past, then flitted along the passage like a graceful bird in flight. Could he really feel another verse coming on, even at such a time?

It seemed to be the only way he could make sense of things.

"We'll talk later," he said severely to the twins, who nodded morosely, sidling out the door. He went with them to the great hall, where they seemed to perk up as they dashed off again, no doubt to interfere in someone else's life.

Alice did not look at him when she walked up to the pianoforte with young Lady Braithwaite, even though her flowing skirts brushed his ankle. Beyond a certain tautness of the skin, her face betrayed nothing of her recent experience. There was no puffiness about her eyes, and if they were a little reddened, it was hardly obvious when she sat down at the pianoforte and lowered her gaze.

As Lady Braithwaite introduced her in glowing terms, she smiled, a faint social smile, while keeping her gaze on the keys in front of her. She held her hands together in her lap, apparently at ease, although her knuckles were white. And when she placed her fingers on the keys, she was still trembling.

She should not be doing this so soon after such a fright. In outrage, he actually started toward her, as though to sweep her away from everyone gawping at her. But then she began to play, a sonata he knew, and he stilled.

There was magic in her fingers, compelling everyone to listen and enjoy. But no, it was not magic—it was sheer talent, skill, a delicacy of touch, a profound love and understanding of the music that allowed her to move her listeners as she was moved. And it must have taken an enormous amount of practice. Her previous upset had vanished. She was assured, absorbed, perfect.

She was spellbinding.

Even after the piece finished, there was an awed silence before applause broke out. Alice bent her head over the keyboard for a moment, eyes closed, then she smiled and rose, curtseying to acknowledge the appreciation.

"My daughter is gifted, is she not?" someone said beside him.

At some point, he appeared to have sat down in the front row of seats, beside no less a personage than the Dowager Countess of Braithwaite.

"Extremely," he managed. "You must be very proud of her."

"I am. In every way. She did not even want a London Season, you know. She would have preferred to stay at home and play the pianoforte, so she did not even try to please the *ton*. And yet she did. London was at her feet."

"And all Blackhaven," he said, although it was hardly so large or important a stage. His mind was more on why the countess was telling him this. She was a formidable lady who appeared older than her years. Most of Blackhaven was terrified of her, whatever the *ton* thought.

She rose, and, of course, he rose with her and bowed as she sailed away with the elder Lady Morgan.

Have I just been warned off? It was oddly flattering to think so. After all, Alice was sister to an earl, and everyone knew she was well dowered.

By popular demand, Alice played another piece. This was her own composition, the one she had begun to play for him the night of the ball. Cornelius stared at his hands in his lap to avoid gazing at Alice as the emotions washed across her face. He realized he had been doing so throughout the sonata. The countess must have noticed. She must have imagined she was warning off a lovesick puppy.

Perhaps I am, he thought ruefully. *But I'm a puppy who knows his limitations.*

Despite his best intentions, the music seemed to wriggle under his skin and flow to his heart. He could not help raising his gaze to Alice's face, intent, impassioned, beautiful. His mind might have known its limitations, but his heart did not.

FOR ALICE, MUSIC healed nearly everything. The few things it could not mend, it made more easily bearable. Once her fingers settled on the keys, they knew what to do. The world receded and she played her heart out. And yet if Cornelius had not been there, she didn't know if she could have played at all. She played for him. Though under the scrutiny of so many, it was his distant, yet intense, eyes that seemed to burn into her, lending her strength and excitement.

She played better than she ever had in her life, and her first reward was Frederick Baird leaping to his feet to applaud her.

"Then you will give me a lesson?" she teased him when he congratulated her.

"I have nothing to teach you," he replied. "Goodbye, Lady Alice. It has been an honor to meet you, and a very great pleasure to listen to you."

When she turned from him, warmed by his praise, she could no longer see Cornelius. Swamped by congratulations and effusive admiration, Alice longed only for his.

The children bolted inside en masse and upstairs for tea in the nursery. The adults enjoyed more civilized refreshment below, while the musicians set up in the hall once more for a little informal dancing.

In a welcome blink of sunshine, Alice wandered outside at last. She needed to be alone now to sort out the confusion of shame, disgust, and anger that had only faded with her playing the piano, not vanished. And yet she wanted Cornelius's peaceful presence by her side.

She smiled as she walked. Why should she imagine he would bring her peace? She always quarreled with him, or he with her. And yet he had been so kind about Daubin's attack and her own quite out-of-proportion reaction. She didn't really want to think about why.

Avoiding the formal gardens, where a few guests walked and flirted, she walked past the orchard and toward the wood. She came to the ancient oak that in her childhood games with Helen and Maria had always been the Guardian of the Forest. And there, her heart broke.

Cornelius and young Lady Morgan stood in its shade, close together and talking quietly. At least, *she* was talking, in a kind of distressed whisper. Cornelius was listening, concern in his furrowed brow.

He loves her still…

He glanced up, and straight at Alice. He did not even look guilty—why should he? He had discovered her in a much more compromising position little more than an hour ago.

"Lady Alice." He almost sounded relieved.

Lady Morgan jumped away from him, staring at Alice in fright.

Cornelius introduced them without fuss, adding to Alice, "I was once steward for Sir John Morgan, Cecily's husband. We are old friends."

Clearly.

"I hope you will not think me fast, Lady Alice," Lady Morgan blurted. "We are such old friends, I was merely asking Cornelius—Mr. Vale—for his advice in a rather private matter."

"Then don't let me intrude," Alice said at once, turning to the westward path.

"Oh, there is no intrusion," Cornelius said quickly. "In fact, your insight would be welcome."

Not to Cecily Morgan, it wasn't. As Alice glanced back in surprise, the other woman was scowling at him in mingled fright and alarm.

"Lady Morgan has a friend," Cornelius said smoothly. "A very close friend who relies on her. This friend made a love match less than two years ago and is now distraught because she has discovered her husband has already strayed."

"I would like to help my friend, of course," Lady Morgan said stiffly, still glaring at Cornelius, "but I would never trouble your ladyship with the problems of people you do not know."

"If I don't know them, I doubt their problems would trouble me at all," Alice remarked. Then, catching sight of the unexpected plea in Cornelius's eyes, she added hastily, "But distance can be useful in matters that might seem too personal. I am happy to help if I can."

"How should Cecily's friend go about winning back her husband's love?" Cornelius asked. He sounded embarrassed, and so he should. No one believed in *Cecily's friend*.

Alice considered. "She probably doesn't need to. Men are odd creatures and seem quite capable of loving their wives while—er… straying with other women. Or perhaps he is only flirting."

"He isn't," Cecily said with such misery that, for the first time, Alice felt sorry for her. Even if Cornelius did still love her.

"Either way, she wants and deserves his attention back," Cornelius said.

"Does she?" Alice met Cecily's gaze. "Then your friend is faithful to him?"

Cecily's eyes flashed in outrage. "Of course she is!" She stalked out of the wood, and Cornelius and Alice went with her, walking back toward the main house.

You are very beautiful, Alice thought, not without a pang. *I cannot imagine you have much competition there.* "Does your friend share her husband's interests?"

Cecily frowned. "Interests?"

"What does he read? Does he care for politics, literature, science?"

"Well, no, not a great deal. He likes horse racing and horrid prizefights."

Alice pounced. "He likes horses? Then your friend must ride with him, take an interest in horseflesh—"

"Oh no!" Cecily exclaimed. She flushed under Alice's surprised gaze. "My friend is rather afraid of horses. And she does not like dogs either."

Alice sighed and tried a different tack. "What made him fall in love with your friend in the first instance?"

"I don't know," Cecily said wretchedly. "Probably just because she was admired by…others."

"If there isn't more to it than that," Alice retorted, "then she is better off without him."

Some of the older children had spilled outside again and were running down the hill toward a meadow where they had played football earlier. The Vale twins peeled off from this group and ran up to Cornelius.

"Ah," Alice said. "Just the Machiavellian minds we need! How should a woman go about winning back the love of her straying husband?"

Cecily made a strangled noise in her throat.

"These are my siblings," Cornelius murmured comfortingly, though Cecily did not look much comforted.

"Make him jealous, of course," Lawrence said. "Worked for—"

Leona kicked him in the ankle, and he broke off.

"Must dash," he said hastily, and they ran back the way they had come, leaving the adults to gaze after them in bemusement.

"He is right," Alice said in wonder. "Your friend must make her husband jealous by flirting with someone else."

And then she wanted to kick herself. Because the ideal candidate for flirtation walked by her side.

As Darcy Daubin stormed back into Cloverfield House, his father called to him from his library, where he was surrounded by ledgers and correspondence. Papa's eyes narrowed above the spectacles perched on the end of his nose.

"Good God. Did you go to the countess's garden party or get sidetracked into a drinking game at the tavern?"

"Very funny," Darcy raged. "Damned brute! It was all going perfectly, too. Another minute and someone else would surely have come along to witness the scene and I would now be introducing you to my betrothed, the earl's sister!"

The spectacles dropped off his father's face. He closed his eyes, pinching the bridge of his nose. "Subtlety just isn't your strong suit, is it, Darcy?"

"I am very subtle," Darcy said, glaring. "No one is subtler." He dropped into the armchair, wincing as he felt around the swollen flesh of his eyes.

"Which of the earl's sisters did you assault?" Papa inquired.

"Lady Alice," Darcy said sulkily. "She would make a fine match. She is addicted to poetry and music and all the things I love. She was perfect. Except she's both haughty and frigid!"

"Which you established by assaulting her," his father said without emphasis.

"Of course I didn't assault her! I merely kissed her, and she reacted as though I was murdering her. It wouldn't have mattered if *he* hadn't been the one to discover her in my arms."

"Presumably he is the one who blacked your eye?"

"I'll get him back for it. Got some brat and two footmen—damned lackeys!—to throw me out." He rubbed his shin, aggrieved all over again. "One of them kicked me."

"No doubt because you assaulted his mistress. Who hit you?"

Darcy shrugged one shoulder angrily. "Some nonentity. Vale?"

His father went very still. "Which Vale?"

"Does it matter?"

"Yes. Sir Julius Vale is our neighbor at Black Hill, whose grazing land we have just appropriated."

"Good!"

"Was he tall? Imposing? Patch over one eye?"

"No patch." Darcy flexed his jaw. "Bloody strong, though. The brat called him Cornelius or some such."

Papa sprang up and charged toward him. "Oh, damn you, Darcy, why can't you leave things alone? We do not want Cornelius Vale as our enemy."

"Don't see why not. He's only a younger son."

"And the steward at Black Hill, which we have been en-croaching upon and embezzling from since we bought Cloverfield."

Darcy blinked up at him. "Why?"

"Because there's no damned money in land, and I won't pour any more of the mill money into it. Fortunately, Norrie's a good man and imaginative, and we'd no idea the Vales would come home when they did." He dragged his fingers through his thinning hair. "You will stay away from the Vales. And the Braithwaites. Until we can find a way to deal with both."

"Actually," Darcy said, brightening, "we're still in with a chance. The footman might tell Braithwaite, and the earl will force Alice and me to marry."

"He's more likely to beat you to a pulp, and right now, I'd probably help him!"

"He wouldn't touch me if it would drag his precious sister's name in the mud."

"Oh, get out of my sight," Papa said, stalking away from him. "Go and change, for God's sake. You look like a scone with jam and cream."

Chapter Nine

T HE FOLLOWING DAY left Cornelius little time to brood on the events of the garden party.

On his return to the great hall yesterday, he had ached to dance with Alice, but, aware of her ordeal and her unspoken fears, he would not inflict himself on her. Instead, he danced with Cecily. After all, he thought wearily, they might as well begin their flirtation before Morgan appeared in Blackhaven.

And shortly after that, he had escaped, with the excuse of matters to see to at Black Hill before the end of the day. In fact, he was so preoccupied with Alice that he failed to pay adequate attention to his siblings.

He knew Roderick was much taken up with a new business venture that Cornelius hoped would prevent him going back to the army. Like the others, he pretended not to hear the anguished cries of Roderick's nightmares, which seemed to be growing less with time. The army was no longer good for his brother.

Julius was still pursuing the horse thieves, who had turned out to be gun smugglers.

Lucy was furious because the man to whom her foolish mother had betrothed her at birth had suddenly appeared at the garden party. Cornelius couldn't see the need for fuss, since no one, let alone Julius, would force her to marry anyone, whatever their parents had agreed.

Felicia bothered him more. He suspected her of a clandestine love affair and didn't know whether to be pleased or afraid for her.

But it was Julius who suddenly upturned everything. A message from the twins was delivered to him in the fields. Antonia Macy was being abducted, and Julius had gone to sea in a borrowed ship in pursuit of his wretched gun smugglers. Dropping everything, Cornelius dashed back to the house, yelled for the carriage, and grabbed a pistol, dagger, and brandy for emergencies. At the last minute he swept an insistent Lucy with him to Blackhaven in search of the twins.

The twins had brought most of the town to the harbor, and poured out their unlikely tale involving Antonia and the cheating administrator of the local charity hospital, who appeared to be in league with Julius's gun smugglers.

Cornelius stood among his siblings—Delilah, Roderick, Felicia, and Aubrey were there too—staring out to sea, willing Julius to be safe. And Antonia. The cold fingers of fear around his heart forced him to acknowledge not just his affection but his need of his family. Julius was his heroic big brother who relied on him to tame the land and nurture it. It was just the purposeful work Cornelius had needed, still so discontented after Cecily, and he had seized Julius's offer with both hands.

It was true that, until the last few months, much of their lives had been lived apart, but Julius had aways been there, a powerful figure to look up to and turn to. To rely on. A world without Julius was unthinkable to Cornelius.

By the time Julius came ashore, his arm around Antonia, Cornelius could not speak for relief. Happiness blazed out of Julius's one eye. Cornelius, almost afraid of his emotion, began to compose wild poetry in his head, though he managed to cheer with his siblings as Julius announced his betrothal to Antonia.

Cornelius needed Julius to be happy. He needed them *all* to be happy.

With the crisis past, he knew he should return to Black Hill, but he didn't. He went with seemingly half the town to the hotel and enjoyed a large, boisterous tea party with champagne and toasts to the happy couple.

For the first time, he felt part of something larger than his own family. They were part of the Blackhaven community. Mr. Winslow the magistrate and Colonel Doverton of the local regiment were celebrating with them. So were the vicar and his wife, the doctor and his. The Vales were more than accepted in Blackhaven. They were *liked*. Even Cornelius seemed to be liked. For once, none of his conversations were about land or building repairs.

It felt a little like a revelation, not least because he liked the feeling. All that was missing was the presence of Alice.

Alice.

He left quietly, clapping Julius on the shoulder on his way past. It was still light outside, which took him by surprise. He had drunk too much champagne and was neglecting his duties. He had been absent all afternoon. Laborers, tradesmen, and tenants would all be going home. Cornelius, leaving the carriage for the others, meant to walk home. And he chose to do it via Braithwaite land. Just in case…

But unexpectedly, he caught up with her before he even reached the castle.

Wearing a rather dull gown and bonnet that might have been left over since childhood, she was marching briskly along the road and didn't hear him coming. He walked beside her for two steps before she became aware of his presence.

He half expected her to start, but instead he thought she smiled before she even turned her head.

"Mr. Vale. Where did you come from?"

"From the hotel. We were celebrating my brother's engagement to Mrs. Macy."

"How wonderful! I heard something of their adventures. Are you coming to the castle to tell us the rest?"

"No, I just decided to walk home. I'll leave Julius and Antonia to tell their own tale." Rather than ask how she was, he searched her face for signs of nervousness or alarm. He found none, only a hint of distracted excitement and a faint, soft flush in her cheeks that made her look so beautiful he ached. He rushed back into speech. "Are you just walking for pleasure, or have you been visiting?"

"Neither, really." She glanced at him. "You are a man used to keeping secrets. Will you keep mine?"

"Yes."

A smile flickered on her lips. "I was at the King's Head, making a few last-minute arrangements with our hired guards."

He blinked. "Hired guards?" It flashed through his mind that Roderick's new business was in such a line, but mostly, he was afraid for Alice. "Why do you need hired guards? Has that scoundrel Daubin dared to come near you again? Because if so—"

She laughed. "Lord, no, it is nothing like that. You are aware of my ambitions. And my sister Helen's."

"Yes."

"Well, we have taken the Whalen theatre for Monday—all day and into the evening. We shall show Helen's pictures in the foyer, offering them for sale, and I will give an evening recital."

"In Whalen?" he repeated uneasily. It was a larger, somewhat rougher town than Blackhaven, with much less in the way of either gentry or employment. Discontent had simmered below the surface and erupted into riots only a couple of weeks ago. "Why not Blackhaven?"

"Everyone knows us in Blackhaven. I told you it was a secret."

He caught his breath. "Your family doesn't know?"

"They would stop us. We want to reach more people. I know Whalen is not as rich, but it does have a higher population than Blackhaven, and it will be good practice for us. If we can arrange something similar in York or even London…"

"And you are hiring guards from the King's Head? At least it's not the tavern!"

She did not rise to his criticism. "You misunderstand. It is a new company of guards, and it just so happens that one of the partners is staying at the inn. Captain Skelton is a former army officer."

Cornelius relaxed. Skelton was Roderick's friend and partner. So it was Roderick who would guard Alice and Helen in their unwise venture. At least they would be safe.

"Will no one miss you if you are gone all day and evening?" he asked.

"I doubt it. The castle is filling up with more guests all the time. It's our grand ball on Friday. All my older sisters are present to help Eleanor with entertaining and so on, and if it comes down to it, Maria will cover for us."

"Why don't you take Lady Maria—and her husband—with you?" Cornelius asked, trying to provide the venture with a modicum of respectability.

"Then who would cover for us?" Alice said. "Besides, we wouldn't drag Maria into this. She does not care for confrontation, and if anything goes wrong and we are caught, Mama will explode. You will see the bodies for miles. And the scorched earth."

"And you will risk that?"

She lifted her chin. "Yes. We need to begin somewhere. We decided in London that Whalen was the perfect place to start. Are you disgusted?"

"No."

"Will you tell Gervaise?"

"Lord Braithwaite? No." *Not yet, at any rate.* "I gave you my word I won't tell anyone."

"Thank you."

She had no idea how her smile affected him. He wondered what she would do or feel if he took her hand. Would she flinch? Pull away in disgust? She had done neither at the ball or the garden party.

It does not matter. She is not for you under any circumstances.

She obviously knew that, for she did not invite him into the castle, merely said she would see him at church tomorrow then hurried off over the bridge while he turned left onto the path that wound past the castle and over the fields and hills.

He could still see her in his mind's eyes, smell her unique scent of freshness and warmth. No, she was not for him, but he could still look after her. She was his friend.

KNOWING HE HAD come from the hotel, Alice would have died rather than ask him about Cecily Morgan. And in fact, from the pleasure in his face when he spoke of his brother's engagement, she thought it was that—plus the champagne she could smell on his breath—that made him so much more…approachable.

She wished the walk to the castle were longer. She wished she had the courage to invite him for tea, but she could not bear an excuse.

What has happened to me? I used to seize every opportunity!

But there was no opportunity here for her. Cornelius was still in love with Cecily. Alice, with her sharp tongue, her temper, and her dislike of male intimacy, could never compete with Lady Morgan. In fact, it was beyond her why she would want to, given her inconvenient dislike that had only been reinforced by Darcy Daubin yesterday.

So, she went home alone, casting only one look back at him before he strode out of sight. She liked the way he moved, economical and decisive yet not without unconscious grace. She remembered how he waltzed and wished he had danced with her yesterday.

Her wishes and fears seemed to go around in circles.

In one sense, church the following day—where the banns were called for Julius Vale and Mrs. Macy for the first time—was an improvement on the previous week. Cornelius actually smiled at her. On the other hand, he was much more attentive to Cecily, whether for his flirtation campaign to make her husband jealous, or just because he wanted to. Alice tried to thrust him from her mind and concentrate on the logistics of their escape to Whalen the following day.

However, in her final pianoforte practice at the castle, she found she played better when his face danced in front of her. Perhaps by imagining him, she could also banish her performance nerves.

EARLY ON MONDAY morning, Cornelius was surprised to receive a visit from Lord Braithwaite, who walked into his office in the wake of Lucy.

Guilt drove Cornelius to his feet, for it struck him he was hiding too many of Alice's secrets from her legal guardian. He even imagined Braithwaite had somehow got wind of his feelings for Alice and come to disabuse him of his pretensions.

But Braithwaite quite amiably held out his hand. "So sorry to interrupt you. I have come with a confession and can only beg your forgiveness."

Cornelius blinked. "You have? I mean, you do? Why?"

"Please, sit down," Lucy intervened, covering Cornelius's lapse of manners. She stuck her head back out the door. "Coffee if you please, John."

Why was she still lurking in the office with them?

"You took on one Rob Smith to oblige me," Braithwaite said.

"I was glad of him," Cornelius replied, sitting back down opposite the earl. "And he is a good worker. It is I who am obliged."

"The thing is," Braithwaite said with difficulty, "I was not entirely truthful. I changed his name to protect him as well as you. In fact, he is Luke Farmer, the son of one of my own tenants, and he had escaped from the town jail."

Cornelius, still unreasonably relieved that the visit had nothing to do with Alice, took a few moments to understand the ensuing story, which seemed to involve Lucy's reviled betrothed, Lord Eddleston. Braithwaite wanted to take Rob Smith, alias Luke Farmer, to Blackhaven to prove false a surely bizarre charge of highway robbery.

The timing was annoying, for Cornelius needed all hands possible today if he was to escape early. However, he could hardly stand in the way of justice and, after a pithy word to Farmer about honesty, wished him luck and sent him off with Braithwaite.

Although Cornelius didn't do quite all he wanted to that day, he bolted home at four o'clock to wash and change into evening clothes. Both the carriages had gone—one with Felicia, the other with Julius and Lucy—so he had to make do with the servants' gig to drive himself to Whalen.

Arriving in the town in good time, he left the tired horse to the tender mercies of a local inn, saying he would be back around nine or ten this evening. In his dreams, he drove back with Alice.

In reality, he enjoyed a bite to eat at the inn and strolled on to the theatre, hoping Helen and Alice would not be too disappointed by a poor turnout. He paused to read the bills outside the theatre, advertising an exhibition of watercolor pictures for sale and a pianoforte recital, by the Misses Connor. The really were incognito. He wondered if it would last all evening.

Pulling his hat down low, he marched up to the doors, which were immediately opened for him by an unknown man with a soldierly bearing, presumably one of Roderick's recruits. The quickest glance showed him a surprising number of people, mostly gazing at the pictures by Lady Helen.

Cornelius had seen some of her work at the garden party, and although he knew little about art, he had been very impressed by both her landscapes and her thoughtful, insightful portraits. Her style was very different from her brother-in-law Lord Tamar, who had apparently become very fashionable in London, but it retained a kind of fresh innocence that he doubted Tamar had ever possessed.

Cornelius could not linger to examine the pictures further, for barely three feet away from him, talking to a prospective buyer, was a masked lady in an evening gown who could only be Lady Helen herself. His lips twitched with as much appreciation as amusement. Perhaps he should do masked public readings of his poetry.

He could see no sign of Alice. Presumably, she was backstage.

He bought a ticket from the little box office—choosing the one seat still available in the front row—and tried to blend with the crowd on his way into the auditorium. Here, he was relieved to see Skelton, watchful and discreet. Roderick was presumably elsewhere, but another pair of eyes would surely do no harm.

Butterflies were swarming in his stomach, more like anxious bees, as he took his seat and waited with tense anticipation for Alice to walk onto the stage and take her seat at the grand pianoforte.

ALICE SAT IN her tawdry little dressing room, frozen by fear. She wore a gorgeous and sophisticated evening gown of pure white, with gold trimmings under the bust, sleeves, and hem. The fabric of the gown was flecked with delicate gold thread and matched by the gold mask covering most of her face. It was held firmly in place so that it would not move and blind her during the performance. Her hair was piled high on her head. Helen had painted her pale lips, and she looked like a stranger in the glass.

Somewhere, she knew this was a good thing. She was barely nineteen years old, but on stage she would easily pass for thirty. She also knew that Helen had been brave enough to stand by her pictures all day and listen to the discussions of prospective buyers—not all complimentary, although much of it had been, and she had sold several pictures. The exhibition was already a success, and she had to do her part.

But she barely heard Helen's encouraging words as she was drawn to her feet. In fact, she clung pathetically to her sister as they walked along the passage to the stage.

From the wing, she glimpsed a terrifying sea of faces. The theatre was full. She had never in her life played to so many people. And yet this was only a steppingstone in her ambition. She wanted to play huge concert halls in the capitals of Europe. Oh God, who was she fooling?

I can't. I can't do it. She had no idea if she said the words aloud. The theatre manager, Mr. Pritchard, was looking anxious. Forcing herself, she let go of Helen.

As if from very far away, Helen said, "Go. Be brilliant. Be yourself."

There is no point. I can't play like this. I'm shaking like a leaf.

Yet she had promised.

Very slowly, forcing every step, Alice began to walk on stage into the glow of the light. A smattering of applause nearly sent her fleeing back to Helen in the wings, but, gritting her teeth, she kept going.

The noise in the auditorium quietened. She could not look beyond the pianoforte. She sat and spread her trembling fingers across the keys. Normally, as at the garden party, when she did this, her fingers took over, and then the music just flowed, banishing the terrible nerves. This time, nothing happened.

I can't remember the notes.

It was her worst nightmare. The audience shifted in their seats, restive. In a panic, she flicked her gaze toward Helen in the wing. But from the corner of her eye, she glimpsed a man at the end of the first row in the audience. Still, handsome, and well dressed, he looked so much like Cornelius that she fixed her gaze upon him.

Dear God, it *was* Cornelius. He had come to listen to her.

Her heart swelled with pride and gratitude. For an instant, his eyes locked to hers, and her fingers began to play for him.

CORNELIUS COULD ALMOST imagine that an unseen hand had pushed her on stage. Her fingers curled stiffly like claws at her side, and her beautiful gown trembled with her shivering. Beneath the beautiful mask, her lips were stretched into a fixed, unchanging smile.

Alice was terrified.

He wanted to leap onto the stage and take her hand, conduct her to her seat, and murmur words of belief and encouragement. She looked so desperately alone. The depths of her courage, her determination, moved him.

Why do you put yourself through this?

He wanted to snatch her off the stage and make her safe. Only, she would hate him for it. Helplessly, he willed her to sit, to play as she had at the ball, at the castle…

She sat, but without her usual elegance—it looked more like a collapse. Now he was truly frightened for her. But somehow, she raised her shaking hands to the keys. The audience waited expectantly. So did Alice, as though the next step was beyond her control.

She can't do it, he thought numbly. *Oh, my poor Alice…*

This would shatter her. Her head moved, as though she were seeking some friend—Helen, perhaps—while members of the audience began to look at each other with annoyance. Up until now, she had totally ignored them, but her downcast eyes must have glimpsed the front rows below her, for, quite suddenly, she saw him.

Behind the mask, her eyes widened. Would she be angry because he witnessed her humiliation? How the devil was he to get her out of here? So many people could turn ugly…

Her lips curved, and in that instant, while their eyes still locked, she began to play.

Cornelius sagged back with relief. The whole tense episode had seemed to last a lifetime, but in reality it could only have been a few moments. As he gazed at her now in wonder, it was as if her fear had never been. The music flowed from her fingers, grasping her audience by the heart and sweeping them into her world of beauty and tragedy and soaring joy.

Apart from the Beethoven sonata, and her own composition, he did not recognize the pieces she played—each was greeted by tumultuous applause—but she ended on a fun, joyful dance that had the audience surging to its feet and clapping wildly.

Cornelius, trying to roar his approval with the rest, found that no sound would come out. It didn't matter. Crying, "Brava!" was simply not enough. He bolted, striding through the nearest door of the auditorium.

Most of the audience would pour out of the main doors at the back, into the large foyer, but one of Roderick's men stood in the side passage, almost next to Cornelius, calling to someone else in the foyer ahead. "…beautiful! Audience are over-exuberant, so watch 'em…"

Cornelius seized his moment and walked swiftly toward the back of the stage, his ears full of music, his heart full of Alice and his need to tell her how wonderful she was. As he whisked past a couple of offices, loud approval still rang out from the auditorium. He hoped to catch her as soon as she came off stage.

But someone else was there, a beaming, oily middle-aged man. The theatre manager, no doubt.

"My dear Mrs. Connor, quite dazzling! A brilliant performance, and they love you! One more bow…"

Cornelius, unwilling for the manager to see a man waiting for her, backed into the shadows. A wall lamp showed him a door with a sign on it saying *Dressing Room*. But the manager was already hurtling away toward the foyer, where there were still Lady Helen's pictures to protect. To say nothing of Helen herself.

From the shadows, Cornelius watched Alice almost leap

down the steps from the stage. She still wore her mask, but her eyes sparkled and her lips were smiling as though they would never stop. She danced the few yards toward the dressing room, and Cornelius, words still stuck in his throat, stepped out of the gloom.

She let out a squeak, but it didn't seem to be of alarm, because the next instant, with a sound between a sob and laughter, she hurled herself against him, both arms around his neck.

"Oh, Cornelius, I did it! I did it!"

"By *God*, you did," he said hoarsely, closing his arms about her and spinning her right off her feet.

She laughed with pure joy, her lovely face turned up to his in the lamp's glow. He forgot everything he knew and acted instinctively from his own elation. He kissed her.

Chapter Ten

I T WAS SO sudden that she had no time to fear it. She was so elated that it seemed perfectly natural. There was exuberance in the first hard pressure of his mouth, which she gladly returned, and then the kiss quickly gentled to something else altogether. Sweet, exciting, melting... His lips moved, parting hers and caressing. His fingers in her hair released the mask, which fluttered to the floor as he cupped her cheek.

Heat and pleasure surged through her, making her gasp, and suddenly the kiss was not gentle anymore. It was wild and passionate, like the most wonderful music.

She gasped into his mouth, grasping the soft hair at his nape. When had her arms gone around his neck? In that first, delighted moment, she had run to him. But this was like no other embrace she had ever known. Not like Glover's fumbling slobber or Atherstone's crushing assault... This was *Cornelius*, and he was...

He was music. She had no other words.

And then, abruptly, the door opened behind her. She all but fell into the dressing room, and he was gone, vanishing toward the stage door.

Stunned, she almost fell onto the nearest stool, touching her lips in wonder, hugging herself to re-create the wonder of his arms about her. It didn't work.

Then she laughed, because it had been such a wonderful

evening, and she was happier than she had ever been in her life.

She was even glad to lose herself in hard work, changing her clothes and then, as the theatre gradually emptied, helping pack Helen's unsold pictures to load into the waiting carriage, keeping aside the bought ones with their tickets to be delivered by Captain Skelton or his men tomorrow.

Helen was thrilled for her. They were thrilled for each other.

"You were splendid!" Helen declared. "You have never played so well! Everyone adored you. I heard them as they left. In fact, you sold me another two pictures by making people so happy."

Alice laughed. "It was well worth the effort, was it not? I think we've done very well, and Captain Skelton says there has been no trouble to speak of."

Captain Skelton, however, spoke too soon. As Alice climbed into the carriage with all their things, there was shouting not so very far away, as if the town was uneasy.

"Time to go," Skelton said a little grimly, squeezing himself onto the bench opposite between the open door and two large picture frames. "There's a large group of men approaching with torches, and there are too many of them. Don't like the look of them. I think we have a riot forming. Where the devil is North?"

North was one of his men, coachman for the night and comfortingly large.

Skelton drummed his fingers on his thigh. "We should go."

"I'll go and hurry Helen," Alice said, reaching for the door.

Skelton blocked her. "Oh, no. Harper and Black will escort her. She's just coming." He peered out of the door up the street. "North!" he yelled, slamming the carriage door, for suddenly the riot was upon them. Yelling men surrounded the carriage, some bearing torches, others, their faces twisted with anger and malice, shaking the carriage as though to overturn it. Only the fact that others were shoving from the other side seemed to prevent its fall.

The horses were screaming, surely ready to bolt, even with

the break on the carriage wheels.

Suddenly, like a thunderbolt, the enormous figure of North exploded through the crowd and leapt onto the carriage box. Alice, angry and frightened, was almost glad to see his whip lashing over the worst offenders.

Finally, Helen walked out of the theatre with her escort, and straight into the melee. Instantly, she was surrounded. Harper and Black fought furiously, but to her mounting horror, Alice saw that her little sister was being separated from her guards. Rough men had taken hold of her arms.

Screaming, Alice lunged at the door again, and was almost thrown back into her seat by Skelton, who had a pistol in his hand, leveled at the rioter trying to wrench open the carriage door.

And then, from nowhere, a horseman rode down the attackers nearest to the coach. He looked very like Cornelius's brother, Major Vale.

"Drive!" he yelled, presumably at North. "Now!"

The rioter at the door vanished, buffeted by the major's horse, and the carriage lurched into motion, immediately hurtling along the street.

Alice cried, "Stop, damn you! Let me out!" For Helen was still in terrible danger.

"She'll be fine," Skelton said, looking sick with relief. "The major has her now."

Through the back window, Alice, sobbing with helpless fear, saw the major laying about him, and then Helen seemed to be leaping through the air, and landed behind the major's saddle.

Alice wailed because she was getting further and further away from her little sister, whom she had always protected—whom she was *supposed* to protect. No obstacles blocked the carriage's advance now.

"Stop!" Alice shouted. "We *must* go back for Helen!"

"There's no need. The major will catch up with us. She'll be frightened but unharmed. Like you."

Shaking worse than at the concert, she fell back against the cramped seat and prayed he was right.

The major did not catch up with them.

When they finally reached the castle, Alice grabbed the first armful of their things and raced through the side door as silently as she could. Since it was after midnight and the guests were saving their energies for the ball, the castle was quiet and in darkness. Alice lit a couple of lamps to make her journey easier. Abandoning her burden in the sitting room she shared with Helen, she found no sign of her sister. Nor was she in her bedchamber, or Alice's.

"She will be safe with the major," Captain Skelton whispered yet again as he and North helped move the carriage load of things to the side door. "Shall we take these inside for you?"

"Better not," Alice said, nervous of strangers being discovered in the castle with armfuls of art. "Thank you for bringing them this far."

In fact, as they crept away to the carriage, Alice was glad to have something to do. Making several trips to return everything to the sitting room kept her busy for a while longer. Then, reluctantly, she doused the lights on the stairs and in the passage and went to her own room.

The flowers that kind people had thrown onto the stage lay on her dressing table, looking a little tired and limp—not surprisingly, since they had been crushed in Cornelius's astonishing embrace and then scattered on the floor when she forgot all about them. She busied herself filling a vase with water from the jug on the washstand and arranging the flowers. Hopefully, they would revive.

She undressed slowly and climbed into bed, alert for every faintest sound, but there were none except the odd creak of timber and a distant snore that was certainly not Helen's. She turned down her bedside lamp and lay down. If she could just fall asleep, she would wake again to find Helen chattering away about her adventures.

She was far too anxious to sleep. She tried to bring back the elation of the concert, her sense of triumph and delight. She recalled the wonder of Cornelius's kiss and her own delicious reaction. None of it was enough to banish her anxiety over Helen.

IT WAS ALREADY dawn before she slipped into exhausted slumber.

She woke with a start to the sound of her bedchamber door opening. *Helen!* But before she could move, her brother whispered, "Alice." And a light shone on her face.

Fear paralyzed her all over again. *Still not home.* She had no idea what to say to Gervaise. She hung on desperately to Captain Skelton's certainty that Major Vale would bring her home safely. And if that was true, then blabbing to Gervaise would cause unnecessary trouble. So she lay still, pretending to be asleep, and Gervaise left again.

Slowly, Alice sat up and buried her head in her hands. How could she have abandoned Helen when she was in danger? Was she wrong to keep this from her family now?

IT WAS THE maid she shared with Helen who brought the news with morning tea.

"His lordship's in a great taking, and poor Lady Helen's in big trouble."

Alice's heart lurched with hope at last. "How? Why?"

"Found her walking with one of the handsome Vale broth-ers..."

Oh, thank God.

Almost sick with relief, she finished dressing hurriedly, while her sister's distinctive footsteps sounded in the passage. Almost running into Helen's chamber, she seized her, almost as tightly as she had held on to her before last night's performance, scanning her for signs of hurt.

For a moment, they clung together before they exchanged news. Which was when Alice realized they were not out of the woods yet.

CORNELIUS WORKED PARTICULARLY hard the day after his visit to Whalen. It began with the return of Rob Smith, in reality Will Farmer, who wanted to marry Betsy the parlor maid and take over the tenancy of a farm at Black Hill. Cornelius, who liked his rough dignity and knew only too well the plight of returned soldiers, gave him work and promised to discuss the tenancy with Julius if he proved himself.

Cornelius raced over the land at top speed, for he planned to walk over to Braithwaite, even to call at the castle, in the hope of speaking to Alice.

In truth, in spite of the wild excitement of holding her in his arms—or because of it—he was thoroughly ashamed of himself. She did not care for that kind of intimacy, and he had forced it upon her, which made him no better than Daubin or Atherstone or any of the others who had frightened her. For that at least, he owed her an apology, an explanation, even, that might just allow them to remain friends.

In his memory, though, she had not objected. But then, he had taken her—and himself—by surprise, and she might have been too frightened or frozen by disgust...

She had not *felt* disgusted. Her soft lips had trembled as they opened for him. He had felt their pressure, their instinctive, passionate response... Or was he fooling himself? Was he remembering what he *wanted* to have happened rather than what actually had? Why had he not stayed another few moments to find out?

Because he had heard people coming and he was trying to preserve her reputation. But he had to see her, had to know, if only to ease any harm he had caused her.

Returning home to change, he found everyone in a state of great excitement because Lucy had engaged herself—in truth this time—to Lord Eddleston. She appeared to be deliriously happy, carrying everyone with her, including Cornelius, who found he could not miss her celebratory dinner.

The next day, he decided to take time off in the middle of the day instead, in order to visit the castle. Having begun the clearing of some good land that had gone wild, and given orders for the necessary work to continue, he left the men to it and rode a little way off to the small headland, from where he could see both the sea and a large part of the Black Hill estate, much of it hills and valleys.

Here, he dismounted, sat on a rock rising from the ground, and delved into his battered satchel for the hunk of bread and cheese he'd wrapped in a napkin. If he meant to go to the castle, he should really go home and change first. Either way, he did not want his stomach rumbling.

However, he had not even taken a bite before he saw a rider galloping over the rise, exactly the way he had come. From the shape formed with the horse, she was female. One of his sisters? Was there trouble? He lowered the bread back to the napkin.

His heart thudded with hope even before he recognized Lady Alice. After re-wrapping his luncheon, he dropped it back in his bag and rose to his feet. She reined in her mount beside Cornelius's horse and dismounted unaided before he could reach her.

"Good day, Lady Alice," he said formally. "May I be of service?"

Her color was high from exertion, or perhaps embarrassment because of the way they had last met. "Actually, yes. I need to ask you something. Am I spoiling your luncheon?"

He blinked. "You rode over here to ask me that?"

Her lips twitched. The tension in her shoulders seemed to ease slightly. "No. It just struck me. Miss Vale told me you where you were likely to be, and your men sent me over here. You probably want peace."

"No," he said honestly, conducting her to his favorite rock and offering her the spot he had just vacated. "Actually, I was about to ride over to Braithwaite to call on you."

Her color deepened. She avoided looking at him, which made him ashamed. He wanted to kick himself. Then, with what seemed to be a gathering of courage, she raised her gaze to his.

She had beautiful eyes, clear and direct. It was not easy to discern the dreaminess behind the wry humor and the no-nonsense air, but it was definitely there. Even if he had never heard her play, he would have recognized that.

"It's as well I came, then," she said. "We couldn't talk in private there very easily. The castle is full of people, and Helen and I are in disgrace. Do you have loom over me like that?"

"No." He just hadn't wanted to sit too close without permission. Assuming he now had it, he lowered himself to the rock beside her. A pulse beat in her throat, just above the collar of her smart habit. When he breathed in, he could smell her fresh, light scent, with a hint of horse. He didn't touch her, instead gazed out over the land to give her time. And to compose an answer. "And your question?"

She took a deep breath. "Is your brother Roderick a good man?"

He jerked around to face her, staring. "Roderick?" Of course she must know Rod—his men had guarded them in Whalen—but he was quite unprepared for the surge of helpless jealousy. Rod was a dashing hero. Though Cornelius had begun to suspect his brother to be taken with Lady Helen. *Not Helen, Alice.* Or was Alice doomed to the same heartache as Cornelius? That would be funny if it did not hurt quite so much.

Pulling himself together, he said, "He is the best of brothers. Why do you ask?"

"I'm afraid Helen is going to marry him."

Cornelius almost laughed with relief. "Well, it is certainly a step down for her. I doubt his lordship would agree to such a match."

"It is his wretched lordship who is insisting on it. Our Whalen adventure is discovered. Worse, it all went horribly wrong at the end, and we got caught up in a riot that separated Major Vale and Helen from the rest of us. The major was injured, and he and Helen had to rest at an inn in Whalen. Gervaise caught them returning to the castle in the morning."

"Rod is injured?" How could he not know that? Because Roderick was barely at home, and kept such matters to himself, including the deeper wounds that troubled his sleep.

"It's minor, I believe," Alice assured him. "But the upshot is, rather than allow Helen to be ruined by scandal, Gervaise is insisting she marry either your Roderick or Mr. Glover."

"Who is Mr. Glover?"

"An old suitor of mine who took a shine to Helen instead. He was with Gervaise when Helen came home. I don't trust him, not least because he was at Whalen with Mrs. Maven."

"I'm lost," Cornelius said.

"Mrs. Maven seems to be someone from the major's unrespectable past."

"Ah. *That* Mrs. Maven."

"I don't trust either of them. But I'm afraid Helen is leaning toward Glover—somewhat bizarrely, because it is your brother she truly wants. To help, I need to know if your brother is worthy of her."

"He is worthy of anyone," Cornelius said at once. "He is brave and loyal to a fault. He is a good musician—you would like him—and he used to be great fun."

"Used to be?" Alice pounced.

Cornelius shook his head. Loyalty kept him silent. "The war has sobered him. He is debating his future, beginning new ventures like the guard service you made use of. I hope it will keep him home, but he still talks of returning to the army."

"Will he be faithful?" Alice asked.

Considering Mrs. Maven and others, it was a reasonable question. Cornelius didn't know the answer.

"If he loves her, I believe he would be. Under normal circumstances, I don't believe he would marry without it, but given your brother is holding a gun to his head…"

"I know," Alice said ruefully. "Gervaise has managed this very badly. Especially insisting that the marriage occurs immediately. He means to announce the engagement at the ball on Friday, which gives no one any time. If we had longer, I would advise her to choose Glover, who is a shocking fortune hunter, and then dangle a richer heiress under his nose so that he will be happy for Helen to jilt him. I thought of asking your twins to find one."

Cornelius's lips twitched. "I'm sure they would be honored. And successful. A good contingency plan, perhaps, but I'm not sure it would be good for Roderick's nerves."

"Does Roderick love her?"

Cornelius hesitated, shifting uncomfortably on the rock, which made him brush against her skirts. She did not withdraw them. "I would say he has a penchant. But he would never take advantage of her. If he stayed in Whalen with her, it was innocently."

"That is what Helen says. She seems to think she would please him by choosing Glover."

"She wouldn't."

"That's what I said." She sighed. "It's all a bit of a mess."

Cornelius reached for his satchel and took out the bread and cheese once more. Breaking it in half, he offered one piece to Alice.

"Thank you." She took it, gazing out across the sea and then inland over the fields and hills.

They ate in silence for a bit. It was curiously companionable and yet… uplifting. The combination of Alice and the land felt *right*.

"You are taming it," she said at last. "I can see the difference already."

"In places," he agreed, and somehow, without meaning to, he was talking about how nature had been allowed to take back previously cultivated fields, and his plans to expand into it and improve the yield of all the land.

He would have forced himself to stop sooner, only Alice asked questions and appeared to listen and understand. Lucy would have told him off for boring a lady with talk of crop rotations and sheep. Alice nodded, looking thoughtful, and did not change the subject.

Eventually, she said, "You love the land, don't you?"

He smiled into the distance. "How can you tell?"

"From your poems," she said unexpectedly. "And from the way you speak of it now. As though Black Hill is your child—or lots of children with their own unique characteristics."

He laughed. "I suppose it is. Like children, it thrives with care and will reward you unceasingly." He felt her gaze on his averted face and turned to meet it.

"Have you always felt like that? About land?"

He shrugged. "A little, I think. I love the beauty, and the rhythm of nature, the fact that the land nourishes us all, human and animal. And… I didn't know it at the time, but I think being dragged around Europe from pillar to post in the wake of my father gave me a yearning for stability. Ever since my first position as a steward's assistant, I've loved making a difference to the land and to the people who work it. Every estate became my home very quickly."

"But Black Hill is different," she said.

"It is. It's in my blood."

"Do you wish it were yours instead of Sir Julius's?"

He smiled again, shaking his head. "It *is* mine, in a way. The better the land, the better my salary, so I am living off it, too."

"Then you plan to remain with Sir Julius?"

"I would like to." Only as he said the words did he realize

how true they were. "Not necessarily in the house," he added. "It's the land that is home for me, and Julius is getting married. Antonia is wonderful, but I can't imagine she will really want us all under her feet forever. I have a notion to build my own house somewhere in Black Hill, or perhaps extend one of the cottages. Sometime."

Again they fell into silence.

"That must seem dull to you," he said, "who wants to travel the world and dazzle music lovers in all the world's capitals. You could do it, too. Such talent deserves to be shared."

Color seeped into her face. "Thank you. I'm not sure my nerves would stand the strain. Without Helen, I would never have got onto the stage. Without you, I would never have played a note."

He was so moved that a lump formed in his throat. "That will get easier with time."

"You are encouraging me to break my family chains and go."

"I am encouraging you to follow your heart."

"My heart holds too much. Our secret little jaunt has been a disaster for everyone. Helen is being forced to marry. I am in disgrace and untrusted. I have to positively *sneak* out of the castle now. Gervaise is distraught. It has made me realize the way scandal would affect the people I love. Especially Maria, who is dependent on the votes that put her husband in Parliament."

"A conundrum," he agreed. "But there is always some middle course."

"What?"

"I don't know yet, but there's bound to be one."

She smiled, and, for a while longer, they sat in silence, appreciating the beauty. She tugged at some moss growing on the rock at her side. "I should go," she said, so reluctantly that his heart beat faster.

"There is one thing we haven't talked about."

"Many, I should think."

He held her humorous gaze. "I kissed you."

"I remember," she said lightly.

"I'm sorry."

She jumped to her feet, obliging him to rise too. "You needn't be," she snapped. "I shan't hold you to marriage. In fact, it is already forgotten."

"You really are mistress of the set-down, aren't you?"

"What do you want?" she demanded. "A medal?"

"No, I want to know that I didn't hurt you, frighten you, or offend you."

A stricken look came into her eyes. Her lips parted as though in shock. She said hoarsely, "You must think me a very poor creature."

"I think you a splendid creature whose trust has been abused along with her person."

She swung away from him as though he was unbearable. "I simply do not like to be mauled. I am not so sheltered that I don't know it could be worse."

"And that is why you don't want to marry?"

"That and my music."

He gazed at her averted face, feeling helpless. "I was so pleased for you, so proud of you, and your elation was catching. It might not have felt like friendship, but it began that way. I'm sorry I mauled you."

"You didn't." She turned back in clear astonishment. Then she flushed to the roots of her hair. "It did not feel like mauling."

A weight fell from his shoulders. He wanted to seize her in his arms and repeat his offense. Instead, very delicately, he took her hand.

"Then perhaps I may do it again some time."

Her gaze flickered to his. "When?"

His breath caught.

Hers rushed out on a laugh as she pulled free and strode toward her horse. He boosted her into the saddle and, when she had donned her gloves, handed her the reins. As she took them, his hand twisted and grasped hers, willing her to look at him.

She said, "You will come to the ball?"

"I will come to the ball."

She smiled so sweetly that all he wanted to say stuck in his throat. Instead, he gently peeled back her glove and kissed the inside of her wrist. She shivered, but not with cold, and certainly not with revulsion. Her eyes were warm, if confused.

"Mr. Vale," she said breathlessly, and kicked the horse into motion.

"Lady Alice," he replied gravely.

Like a lovesick schoolboy—*or poet*, he taunted himself—he watched her until she breasted the hill and vanished from view. Then he started walking back to where he had left the men laboring and had to go back for his forgotten horse.

Chapter Eleven

WHILE ALICE FELT wild new emotions opening up like a flower in the sunshine, she was increasingly worried about Helen, who grew wan and pale. She seemed to have decided on taking Glover rather than Roderick Vale, so when Cornelius duly sent the twins to Alice at the castle, she tasked them with finding a massively rich heiress to distract the prospective groom.

"She definitely shouldn't marry Glover," Lawrence stated.

He and his sister exchanged glances, and then Leona said, "Roderick loves her."

Alice was sure that Helen loved him too, but she was too confused by her own emotions to understand Helen's.

The castle ball was to be a masquerade, but neither Helen nor Alice could bend their minds to costumes. Defiantly, they settled on the masks they had worn at Whalen, together with domino cloaks to keep to the spirit of the occasion. But if Helen was dreading the ball as though it were her doom—her engagement was to be announced at the end of it—Alice was looking forward to it merely because Cornelius would be there.

On the morning of the ball, she woke with butterflies in her stomach and happiness in her heart. She liked the feeling so much that she refused to overthink it in case it went away.

However, she could not help wondering what he felt for her.

He had gone to Whalen to listen to her, had come backstage to compliment her, and apparently he had liked kissing her. He had threatened to do it again, and Alice, once so certain that any physical intimacy disgusted her, could not wait.

She spent the day being a dutiful sister, helping Eleanor entertain the castle guests and resolving the issues of the servants, from ballroom decoration to kitchen logistics. She and her sisters were still a little wary of stepping on Eleanor's toes in such matters, trying to balance helpfulness against giving her her deserved place as lady of the castle.

They had been rained off a pall mall competition and were all rushing back inside for tea when the Duke of Atherstone strolled across the hall with her mother on his arm. Behind them walked a rather bowed man carrying a prayer book, presumably the duke's chaplain.

Abruptly, Alice's hopeful new feelings shattered into the distasteful memory of old ones. During one of the early balls of the Season, a man she had rather admired, mature, erudite, and handsome, had singled her out for his attentions. She had been undeniably flattered, and because he was a friend of her brother's, she had walked happily with him into that anteroom. And then he had changed from un urbane, agreeable admirer into an attacking beast.

Immediately the door was closed, his mouth had been mashed to hers, his tongue, hard and disgusting, halfway down her throat, making her gag and silencing her scream of rage and fear. His hands had been everywhere, the neck of her gown pulled down off her shoulders and impeding her arms as she tried to escape.

That was the worst part, the realization that she could *not* escape, that there was nothing she could do to halt the nightmare. No one had ever touched her with such roughness, such violence. She had hated the male body rammed against hers, its nasty, hard bits moving so revoltingly as his leg forced itself between hers. She had been helpless against his strength, trapped, her body pained, her mouth bruised.

It had seemed to go on forever, though when he had finally, casually, released her, the hands on the mantel clock had not moved. And yet for her, everything had changed.

"What are you crying for, silly little girl?" he had said indulgently, strolling toward a brandy decanter while she cringed back against the wall, tears streaming down her face, her legs too weak even to run. "Don't make such a fuss over a kiss. You must get used to a man's passion to be any use to him as a wife. You have advantages, you taste sweet, and you have a rather delicious body. I shall enjoy teaching you to kiss properly and please me in the marriage bed."

Somehow, she had fled from the room and found the cloakroom unseen to wash the tears from her face and re-pin her hair with shaking hands. She had married sisters; she had listened to debutante whispers of stolen kisses. But dear God, she would *never* submit to that—or worse! Her Season was wasted, for she would never marry.

All of that came back to her now, along with the knowledge that the fault was hers that she could not bear the intimacy of men. She had turned down the duke's offer of marriage. Yet here he was making up to her mother, as though her refusal had never been. As if her answer, her wishes, counted for nothing.

As Helen's counted for nothing, even with Gervaise, who was a kind and honorable man and the best of brothers.

A new fear was added to the old—that despite everything, she would be forcibly married and given into the power of this man.

It froze her to the spot. For a second, her gaze met the duke's and she knew he had seen the loathing she could not hide. Did he see the fear as well? Amazingly, a spark of warmth lit his eyes, as though her reaction pleased him, or at least excited some emotion in him.

Her mother released his arm with a smug smile, and he strolled forward, his hand held out to Alice as though they were old friends.

"Lady Alice, what a delight to see you again. I have spent a most pleasant week up in Scotland, but none of their conventional beauties could hold a candle to your charms."

She could not ignore his hand without causing talk. And he knew it. So, with a spurt of anger, she took a leaf out of his book and shaped her hand so that he received a mere two gloved fingers sliding off his as soon as they touched, and she sank into a curtsey.

"Your Grace. What an honor to see you back so quickly. You must excuse me—we have been caught in the rain and must change."

Although it was clearly a retreat, she refused to flee ignominiously. Instead she strolled upstairs with the others. Only when they parted ways did Alice seize Maria's hand.

"Whatever happens, don't leave me alone with the duke," she hissed, and fled into her own chamber.

WHEN SHE WAS very small, Alice had hidden in the gallery with her brother and sisters to watch the beautiful ladies and gentlemen dancing at her parents' spring and summer balls. The joyous music, the bright colors, the sparkling jewels, and the graceful, stately measures had seemed part of a fairytale, and her greatest ambition had been to grow up and become part of it.

Well, now she was, and her heart was not remotely given over to carefree enjoyment. Mostly, she was worried for Helen, who, despite all the advice of her sisters, seemed to have opted for the untrustworthy Glover. But Alice also longed to see Cornelius, and wished desperately for the Duke of Atherstone to be somewhere else entirely.

During tea, she had flitted about far too much to speak to anyone for longer than a moment, and at dinner—which had been earlier and lighter than usual—the higher precedence of her older sisters had kept her well away from His Grace.

She did, however, sit opposite the man who had arrived with Atherstone. He appeared to be a humble, somehow downtrodden man who said little after revealing to his dinner companions that he was the duke's chaplain and agreeing with them that he was extremely fortunate in his post.

And if ever a man needs to be reminded of God, Alice thought, *it is the Duke of Atherstone.* On the other hand, she was fairly sure Atherstone kept a chaplain merely to add to his consequence.

At the ball, Alice knew, the duke would be harder to ignore. She could hardly refuse to dance with him if he invited her, and she was unlikely to elude him all evening. Her best hope was that he would not cause trouble, considering the approval of her mother and brother to be enough to secure her hand.

As she changed after dinner, the dowager countess swept into her bedchamber to approve her gown and jewels for the ball.

After looking her up and down, Mama nodded grudgingly, much to her maid's relief.

"You should be a little more welcoming to the duke," she told Alice severely. "It is a great honor that he has come to Braithwaite Castle."

"I don't like him," she replied.

"Nonsense. You hardly know him, though even you must be aware he is the most eligible prize on the Marriage Mart. He showed no interest in Frances or Serena when they came out. His attentions to you are most flattering."

"I shall be civil to him, of course," Alice said. "But I have already told Gervaise I will not marry him."

"You might change your mind."

Alice scowled. "Because you did? Before we left London, it was Mr. Glover you wished me to marry!"

Mama waved one dismissive hand. "Well, Helen may have him if she chooses. Atherstone is by far the better match and, I don't mind admitting, much more than I had hoped for you. You will have precedence over me. And Serena."

"Much as I would enjoy jostling you out of my way—"

"Alice, I am serious."

"So am I," Alice said so grimly that her mother glared.

"Keep an open mind," she instructed her. "And remember what you owe to your family. Particularly now."

The conversation only added to Alice's anxiety, but at least it meant she entered the ballroom with her mother and Helen, and, masked or not, there were soon so many old Blackhaven friends to recognize and greet that she began to relax.

The Vales, who would have needed at least two carriages to travel in, caused a bit of a stir by their arrival—four tall, dashing men, accompanying two elegant ladies. Even masked, Alice knew them at once. The ladies were Delilah Vale and Antonia Macy.

Did she imagine Cornelius's searching gaze on her? No, for he was walking directly toward her! Her heart turned over with anticipation—but it seemed he was not approaching her at all.

He stopped beside a handsome couple and an elderly lady, and bowed. The gentleman held out his hand to Cornelius in easy friendship, and the younger lady smiled dazzlingly. Only then did Alice recognize her as Cecily Morgan. The man with her and her mother-in-law must be the straying husband.

Of course. Cornelius was to make him jealous. Alice had forgotten about that since he had kissed her...

How can I win against someone he already loves? Someone as beautiful as Cecily...

We are hardly in competition for him! She is married, and he is helping an old friend. And I...

The orchestra stopped playing, interrupting a thought that remained unfinished in Alice's mind. The musicians retuned quickly and began to play the introduction to a country dance.

As was the custom at castle grand balls, Eleanor opened the dancing not with the highest-ranking gentleman but with the squire, Mr. Winslow, leaving the duke dangerously free to choose. However, always conscious of his own consequence, he chose Serena, who was a marchioness, and Alice breathed again.

She watched Cornelius lead Cecily onto the floor, and wished it were her.

But she smiled at Colonel Doverton when he asked her to dance, for he was an old friend whom she liked very much. She enjoyed catching up with news of his wife—not a gentlewoman by birth but someone Blackhaven had taken to its heart—and family, and promised to attend the regimental ball at the end of the month.

As the dance came to a close, they giggled together at the entrance of the most stunning costume of the night—a young lady in the garb of the previous century with the widest hooped skirts imaginable and a massive headdress that she could only support with an odd, rigid walk.

The young Earl of Eddleston—Lucy Vale's betrothed—instantly asked her to dance, which caused a great deal more hilarity. Fortunately, it was a waltz and would require no energetic movement.

"What has she got inside that headdress?" Alice demanded. "It cannot all be hair!"

"We could dance close to her and find out," a voice murmured beside her, making her jump.

Instantly, her heart was drumming because the voice belonged to Cornelius. Tall and handsome in evening dress, his black domino hanging over one shoulder, he did not smile. His eyes were not distant at all but focused entirely on her. The mask lent him a new air of mystery, and emphasized the lean, sharp cheekbones. Butterflies soared in her stomach.

"If you are not spoken for," he added humbly.

"I am not," she managed, throwing a last smile at Colonel Doverton and curtseying to Cornelius, who bowed in return before offering his arm. She wondered if he remembered as vividly as she that the last time she was masked, he had kissed her.

"It is the same mask," he said softly, placing his arm at her back and taking her hand in his.

Oh, yes, he remembers! She hoped her flush was hidden. "It matched my gown."

"Beautifully. How are you?"

Right now, I could not be better. "I think Helen will take Glover. And Atherstone is here."

"So are both Daubins. I recognized the younger's golden locks. I'll try to keep an eye on both."

"Thank you, but you won't make Lady Morgan's husband jealous by watching my affairs."

"He is already jealous. She was smiling and clinging to my every word."

"Then you must keep up the momentum," she said, determined he should never know her own petty jealousy. "Oh my, *look*," she added, catching sight of the lady in the headdress who had stopped even pretending to dance and raised her hand to her hair. She opened a hidden door in the head contraption, and a small puppy leapt out, landing on Lord Eddleston's chest and then tumbling to the floor and running with both Eddleston and his partner in laughing pursuit.

Several couples left the dance floor, surging after them with delight.

"Bless her," Cornelius remarked. "She believes she is incognito."

"Who is she?" Alice asked, intrigued.

"My sister Lucy, of course. Purely for Eddleston's amusement. Don't say a word to anyone."

"Does it ever strike you that you don't have to tell your siblings your big secret, because they already know?"

"No. And I shan't quarrel with you, Alice Conway, so you needn't provoke me."

"It will be a novelty on both counts."

"We didn't quarrel in Whalen," he pointed out, and heat rushed up into her cheeks.

She liked waltzing with him, aware of his every movement and change of direction. She loved the feel of his hand at her back, and his light, firm clasp of her fingers. He held her at a proper distance too, though for the first time it struck her that she would be perfectly happy if he drew her closer…

She was perfectly happy now. All her anxieties seemed to have vanished into the soothing pleasure of his company. There may have been a novel excitement in his presence, but he made her feel safe. Not only that, she felt she was *Alice* to him, not the marriageable sister of the influential Earl of Braithwaite, not a mere dowry who had to be spoken to until she was safely married and under her husband's thumb.

His thumb brushed against her palm, making her shiver.

"What are you thinking?" he asked softly.

"That I have so many things to tell you."

"Is there somewhere we can talk in private? After the waltz."

Of course there was.

As the dance ended, protected by the milling throngs returning and seeking their next partners, Alice led Cornelius out on to the terrace, then swiftly down the step to a path that was not lit and to the ornamental pond overhung by a weeping willow and a covered swing-seat.

Cornelius flicked the seat with his domino, and Alice sat. After a moment's hesitation, he lowered himself beside her, not touching.

"Are you troubled?" he asked.

She shook her head, smiling. "No, not now."

Drifting on the breeze, music mingled with laughter and chatter. It was not totally dark yet, and the distant glow of light from the house lent the surrounding leaves a silvery hint, almost like one of Helen's more fanciful paintings. Here, in this little nook, only yards from the ball, it was as if they were in a separate world, safe and comfortable yet surrounded by an indefinable air of excitement.

"You wanted to tell me something," he reminded her.

She opened her mouth, frowned, then closed it again. "I did. I do. But now we are here, I don't know how to put it into words. I could do it with music."

"*You* can do anything with music. Such delicacy and passion together seems impossible, but you achieve it. And in your own piece, there is so much feeling bubbling beneath the surface—like poetry, I suppose."

"It is yours," she blurted.

Even in the gloom, she could make out the twitch of his frown.

"Your lament that Helen read so wonderfully that everyone cried at the garden party. From the moment I read that poem last winter, it obsessed me until I could put it into music that broke my heart all over again. It still breaks my heart as I understand it more and more… I'm sorry, you must hate that I stole your poem."

At least his face was still turned toward her and he did not appear to be appalled.

"Of course I don't hate that." He touched her hand as lightly as a moth wing, and she curled her fingers around his in gratitude. "I'm stunned that such beauty comes from my scribblings. Flattered beyond… What loss is it that moves you so?"

"I don't know," she said helplessly. "I'm afraid of losing the music, or love, or both, of losing the closeness of childhood with my sisters… And then in London this spring I knew I would never have the kind of love I had secretly dreamed of, because I am not made for marriage and children. I *only* have the music." She let out a breath like a sob, although it was also laughter. "I'm not making any sense, am I? Sorry, you must ignore me."

"I will never ignore you," he said slowly. His thumb brushed over her gloved knuckles. She didn't know if he was even aware of the movement, but she longed for it to be a caress. "Atherstone's assault convinced you of this loss."

She had never told him in so many words, and yet he understood. "I was never sure before."

"I don't believe you should be sure now. I don't know *any* women who enjoy being assaulted. It sounds to me like the man forced his attentions on a sheltered young girl in a particularly brutal fashion. Were you just being polite when you kissed me back in Whalen?"

Heat flooded her. "Of course not!"

"Then perhaps we should experiment," he said softly. "You were in an emotional state because of the music you had played, rightly triumphant because of your success. You threw yourself into my arms. Perhaps you were not frightened because you acted first."

"Perhaps."

His fingers slid over her hand and wrist and upward until he found the fastening of her glove, which he began to draw off.

"What are you doing?" she asked without fear.

"I want to kiss your fingers. And then, if you like, you can touch me and see if it disgusts you."

She wanted to laugh, but in truth, it felt curiously exciting to have a man—this man—remove her glove. He tucked it half into his jacket and raised her hand to his lips. She shivered, but it was certainly not with disgust.

"Take your hand back whenever you like. I won't try to stop you."

She had no desire whatever to take it back. Slowly, tenderly, he kissed each fingertip, then brushed his lips across her knuckles. She shivered, watching his bent head with something like awe. He turned her hand and kissed her palm, sending a thrill through her veins. Then he moved to the inside of her wrist, and the gentle pressure of his lips deprived her of breath. Was that his *tongue?*

She twisted her hand, and, immediately, he released her. But she only wanted to touch his cheek in the darkness, and when he raised his head, her fingers followed, tracing the line of his cheekbone beneath the mask, feeling the faint roughness of stubble on his jaw.

She couldn't help the smile flickering across her lips. Cupping his cheek, she leaned closer and softly kissed his mouth. Instantly, yet gently, his lips returned the pressure. Unsure, she withdrew enough to peer at his face. He followed, and just as gently took back her lips, parting them with the caress of his own and fastening there so sweetly that her heart seemed to drop into her tingling stomach. The warmth of his thigh burned through her skin, and that pleased her too.

"Correct me if I am wrong," he said huskily, "but you do not appear to be revolted or frightened."

"I'm not," she whispered. "Would you please kiss me again?"

He did, with infinite tenderness, his mouth moving on hers, his tongue just flickering over her trembling, wondering lips.

"I like your kisses," she whispered. "I like you, Cornelius Vale. Simon Sachev…" The rest was lost in another kiss. She had no idea and less care who began it, just that it was blissful and arousing and utterly overwhelming. Her hand had long since stolen around his neck, clinging to his nape.

Still kissing her, he rose, drawing her to her feet and then slowly releasing her. Silently, he took her glove from his lapel and began to slip it over her fingers. It wasn't easy in the dark, and it made her laugh. Smiling, he let her finish the task herself, then drew her hand to his arm.

She hated to leave the magical place this had become, but with him by her side, close enough to brush against her skirts, it did not seem so bad. In fact, life was rather wonderful.

Chapter Twelve

CORNELIUS FELT AS though he were walking on air as he returned to the ballroom with Lady Alice on his arm.

She might not love him, but she certainly liked him better than any other man of her acquaintance. Rage against the insensitive hurt done to her by an entitled—and titled—brute was lost in the wonder at the passion he had begun to ignite in her. God, she was delicious, desirable, delightful… She would let him away with nothing. She would scold, argue and defy, holding him to account and to the highest of standards. And she would expect no less from him. From the beginning, she had accepted criticism and apologized when she was in the wrong, which was something Cornelius would need to practice…

But he was rushing ahead of himself. A few kisses and a certain profound affinity did not mean marriage! The difference in their rank would never go away, and he would never be a wealthy man. He was the poorest of catches for an earl's daughter, and yet the possibility of Roderick's betrothal to Helen had given him hope. If Braithwaite was prepared to tolerate an alliance with one Vale, why not another? They were both younger sons.

One thing was certain—even if Cornelius had to run away with her and live on his wits in poverty, he would not allow her to be married to Atherstone. Or Glover, supposing Helen rejected him and he returned to Alice's court. In fact, he wondered if anyone would ever be good enough for her. *He* certainly wasn't! But if she loved him…

He was rushing too far ahead again. Politely, he bowed her through the French door into the ballroom, where the next dance was already underway. He strove to put distance between them, to protect her reputation, and immediately saw the hurt register in her eyes before her long, luscious eyelashes swept over them.

Snatching up a glass of champagne from the table, he presented it to her, making sure their fingers touched, and a smile trembled on her lips. He flicked one eye closed, so quickly no one else could have seen it, then escorted her to one of her sisters and bowed before walking away.

The first person he noticed was Darcy Daubin, dressed as a cavalier, striding purposefully toward her. A lady was obliged to dance with whoever asked her, and dogs like Daubin should not be allowed near her. On impulse, Cornelius seized Daubin by the elbow and led him away to a quiet corner by the gallery stairs.

They probably looked like friends conferring, since Daubin was too stunned to object until, just as Cornelius halted, he wrenched his elbow free.

"What the devil are you about?" He peered at Cornelius as though in an effort to recognize the man who had accosted him.

"Lady Alice does not wish to dance with you or even see you here. If you go near her, I'll black your other eye."

Daubin's lips fell open, as much in fury as in fear. "You're that steward fellow again! You're lucky I have not charged you with common assault! Who do you think you are to tell *me* what to do?"

"I am a gentleman, sir, which you most certainly are not. And I do not refer to your birth. You are a fraud in every way, and if you annoy me, I will make sure everyone knows it." With that, he bowed ironically and walked away.

DARCY DAUBIN SHOOK with rage, mostly because there was nothing he could do about it—not in the short term, at least. He was only too aware that Cornelius, as a Vale, was considered to be a gentleman, even when he was a mere steward of the land for his brother, while Darcy, as the son of a mill owner who had made his own fortune from nothing, was not and never would be. Even married to Lady Alice Conway, he would be whispered about behind aristocratic hands. But no one would malign him to his face as Vale just had. He would have influence and power through Lord Braithwaite, and by God, he would use it against the Vales.

He had a damned good mind to resume his journey to Alice's side and invite her to dance. If she claimed to be already engaged, he would ask for another. Only…

Only, Vale had called him a fraud. Had he discovered the appropriation of the sheep field bordering their properties? Which was really his father's business. Or had someone spotted the likeness of his poems to lesser-known works by Simon Sacheverill, Lord Byron, and others? The latter would be much more awkward for him socially. He needed a way to silence Vale. *In every way*, he thought viciously.

"You are happy to let that fellow dictate to you?" a smooth, quiet voice inquired close by.

Daubin blinked himself back into the real world to see an elegant gentleman emerge from the shadows of an alcove beneath the stairs. A few years older than Daubin, he was still handsome and fit apart from the shadows of excess about his eyes and mouth. He wore a purple satin domino carelessly hanging off one shoulder, while his mask dangled from a long, thin finger.

"I have too much respect for my host and hostess to indulge in a brawl beneath their roof," Daubin said grandly.

"Very commendable. I daresay a word with our host would

be a better choice, since his sister entered from the terrace with the scoundrel in question."

"Perhaps you are right," Daubin said thoughtfully.

"Who is the wretched fellow?"

"A brother of Sir Julius Vale of Black Hill. He acts as his steward." He didn't trouble to keep the contempt from his voice, which appeared to amuse his companion.

"He is probably illegitimate," the gentleman said. "Old Sir George Vale was an excellent diplomat but quite indiscriminate where he planted his seed, if you grasp my meaning."

"Sadly, this one was born on the right side of the blanket," Daubin said. "They are quite open about which of them are bastards."

"A pity," the gentleman agreed. "You are at something of a disadvantage. Although, to be perfectly frank, Braithwaite will consider neither of you. He indulges his sisters beyond what I find reasonable or advisable, but even he will not cross certain lines."

"You are saying I have no hope," Daubin said bitterly.

The gentleman smiled. "By no means. In fact, I am prepared to help you. Ah, I suppose I should introduce myself." He held out one thin, languid hand. "I am Atherstone."

Daubin's jaw dropped. He grasped the somewhat limp hand and gave a jerky bow. He almost felt he should drop to hie knees and kiss the man's rings. "Your Grace! Darcy Daubin, very much at your service."

"And I at yours," the duke replied, sliding his hand free. "A game of piquet, perhaps, to cement our new friendship."

"I would be honored," Daubin said. He would be seen with Atherstone, recognized as His Grace's chosen companion. And surely with a duke on his side, he could not fail. As they strolled together toward the card room, he asked, "What exactly do you have in mind?"

"Nothing we can discuss under this roof," Atherstone said blandly. "Perhaps we may meet tomorrow at the hotel…"

FOR ALICE, THE incredible truth, that she did not hate this much intimacy with a man, got lost beneath the wonder of Cornelius himself and the sheer happiness he brought her. Elated by their better understanding, she danced happily with old friends Bernard Muir and Tristram Grant, the vicar. They both remarked how radiant she looked, so she was probably smiling too much, like a cat with the cream, but she could not help it. Until Cornelius waltzed past with Cecily in his arms.

They were gazing adoringly at each other as though no words were necessary.

Alice missed a step and had to catch up. *They are playing their parts*, she told herself. *They are only trying to make her husband jealous.*

And yet it was Alice who was jealous. If he acted so well, how could she believe anything he said to her?

"Have I said the wrong thing?" the vicar asked lightly.

Alice forced a smile, the same kind of fixed, hectic glaze that had, in between witty retorts and sharp set-down, got her through an apparently successful London Season. "Of course not! I am just a little worried about Helen."

She should be. Gervaise was determined to announce her betrothal to either Glover or Roderick Vale before the end of the ball. No one could talk him out of it. Alice felt ashamed to have almost forgotten this much more important problem just because of her own chaotic feelings.

As soon as the dance ended, she dashed off in search of Helen, and instead ran into Cecily, who grasped her arm.

"Oh, Lady Alice, thank goodness. Do you mind pretending we are better friends than we are? My husband is approaching, and he won't scold if I am with you."

"I thought you *wanted* him to scold you?" Alice said acidly. "Is that not the point of your charade?"

"Pray, hush," Cecily said nervously, glancing around her. "Cornelius certainly flirts outrageously. I had forgotten that about him! Shall we walk a little?"

With odd reluctance, Alice complied. Her companion's beauty had taken on a livelier quality than before. She almost sparkled, as though thriving on this teasing of her husband—or the flirting with Cornelius.

"I had forgotten what pure fun Cornelius can be," Cecily confided. "He always puts his whole heart and all his attention into whatever—or whoever!—is before him. Do you think he might still be in love with me?"

It felt like a dagger in her heart. "He does not confide such things to me."

Cecily smiled tenderly. "He is not a great confider. But one can always tell by his eyes…" She sighed. "I was unkind to him. I miss him. Seeing him again even makes me wonder if I made the right decision in choosing Jack over him."

Alice could not speak, but then, she was not expected to.

"I am being unkind again, am I not?" Cecily said. "He is one of those rare, faithful men who love forever."

Sir John Morgan had apparently given up his direct pursuit of his wife and joined a conversation on the other side of the room, from where he cast occasional, brooding glances toward them.

"What should I do?" Cecily asked.

It crossed Alice's mind that Cecily loved this situation. From betrayed and neglected wife, she had become the object of attention for two men. Alice was saved from total misery only by irritation.

"I should remember why you chose Sir John in the first place," she said flatly.

"He has given me much," Cecily allowed. "Position, a beautiful home, wealth… and Lady Morgan. One is never warned about mothers-in-law when one considers marriage. She is a terrible old harridan."

"She is a friend of my mother's," Alice said, not without relish.

Cecily flushed. One did not, after all, offend the Dowager Countess of Braithwaite. She had probably forgotten who Alice was.

"I daresay it is my fault," she said with humility. "I have too much spirit. Cornelius always liked that in me… And I can see he has a position of respect here in Blackhaven. See how Lord Braithwaite himself is laughing with him now? Of course, Cornelius is brother to a baronet… I wonder how I might reward him for hurting himself like this just to help me?"

By leaving him alone. "Perhaps you should have decided what you wanted before you began quite such a public flirtation," Alice snapped. "A discreet affair must now be out of the question for you. You will excuse me."

She wanted to march away from the cloying, selfish creature who had won Cornelius's heart, but somehow she forced herself to stroll, smiling at acquaintances as she went.

And then a sound like a shot rent the air, followed by a scream of desolation, and the music stopped.

CORNELIUS KNEW A gunshot when he heard one. Though muffled by distance and music and chatter, he recognized it immediately. Even before the guests surged toward the French doors to the terrace, he was desperately searching the crowd for Alice. At the same time, other anxieties whipped through his brain—not least the effect of the shot on Roderick, who had come home from Waterloo with an aversion to loud noises. He had locked himself in his room during last week's thunderstorm.

"Thank God," he uttered, all but bumping into Alice, who was gazing with trepidation toward the window. The music had stopped, leaving the dancers in limbo, or pushing out on to the terrace to see what had happened. At her side, he felt for her hand, squeezing it in his relief. For an instant, her fingers clung, and then she pulled free, creating a more decorous distance.

"I am safe, Cornelius," Cecily said. "You need not worry."

Cornelius blinked. Cecily had never even entered his head, but he saw the stricken look in Alice's eyes before she grasped the arm of her passing brother-in-law, Lord Torridon.

"What is it? What has happened?"

"Eddleston is shot," Torridon said in his curt way. "He's alive, though, and the gunman was caught." His gaze flickered to Cornelius with approval. "By your brother, the major."

Cornelius felt a glow of pride in Roderick, not unmixed with relief that he was behaving more in character. Torridon hurried on, and then Sir John Morgan appeared at his wife's side.

"Oh, there you are, Jack," Cecily said carelessly. "Cornelius has been looking after me."

"Vale, my thanks," Morgan said, a little more coolly than usual.

The plan must have been working, though Cornelius found it hard to care when Alice had vanished from his side. When, the waltz resuming on the young countess's instructions, he glimpsed her laughing up at a dashing young officer of the local regiment, he felt an intense needle of jealousy. It struck him that the trick they were playing on Morgan was unnecessarily cruel.

It also struck him quite suddenly that he only had Cecily's word that Morgan was unfaithful.

His Grace of Atherstone was enjoying his evening. Observant and Machiavellian by nature, he was happily sowing chaos around the man for whom Lady Alice appeared to have an incomprehensible preference.

He had come north to this barbaric part of the country with the intention of taming her, for he most assuredly meant her to be his duchess. Not just because of her birth, dowry, and looks—all impeccable—or even because her brother's political influence might prove useful. Those things had certainly attracted him in the first place and made her eminently suitable. Her unexpected rejection of his marriage offer had certainly sparked a greater interest, but what mainly drove him was her frantic fear when he had stolen a small taste of her.

Atherstone liked creatures that were afraid of him. Dogs, horses, women—they all tended to behave in the same way, if they had any spirit, as Alice so clearly did. The combination excited him to try harder, and he always won. He would not only marry Alice Conway but tame her utterly.

Once her spirit was broken, he would no doubt lose interest, as he had with every other woman who had attracted his erratic attention, but she would still be Duchess of Atherstone and, hopefully, the mother of several children by then. He was a man who knew his duty and would carry it out whether with pleasure or with distaste. As Alice would learn to.

It was a long time since a woman had excited him to this degree. He hadn't expected it of his future wife. She was far, far more enchanting than he could have hoped from such a suitable alliance.

Many plans spun in his head. He had just set the amorous tradesman's son on one course, but there was never any harm in others. Having noted, with the rest of the ballroom, Cornelius Vale's flirtation with the insipid Lady Morgan, he was delighted to run into her husband in the card room.

He knew Sir John only slightly, but everyone was gratified to be noticed by a duke, so he wandered up to him as he stood watching the play at the whist table.

"Ah, it's you, Sir John," he observed after several minutes, as though he had just recognized the man behind the mask. "A curiously enjoyable evening, is it not? An unusual amount of excitement, although I am assured poor Eddleston will survive."

"One must hope so. Terrible thing to happen in a nobleman's

home."

"Absolutely. Though, of course, the Braithwaites are a little lax with their company. One meets all sorts at their parties. I was introduced to a dashed mill owner—give you my word! And a steward who imagines his gentlemanly ancestors make him worthy company."

That focused the man's eyes. "Can you mean Cornelius Vale?" he said a little stiffly. "He is a friend of mine."

"Really?" Atherstone allowed incredulity into his voice. "You are a most tolerant husband."

The tolerant husband's eyes narrowed.

"I speak as a man contemplating matrimony myself," Atherstone said, flipping open his snuff box and offering it to Morgan. "And learning from those who already enjoy that happy state. My trouble is, I am not sure I could tolerate quite such public displays of affection to another man. But then, I have always been selfish. Hand of piquet?"

THE INJURED LORD Eddleston, tucked up in a castle bedchamber after being treated by Dr. Lampton, was expected to live, and the culprit was already locked up in Blackhaven gaol.

Less welcome to Alice was the approach of the unmasking, when she fully expected Helen's betrothal to Glover to be announced. She was so anxious about that and trying so hard to keep her wayward mind off Cornelius and Cecily that, as the supper dance approached, she forgot to be vigilant and avoid the Duke of Atherstone.

Worse, she was with her mother when she finally saw him walking unhurriedly toward her, and Mama had spotted him also. She would not be permitted to run away or reject him. He knew she had seen him, too, for a faint, triumphant smirk curled his lips.

And then, behind her, a voice that melted her bones said, "Lady Alice, may I hope for this dance?"

Because of Cecily, she wanted to say no—although that would be as rude as refusing Atherstone. It would also be cutting off her nose to spite her face. Her mouther scowled with annoyance, but Alice turned immediately, already taking his arm.

"Thank you."

Cornelius bowed to the countess, and they joined the nearest set.

Conversation was difficult during a country dance, when you could only exchange words with your partner at the odd moments you came together.

"I am worried about Cecily," Cornelius said, like another thorn in her skin as they joined hands, turned, and separated.

"I wouldn't be," she said when they met again, adding the next time, "She is cleverer than she looks."

They turned together. "That is what worries me," Cornelius said.

And then it was their turn to dance all the way down the set, and any further speech was impossible. She could not help rejoicing that she would have his company for supper too, but she did wonder if she was only hurting herself. Every instinct told her to trust Cornelius. And if nothing else, she knew him from his poems.

Many of which were written for Cecily, her wary brain reminded her. Shaking off the warning, she focused only on Cornelius and began to simply enjoy the dance.

When it ended, she and Cornelius joined the laughing, excited circle for the unmasking. Atherstone, who had never troubled to wear his mask, lounged on a chair outside the circle, looking tolerant and superior. Alice insinuated herself next to Helen and Geoffrey Winslow, afraid Gervaise might announce her engagement to Glover.

Helen's eyes darted all around the masked circle.

"Who are you looking for?" Alice whispered in her ear.

"Meg Maven is here. I saw her."

"Seriously?" Meg, for some unclear reason, had apparently paid for the riot that had threatened them in Whalen and led to all this mess. "How? She would never have been invited, and the staff are strict now about collecting the cards of all the guests. Someone must have brought her. Or let her in. You know, I don't like the way she is always behind trouble—"

"There she is," Helen murmured, nodding a few places to the left of Alice. "Cleopatra. Next to Bernard Muir."

Alice followed her sister's gaze. While Eleanor was congratulating her guests on their marvelous costumes and general mysteriousness, Cleopatra was watching Roderick Vale. This, surely, was the root of the trouble, and she was here purely to upset Helen further.

Under Alice's watchful gaze, Meg slipped out of the circle and around the outside. Suspecting she meant to pass them to Roderick's side, Alice refused to allow it.

As the woman passed, Alice whirled and caught her, sweeping her back into the circle between herself and Cornelius, who blinked in surprise.

But Eleanor had issued the command: "Unmask!"

Cornelius stepped behind Meg and began untying Alice's mask. Though her whole body tingled at his touch, she noticed at once that Meg was trying to slip away again. Alice pounced and twitched the mask off her face.

"Madam," Alice said icily, pretending surprise, "I do not believe you were invited."

But Meg was a worthy opponent. With a dazzling smile, she said loudly, "Your ladyship is mistaken. I entered on the invitation of my betrothed, to the gracious welcome of Lady Braithwaite herself."

Helen went rigid.

"My betrothed," Meg stated with even greater clarity, "Major Vale."

Alice wanted to smack both of them for what they had done

to Helen. In the sudden silence, as everyone tried to work out what on Earth was going on, Roderick crossed the circle toward Meg.

Meg had forced his hand, Alice saw suddenly. Afraid he would marry Helen, Mrs. Maven was publicly making her claim to a man who would be too honorable to deny her. Well, she wasn't getting away with that. Helen should at least have the choice of Roderick.

"Major Vale is your betrothed?" Alice said with blatant disbelief.

Meg laughed and opened her mouth to reply.

"Of course not," Roderick said clearly. "Mrs. Maven jests. She knows perfectly well that I cannot be betrothed to her, charming as she is. For I am already betrothed to Lady Helen."

Oh, well done, sir! Alice smiled at him radiantly.

But Helen had half turned away from him, poised for escape, as though his claim changed nothing. Surely, loving Roderick, as it was clear she did, she could not now take Glover? Helen paused and turned slowly back to face Roderick.

"Oh, thank God," Alice muttered.

Gervaise all but galloped up to them. "Is this true, Helen? Do you wish to marry Major Vale?"

"Of course I still wish to marry Major Vale," Helen said in a rush. "We are indeed engaged—with your approval?"

"Of course with my approval," Gervaise said, grinning, and shook hands with Roderick, before taking Helen's hand and placing it in that of her betrothed instead.

Cornelius thumped his brother on the back. "You old dog! Kept that very quiet! Congratulations, big brother! Lady Helen, welcome to the Vales."

Bernard Muir, that stalwart friend of the Conway family, was turning the previous little drama into a joke, laughing while he swept Meg away as though to supper.

It was not total victory for Roderick, however. "Shall we go into supper?" he asked Helen. "Or shall we go somewhere quieter to talk?"

"I am promised to Mr. Winslow for supper," she said perversely. "Excuse me."

As she flitted away with the rather surprised Geoffrey Winslow, Cornelius murmured, "Have you made a mess of this, Rod?"

"A huge mess," Roderick said.

Alice took a deep breath. "She thinks you don't love her. She thinks you are doing this merely for honor. And by the way, how *did* that woman get in here?"

Roderick stared at her. "What in God's name do you take me for?"

"Rod," Cornelius said warningly.

But Alice suddenly understood and smiled. "*Glover.* Of course—he brought her in to scupper your chances. Don't give up, major."

Chapter Thirteen

"WHAT A CONVOLUTED life our families lead," Cornelius remarked as he led Alice in to supper.

"Helen and your brother? Perhaps they have not been honest with each other."

Cornelius cast her a quick glance as he though he knew it was a barb, but he seemed more curious than ashamed. There were far too many people around then to discuss anything personal.

As they approached the buffet tables, Cornelius suddenly grabbed the arm of Sir Julius. "Where is Lucy? How is Eddleston? Have you heard?"

And Alice immediately felt guilty she had barely thought of the young earl once she had heard he was alive. She had been too taken up with the problems of the living—namely herself and Helen—to consider Eddleston's injury.

"They expect him to live," Julius said. "Lucy must still be with him. I don't see her here." His one eye fixed on Alice. "Shall we sit together, and we can gossip about our brother and your sister?"

"We could just sit with my sister and ask," Alice said, but Helen was already seated with Mr. Winslow at a small table where no one else could join them.

"Repelling all boarders," Sir Julius remarked.

Hastily, Alice changed the subject. "When does your own

wedding take place, sir?"

His rather harsh face softened. "In about a fortnight."

"I wish you very happy," she said genuinely. He had the face of a man who had suffered much and could not quite believe in his current fortune. But when they sat down with his betrothed and Roderick, it was obvious that Antonia adored him. Roderick and Cornelius seemed also to have taken her to their hearts, for they laughed with her and teased her as though she were already one of them, and Antonia bantered back. When Lucy rushed in, both smiling and tearful, the whole family gathered her in, shielding her from the curious and comforting her.

They were good people, Alice thought with a lump in her throat. Kind people. Amusing people. So why did she doubt Cornelius?

Because he had said nothing that could not be construed as mere flirtation? In all honesty, he had offered nothing else, and yet...

"What did you mean about Lady Morgan?" she murmured as they returned to the ballroom at some distance from other people.

"I'm not sure," he said. "Just that Morgan looked upset very quickly when I danced with her. Did he look like a guilty man to you?"

"No. But I believe men—some men—regard other women as their right, but do not accord the same to their wives."

Cornelius grunted, obviously distracted, though his gaze remained on her face. "What did she say to you?"

Alice's cheeks burned. "That she doubted the wisdom of her choice when she dismissed you. I don't know how serious she was." Miserably aware that she could be driving him into Cecily's arms, she refused to be less than honest. "That she values your friendship and loyalty."

His lips twisted. "I may not dance with you again, may I?"

"No, my mother would have an apoplexy, and in Gervaise's current form, he would have us married by the end of the week."

Cornelius laughed, and Alice's heart lightened, especially when she felt the secret brush of his hand on parting. It gave her the strength she needed when she could no longer avoid the Duke of Atherstone.

She was with Serena and Lord Wickenden, an old family friend, and several others when she saw the group parting as if of one will. She knew Atherstone was coming. Well, it had only ever been a matter of time. She could not avoid him forever. If he offered again, she would refuse him again, and now she knew better than to go anywhere alone with him.

So she curtseyed to his bow, and, as he exchanged pleasantries with Serena and Wickenden, who were old acquaintances of his, she began to hope that he had not come for her after all.

But he had. "May I hope for this waltz, Lady Alice?"

"Thank you," she said graciously, glancing at Serena as her nominal chaperone. The duke should really have asked her permission, but such conventions were relaxed at a masquerade, she supposed, even after the unmasking. However, she doubted the duke, so exalted and toadied to by Society, ever asked permission. Even his invitation to her sounded more of a command.

"You have become quite the belle of the ball," he murmured as the orchestra struck up their introduction, and he placed his arm at her back and clasped her hand.

Her flesh crawled, though she refused to show it, "It is my family's ball," she said wryly. "Everyone feels obliged to dance with me."

He waltzed her backward and turned, maintaining the perfect distance between them, for which she was grateful. "Yet you danced twice with the same man. I do not like that."

"Oh dear," Alice said with no pretension whatever of regret. "But then, Your Grace's permission is not required."

"It is now."

"I fail to see how," Alice said frigidly.

"We are betrothed."

Fear churned her stomach, but she would not give in to his mocking, overwhelming gaze. "I missed that announcement."

"It was lost in your sister's to the obscure officer."

"You are deluded."

"They are *not* betrothed?" he asked derisively.

She smiled. "He is not obscure, but a decorated hero praised by Wellington himself."

"Braithwaite could look higher."

"Braithwaite is already married."

"You have humor," he observed glacially, although she did not like the spark behind the ice. "And a certain vivacity that I enjoy. Neither should be overdone."

"In the opinion of Your Grace, which, of course, must weigh with me, because you are the guest of my family."

He smiled, the spark stronger and oddly terrifying in the cold face. "Oh, I shall enjoy schooling you. For a time, at least. Shall I push Braithwaite for an early wedding? Or should I allow us time to enjoy the anticipation?"

Her blood chilled. "The only say my brother will have is to refuse any offer you make for me. I have already told you my answer, and so has he. I would be grateful if you did not press me further."

"Oh, my sweet child, I shall press you a great deal further," he mocked. "But the wedding is already decided. *You* have no further say in that."

"I shall not marry you. Ever. I would like to return to my sister."

Rather to her surprise, he stopped dancing and placed her hand solicitously on his arm, walking her off the dance floor.

There, she thought in relief. *Like most bullies, all he needs is someone to stand up to him.*

But he was not walking toward any of her sisters. He had her hand clamped under his on his arm, and his much larger body was pushing her away from the dancers and toward the door into the part of the castle that was not open to the public.

She halted, digging in her heels in, but he merely pulled her on, his strength frightening.

"Don't make a fuss," he said in in light, conversational tone. "I shan't touch you unless you provoke me beyond endurance. But we need to talk, to clarify a few matters."

"Talk to my brother," she snapped, though a pulse had begun to beat hard in her throat, making it difficult to speak.

"Oh, I shall, I shall," Atherstone said, pushing open the door at the end of the passage.

She tried to bolt, but somehow he had got behind her and pushed her inside with his body. The door closed, sending memories spilling through her brain, paralyzing her. She could already feel, again, the terrible suffocation of his mouth, his hard, cruel grip that she could not break...

But he liked her fear. *That* was the spark she had recognized in his eyes when they danced.

So, as she had done so often during her Season, to cover her discomfort and the fact that she did not wish to be there, she raised her head, produced a distant smile, and pretended to wait patiently for him to say something interesting.

"Braithwaite is an unusually indulgent brother," Atherstone said, walking up to her. Instead of halting in front of her, he walked around her in a circle. "So it is likely that you do not appreciate how little power young ladies of your class possess in the matter of marriage. It is all with your brother and me, not with you."

The back of her neck pricked, but as he re-emerged before her, she shrugged elegantly, a mixture of her haughty mother and Frances. "If you imagine so, by all means go ahead and tell Braithwaite—and the world, if you are silly enough—that we are betrothed. I shall still deny it, even if by some miracle you get me to the altar. I have a remarkably clear and carrying voice."

Her words did not appear to surprise him, let alone upset him. Instead, he smiled. "You are a unique case," he allowed, rather like a doctor diagnosing a rare illness. "Which forces me to take other steps. If you defy me, I shall simply ruin Cornelius Vale and his entire family. Financially and socially."

Her lips parted in shock. "You can't!"

He laughed. "Don't be silly. Of course I can. I might even enjoy it."

She couldn't breathe. Blindly, she tried to walk past him, but he would not stand aside, even mirrored her every step, demonstrating his implacability and the futility of defying him.

"I don't suppose you have considered," she said, proud of the steadiness of her voice, "all the ways a wife may find to kill her husband."

At last she had shocked him. She saw it in the momentary widening of his cold eyes. And then the door suddenly opened and Delilah Vale almost tumbled into the room with Antonia Macy, Lord Linfield the diplomat, and his sister Miss Talbot. All the ladies were laughing.

"Oh, Lady Alice," Delilah said in apparent surprise. "Just the person we were looking for. Your mother wants you."

Since Atherstone had turned haughtily toward the newcomers, Alice walked straight past him. But he still imagined he had a victory.

"I trust I may rely on your discretion, ladies, my lord," he said in his smooth, hateful voice. What he clearly meant—and assumed would happen—was that they would shout Alice's *in*discretion from the rooftops, providing yet another reason for her to marry him.

"For what?" Linfield said. "We were here all the time. Your Grace."

He bowed. The ladies all curtseyed. Alice did not. She merely walked out of the open door.

Delilah caught her hand as Linfield closed the door on the duke. "Are you well?" she asked, her voice casual, though her eyes were piercing.

"Quite." Alice swallowed. "How did you...?" she began shakily.

"Cornelius was worried but thought it best we find you by apparent accident. Cornelius cannot act to save his life."

Then he was not acting with Cecily…

The ball, which had begun so excitingly, so blissfully, had turned into a nightmare. Like so often before, she just wanted it to end.

And yet she was ridiculously grateful when Cornelius made a point of seeking her out as his family took their leave. Having thanked Eleanor, he stepped back to allow Lucy, Felicia, and Sir Julius to discuss Eddleston's care with Eleanor and Maria, and her heart leapt pathetically as he came directly to her.

"May I call tomorrow?" he murmured. "Or would you meet me outside?"

"Outside," she said at once, for she wished to be under the same roof as Atherstone as little as possible, and she was sure there were fierce family quarrels to come over Helen's betrothal.

"You're liable to get caught in the rain… Do you know the old chapel near the Black Hill boundary?"

"Of course. Two o'clock," she said, and walked away to speak to Delilah.

BY THE TIME Alice discreetly left the castle the following day, she was in a state of deep confusion over her own life and profound anxiety over her little sister's. Oddly, the person she wanted to talk to, to help her sort everything out, was Cornelius, and yet there were too many things she could not tell him.

He won't even be there. It will be best if he isn't. I'll give him a quarter of an hour, and then I shall simply ride home again.

The old chapel was a small stone ruin next to a stream. Though local people said it was an abandoned church, it was so ancient that no one actually knew what its original purpose had been. It had four walls up to about shoulder height, and someone, perhaps a vagrant or a courting couple, had placed what looked like a large wooden headboard on top of the walls, lashing it in place with frayed ropes wrapped around the window hole on one side and the space left by a broken stone on the other. It didn't add to the place's beauty, but Alice supposed it was practical, if precarious.

He won't be there.

He stood between the chapel and the stream, gazing at the flowing water, so deep in contemplation that he didn't notice her presence until she dismounted. At the thud of her boots on the damp ground, he turned and smiled, a spontaneous, welcoming smile that melted her bones, particularly as he strode at once to meet her. His fingers brushed hers as he took the reins from her and tied her horse next to his at a fallen tree that must have come down in last week's storm.

"I was afraid you wouldn't come," he said.

I was afraid you *wouldn't.* "I nearly didn't. Everyone in the castle seems to have run mad. Eddleston is shot yet merry as a lark, and even my mother, a high stickler for propriety, does not object to your sister Lucy haunting his bedchamber. Admittedly, her focus is on other things, since Helen is to be married within the week."

"A *week*?" Cornelius repeated, clearly startled. "Why the rush?"

"Presumably because Gervaise does not believe in her and Roderick's innocence after the Whalen disaster."

"Don't call it that," he said quickly. "It was not a disaster but a triumph for you both."

"And yet Helen is to be rushed into a marriage she is not ready for just because your brother was injured saving her from a riot." She broke off, swallowing. "Sorry. She is younger than me. We did everything together, but I always tried to look after her."

He took her hand. It jumped in his hold, but she did not withdraw it. "If it helps, I have never known Roderick to be pushed into anything he did not want. It may be going faster than he had planned, but I think he always meant to marry Helen."

"Always? They have only known each other a fortnight! And no one can change my brother's mind. I have never known him so stubborn."

He tugged her by the hand, encouraging her to walk with him by the stream. "The twins approve," he said lightly. "And Lucy likes Lady Helen. She has an odd gift of reading character from very little. If she thinks Helen and Rod are suited, they probably are. The timing may seem wrong, but I think we have to leave that to the happy couple to sort out."

"But that's the problem!" Alice exclaimed. "She is *not* happy! Just determined to go through with it."

"Are *you* happy?" he asked.

"What?" She glanced up at him, flustered. "We are not talking about me."

"I am." He halted and, with one light hand on her shoulder, turned her to face him. "Delilah thought Atherstone had not touched you last night. Did he?"

"No. He is nothing, and I don't even want to think about him. Helen is much more important."

"So are you." Without warning, he bent and kissed her parted lips.

Her heart fluttered. Her thoughts scattered, and yet it lasted only an instant.

"I want to show you something," he said, and dragged a scroll of paper from his pocket.

Intrigued, she released his hand and unrolled it. As she read, she leaned back against the tree next to her, vaguely aware of the gurgling of the stream water, the singing of a blackbird, and Cornelius, standing very still, staring into the stream as though he could not bear to see her reaction. That trust touched her more than anything. She realized he had never shown his poems to anyone, apart from the publisher who had been hundreds of miles away when he read them.

This poem was about a woman, full of fun and wit, life and longing. His woman leapt off the paper, vital and fascinating, sweet and desirable, brave, talented, and true to her dreams.

It moved her to smiles and almost to tears. *If I could only inspire a quarter such joy in him...*

"Is it new?" she asked, aching because it must have been inspired by meeting Cecily again.

"Yes." He looked up from the stream and met her gaze. Color stained his weather-beaten skin. "I wrote it for you."

"Me?" Her voice squeaked, and his lips twitched.

"You told me you put my poem to music. I can be no less honest. Don't you recognize yourself?"

She shook her head, unable to speak. Blindly, she let the paper roll back up and handed it back to him. "It isn't signed," she said gruffly.

"I didn't know how to."

Cornelius and Simon... Does one love Cecily and one me?

His smile had grown rueful. "No criticism?"

"It is beautiful," she managed. "Wonderful. But it is not me."

"It is how I see you."

Heat flooded up from her toes, burning her face, and all she could think of to say was: "You wrote poems to Cecily, too."

He considered. "I wrote poems of love and loss. Emotions she inspired in me. But they were not *her*. I don't think I ever knew her."

He had not taken the scroll from her, and her hand fell as she gazed at it. "And this is *me*?"

"Don't you recognize yourself at *all*?"

She shook her head, then frowned and unrolled the paper again. A smile flickered across her lips. He saw the vulnerability beneath her brusque tongue, her chafing at the bonds of propriety that confined her nature as well as her talent. It was too intimate, too *terrible*, to be so easily read. And yet it was beautiful...

She was afraid to look up.

"Keep it," he said lightly.

And because she could not bear him to think she was disappointed—God knew she was not!—she took a step closer.

"Thank you," she whispered, and stood on tiptoe to kiss his cheek. And then, because it was so close, his mouth. She let her lips linger, softly caressing his. He felt so wonderful, especially when his arms closed loosely around her and he kissed her back.

She slid her free hand up over his broad shoulder to his nape to draw him closer, and now the whole length of his body touched her. Feeling a surge—not of fear but of excitement—she pressed closer. Still the blissful kiss went on and on while he softly stroked her back, her cheek, her nape.

When he swept his hand down over the curve of her rear, she gasped with more pleasure than shock, and he deepened the kiss, not with force but with leisurely, sensual coaxing. Fire licked through her whole body, even in places a lady did not think about. *Especially* in those places.

Oh, help me... She wanted it to go on forever. She wanted more. He stroked her waist, and upward, brushing the side of her breast, spreading his caressing fingers until she moaned, gluing herself to him, and the hard column against her abdomen was not remotely disgusting, but elating and wonderful...

He let out a groan, dragging his mouth free and pressing his cheek to hers. She could feel his heart thundering above hers.

"You are too beautiful," he said unsteadily. "Did I hurt you?"

"No," she said, bewildered by the question. "You may kiss me again if you like."

"Oh, I like," he said fervently. "But in truth, I daren't. You are much too tempting." He glanced upward at the sky. "And I think it's going to rain."

They went into the chapel, even Alice having to duck beneath the makeshift roof. It stank a bit as if animals had sheltered there too, but when Cornelius spread his overcoat for them to sit on, and lounged against the damp wall with his arm loosely around her shoulders, she was utterly content.

But she never dodged difficult issues. And this was one she had to know.

"Tell me about Cecily Morgan."

Chapter Fourteen

DARCY DAUBIN STRUTTED into the Blackhaven Hotel and took some considerable pleasure in asking for the Duke of Atherstone. Rather to his disappointment, he was taken not the main dining room, where he might have been seen with the great man—he was ushered into a small salon more like a private parlor. And the duke was not even there.

"Where is His Grace?" he demanded.

"I could not say, sir. He instructed me to show you in here. May I fetch you refreshment?"

"A brandy, if you have a decent one," Daubin said ungraciously.

Ten minutes later, he had almost finished it when the duke sauntered in.

Daubin sprang to his feet, bowing.

"Ah, Daubin, there you are," said Atherstone, as if he were not the latecomer. "Such excitement at the castle. It's quite exhausting. What with Eddleston fighting off all the ladies who wish to nurse him, and an extraordinary number of Vales floating about the place as though they are guests, I don't know whether to be fascinated or appalled."

A glass of brandy was placed reverently in front of him by the same footman, who bowed and departed, closing the door behind him.

"Vales?" Daubin repeated uneasily.

"Young, pretty girl who appears to be engaged to Eddleston. The major who claims to be betrothed to Lady Helen—who hardly looks charmed by the prospect, and who could blame her? Sir Julius called too, apparently to make arrangements for moving Eddleston—poor fellow—to the Vale hovel. I have even seen a pair of children with Vale characteristics who look so damnably alike that one cannot tell boy from girl."

"But no Cornelius Vale?" Daubin asked.

"Not when I left, but there could have been more of them skulking in closets or hiding behind doors. And so you have a *tendre* for Lady Alice?"

Daubin blinked, trying to catch up with the duke's shift between contemptuous commentary to serious question. Once more, he took in the haughty, aristocratic features and the cool, clever eyes. It would do no good to pretend any kind of equality with this gentleman. Daubin must be the supplicant, humble and grateful for the great man's assistance.

"My birth is not worthy," he said sadly. "Although I have been educated as a gentleman, with all a gentleman's circumstances, my father is a mere mill owner. And yet I have much to bring to an alliance. To be vulgar, Lord Braithwaite would not object to my wealth, encumbered as he is with impoverished sons-in-law. Tamar must cost him a fortune. Hanson is a nobody, and I don't believe Roderick Vale has a penny to his name."

"The perils of allowing one's womenfolk to choose," Atherstone said with a curl of his lip, "when they do not have the brain necessary to do so. Most assuredly Braithwaite would be happier with your good self than with the land steward. But I know for a fact that if Lady Alice rejects your offer, so will he."

Daubin sighed and finished his brandy. "Your Grace will forgive me if I say I found her quite rude. Devoted as I am, I cannot help feeling she needs to be taught who is master."

"Most assuredly not the females of the house," Atherstone said.

Daubin waited, but the duke said no more, merely looked thoughtful while he swirled the brandy in his glass.

"And yet you implied last night that there might be hope for me," Daubin urged.

"Oh, there is always hope," Atherstone said blandly. He glanced up. "For those with the courage to flout convention and act decisively."

"Meaning…?"

The duke flipped open his snuff box and took a small pinch. "Meaning, abduct her, my friend. Elope. Marry her out of hand. The Braithwaites will cover it up and, for appearances' sake, welcome you to the family."

Daubin's mouth fell open. But fantasy was already flying. Alice at his mercy, in his power and in his bed. Her beautiful dowry his, along with her family and all their influence. His future was assured.

He began to smile.

Atherstone allowed himself a mere twitch of the lips. "You see the advantages?"

"Intimately."

"Then go to it, my friend. There will be many opportunities. Lady Alice rides out alone and frequently walks to Blackhaven by herself or with one sister. It is a form of arrogance on the Braithwaites' part, but I see no reason why you should not take advantage of it. In fact, when you have made your plans, inform me of the details and I shall endeavor to—ah—put his lordship off the scent until you are clean away."

"Perfect!" Daubin exclaimed.

"Perfect indeed," Atherstone murmured.

"CECILY," CORNELIUS REPEATED, with a sort of rueful nostalgia. "I could not believe my luck when she danced with me at the local assembly. Sir John was kind to me. I dined at his table, was invited to his mother's dinner parties. Cecily's family were neighbors, so I saw a good deal of them. She was everything I thought I wanted, more than I had ever dreamed."

Feeling Alice's stillness, he turned her face up to his, reading the pain in her eyes.

"I was lonely," he said more urgently. "This was my first post as chief steward. I no longer had a mentor or his family. I felt desperately alone, and I was dazzled by Cecily's beauty, and more than anything by the fact that she had chosen me. I knew her father would not be happy, but he was an amiable man, and I *am* a gentleman. She had no brothers, and there was no entail, so if we had married, in time we would have inherited his land. It was enough for me to hope. In the meantime, we met often, and then, on the day I had plucked up the courage to speak to her father, Sir John stepped in and did so."

"Did he know about your understanding with Cecily?"

"No, I don't think so. To be honest, I think my understanding was different to hers. But he must have seen my preference for her. At any rate, he was very kind when I sought another post, gave me a glowing reference."

"You love her still?"

He shook his head slowly. "No. That part of my life is over. We have both grown up, I think. I could never refuse to help her, but, to be honest, I wonder now how I could have found her so fascinating. She seems...bland, almost shallow, with occasional blinks of cleverness. I don't think she is being honest with me."

"She wants you back," Alice said.

He frowned, searching her eyes, which were clear and determinedly brave. He could not help drawing her closer until her head rested against his shoulder. "I have nothing that she wants."

"She wants adoration."

"Perhaps." It felt disloyal to say so, but he suspected Alice was right. In any case, he did not want to think of Cecily and the past, not when he had the wonder of Alice in his arms. Her kisses, so shy and so passionate, intoxicated him. He could not help taking another, even though the temptation to teach her more, much, much more, clamored within him. She was too enticing for his willpower, all the more so because she seemed to have no idea of her effect, of her attraction.

Whoever won her in the end, whoever married her, would be a damnably lucky man.

The very thought enraged him.

He pulled back a little too abruptly. "The rain is off, and you should go home. I have work to do." Was that hurt in her eyes? He could not help kissing it away. "I will see you at church tomorrow."

She nodded dumbly, and he led her back outside to the horses. After drying off her saddle with his abused overcoat, he helped her to mount and kissed her wrist as before. She swooped, kissing him on the lips in return, and then she galloped off, the bright, vital spark to his life.

I am doing it again, he thought. *Falling in love with a girl I cannot have.* Only Alice was so different. Unlike Cecily, she was his friend, his critic. And somewhere he knew that when they parted—as part they inevitably must—his pain and loneliness would be far, far worse than ever before.

Walk away while you still can, he urged himself. And knew that he would not. *Let the poem play out until the end.*

Having checked that the work he had ordered was in full swing, he rode home. He was just unsaddling the horse when his sister Felicia strode purposefully in.

"Don't," he said, guessing immediately what she wanted to discuss. "Leave Roderick to his own marriage. She's probably the best thing for him."

"Why do you think so?" Felicia asked. "Do you know her well?"

"I know Roderick. And I have it on good authority that Lady Helen is devoted to him. Is that all?"

"No, grumpiest of brothers," Felicia replied. "It is not. In fact, it's not at all what I came to ask you. You know the land around here and all around Blackhaven. Can you tell me where there are disused buildings?"

Remembering the ancient chapel, he felt a guilty flush rise to his cheeks. Could she possibly know? Hell, had the twins been lurking about the area unseen?

"There would have to be lockable doors," Felicia continued, frowning, "probably boarded or shuttered windows, and be far away from other dwellings, roads, and pathways."

Cornelius, still clutching his saddle, turned to stare at her. "Why the devil do you want to know that?"

"I'm trying to help a friend who is in trouble."

Felicia had been worrying him. He had the feeling she had begun some liaison that involved secret assignations in the summer house. God knew she deserved any happiness she could find, but Felicia, like the rest of the family—except their reprehensible rake of a father—was too loyal by nature to indulge in lighthearted affairs. She could only be hurt. Especially by liaisons in disused, lockable farm buildings.

Hiding his unease, Cornelius strode past her and deposited the saddle. "Is it the sort of trouble that needs us all to help?" he asked quietly. He would tear apart anyone who threatened harm to his sister. More than anyone, it was Felica who had always held them all together.

Her eyes softened. Perhaps he was wide of the mark.

"Thanks, Cornel," she said. "It's just information, really, to pass on."

So, he named all such buildings he could think of. Fortunately, he did not have to mention the chapel, which had no lock and no door.

THE COMPANY IN the castle drawing room was enlivened that

night by the unexpected visit of Bernard Muir. Bernard and his married sister, Lady Wickenden, were the children of a local army officer, and Alice had known them forever, so she was happy to exchange waves and grins, as well as more formal bows, with him. However, after making sure they all intended to come to the charity card party at the King's Head at the end of the week, he took the seat next to Mama and seemed to be having a quiet but intense conversation with her. Mama's eyes sparked.

Oh dear, what has Bernard said to set off that humor?

Mama rose to her feet. "Frances, Serena, accompany Bernard and me to his carriage to wish good evening to Mrs. Muir, his stepmother."

Serena, who was sitting beside Alice on the pianoforte stool, rose to obey. As though intrigued, her husband went too, followed by Lord Torridon. It thinned out the company some-what, but no one minded the lack of conversation. After last night's ball, most people were looking forward to an early night.

On the other hand, it gave the Duke of Atherstone the space to sit next to Alice on the stool.

"What will you play?" he asked mildly. "Will you allow me to turn the music for you?"

"I don't believe I am in the mood to play after all," she said, letting her hands slip from the keys, but before she could stand up, he spoke quietly and quite without his usual arrogance.

"Perhaps I owe you an apology, my lady."

She did not dispute it.

"I am too full of my own consequence," he said. "My mother died giving me life, so I had no one to teach me the respect due to a gentle lady. Added to which, no one ever denies me, so I have grown too...entitled to whatever I want. But there is no excuse for my brusque manners or my threats. I beg you to forgive me."

Stunned, Alice stammered, "D-does this mean you withdraw your...offer?"

He smiled, and for the first time she saw something in him that might have been charm.

"No," he said, "but it means you need not fear me. Let us start again and be friends. Tomorrow, I shall remove from the castle to the hotel, to make you more comfortable, but I would like to call, to walk and talk with you. I am hoping that by the time I have to leave Blackhaven, you will agree to be my wife. But if you don't, I shall, finally, accept my fate."

"That is very gracious of you," Alice said, so relieved to have the threat to Cornelius and his family lifted that she looked no further. "I should warn you, though, that my mind is made up, and advise you not to waste your valuable time on me."

"It is my time to waste," he said. "Play something for us now. You are so gifted…"

SINCE SHE HAD never told Cornelius about the duke's threat against him, she saw no point in discussing its withdrawal. Instead, when they met at church the following day, they discussed the banns for his brother Julius's wedding, and for his sister Lucy's.

"No banns for Helen and the major," Alice said with disapproval. "Apparently Roderick has gone to obtain a common license, and they will be married on Friday. They don't even have anywhere to live."

"There is room at Black Hill."

"There is room at the castle," Alice snapped. "That is not the point."

"No, it isn't," he agreed, "but you needn't take it out on me."

"Sorry," she whispered. "I am too comfortable with you."

"Good. Can we meet later?"

"At the chapel?"

"Why not? I'll bring you some more poems to criticize." He must have seen the look in her eyes, for he muttered something under his breath, then, "It was a joke, Alice. I truly value your opinion."

And from the warmth in his eyes, she rather thought he might. A haze of wonder gathered about her. She didn't even mind when she saw him a few minutes later with Cecily at the gate.

It was the beginning of the happiest week she could remember, full of fun and laughter and the wild excitement of Cornelius's kisses. The feeling never seemed to go away, only intensify whenever she was with him. There was new pleasure in simply getting to know him, learning his opinions on many things and arguing her own. She loved discussing his poetry—occasionally she won arguments over a word or two—and that of others. And one day they went through Daubin's book, marking all the stolen lines and verses and ideas.

"I don't understand," Alice said once. "If he cannot be bothered writing it, why does he bother publishing it? Perhaps he steals it quite unconsciously."

"He might, but I don't think so," Cornelius said. "I think he learned to steal from his father's sharp practice. Daubin Senior has appropriated a Black Hill field that I am sure was never sold to him. I have documents meant to prove its purchase by Daubin, and the signature certainly looks like my father's, but I think it was forged when Julius came home and it became clear we were staying. I suspect from time to time they used some other fields, for there is no record of our harvest there. I fear they appropriated that, too."

"But that's shocking!" Alice exclaimed. "You will not let it lie, will you?"

"No, I have written to our man of business in London. Which is another thing—why use him when it is a local matter that would normally be handled by our solicitor in Blackhaven? Anyway, I await his answer with interest. I would like to give Julius back the top field as a wedding present, if nothing else."

Once, when the weather was kind, they rode together over Black Hill, and he explained the work they were doing, improving the land under cultivation and reclaiming fields that had so been badly neglected over the nearly twenty years since his father had left.

She loved to watch him at some times, the contentment and appreciation of beauty always behind his critical observation and whatever decisions he reached. He always stopped to speak to the farmers and laborers encountered, listening to whatever they said. For their part, they showed him respect but no servility. They already understood they were dealing with a man who knew the land, even if they were occasionally suspicious of the newfangled methods he advocated.

"We were hoping for a good harvest as a beginning to build on," Cornelius told her, "but if the rain keeps up, it will be poor. All we can do is hang on, make sure no one starves... Do you think this would be a good place to live?"

Alice followed his pointing finger and regarded the abandoned cottage with doubt. The roof was still there, if damaged, as were all four stone walls, though it had no glass in the windows, and any garden had long since been taken over by nettles and thistles. It was quite a large house, though, with windows in the eaves. Once, it had probably belonged to a well-to-do farmer.

"Do you mean to get a tenant in? Does it come with land? Oh, goodness, the view is beautiful!" Black Hill was spread out before her, green fields and woods and rocky cliffs dropping down to the sea. Streams glistened all around the landscape, between dotted cottages and the tiny figures of working men and animals.

"I thought I might live here," Cornelius said dreamily. "If Julius permits."

"It's peaceful," Alice replied. "You could write wonderful poetry here." Bending in the saddle, she peered in through the nearest window. "Large and surprisingly gracious in proportion, but the walls and the floor... It would be like starting again."

"I think that's what I like. And yet it's as if the building has already grown into the landscape."

Alice had a sudden vision of this space as it should be—a

comfortable yet elegant drawing room, with paper on the walls and shiny new floors, armchairs and sofas scattered around the fire, a pianoforte and perhaps a guitar or a violin, lots of books on shelves, children playing among the feet of contented adults…

She blinked and straightened. "Have you seen Helen and Roderick's house in Blackhaven? She is working miracles to have it ready by the time of the wedding on Friday."

His eyelids swept down, and he turned his horse back to the road. "No. Not yet. Rod seemed content enough with it, though it's hard to tell. He is away again, until tomorrow."

Somehow she had offended him. By not showing sufficient interest in the cottage? How could she tell him she had so vividly imagined herself living there with him and their children? Heat flooded her at the very thought. And as usual, when she was nervous, she tried so hard to cover the reason that she said exactly the wrong thing.

"You would obviously be much more comfortable in Black Hill House than *here*. I think you would be merely hiding to live in such a solitary place. You are afraid they find out you are Simon Sacheverill, aren't you?"

"Most of my siblings don't know who that is," he said shortly.

"You should tell them. Tell everyone. It is something to be proud of, not—"

He interrupted with a bitter laugh. "At least I have something to be proud of. We had better gallop on the way back. I have much to do now that I've wasted so much daylight."

Wasted? If he had struck her, he could not have hurt her more. "I'm sorry to have held you up," she said between stiff lips.

Neither of them spoke until they reached the boundary wall between Black Hill and Braithwaite. Appalled to think she had been distracting him from what he really wished to be doing, that he was bored with her and impatient to be rid of her, she was afraid she would cry.

So she did not look at him at all. "What a pleasant afternoon. I suppose we will meet again on Friday at the wedding. Good-bye!" And she set off at a canter without looking back.

Chapter Fifteen

CORNELIUS'S HEART TWISTED with misery as he watched her go. He had reached out his hand to her as soon as they halted, to try to repair the foolish breach that had opened so suddenly. But she did not even glance at him, so she didn't see. He knew he had hurt her appallingly, a snapped response to her implication that his poetry was the one thing in his life he could be proud of.

That had hurt too, to have his inferiority rammed in his face. He was merely the steward of his brother's lands, largely unpaid until he could make the estate profitable again. She was an earl's daughter, immeasurably above him. Even Roderick, with his commission in the army, and his new business ventures, had better prospects than Cornelius.

And yet he knew she had not meant that criticism. She said the wrong thing, as she often did when anxious or thrown off stride. He had frightened her, showing her the house. Had she guessed his dream was to live there with her? He had barely guessed it himself, so it was unlikely, but either way, it had clearly appalled her. And now he had let her go with no prospect of seeing her tomorrow.

Perhaps she would come to the chapel anyway. He would.

Forcing his mind to the tasks still to be completed, he turned away from the unbearable sight of her vanishing, somehow vulnerable figure, so straight in the saddle and yet so frail. He rode down to inspect the troublesome drainage in the bottom field.

By the time he reached home, he was tired and short-tempered. He wanted only to wash, change, eat, and write a letter to Alice, which he would try to induce the twins to deliver for him the following day. But a different letter entirely waited for him in the hall.

The handwriting looked familiar, though he could not place it, so he seized it on his way to the staircase and broke the seal as he entered his bedchamber.

Cecily. Of course. He groaned and read it hastily while unbuttoning his coat and tearing off his necktie at the same time. Almost hidden amongst a lot of conventional greetings, inquiries, and farewells was the urgent message that she needed to see him, and he should come to the hotel at his earliest convenience. Jack had apparently taken his mother to the theatre this evening, a treat from which Cecily had cried off with a migraine.

Cornelius groaned again, for he could not let her down. Besides, it was time to end the stupid charade. He should do what he had almost meant to and simply talk to Jack Morgan, for he had come to doubt the veracity of Cecily's claims. It would be like her to exaggerate a minor flirtation into a series of infidelities. But one way or another, they had to sort their own marriage out, as he would tell her, kindly but firmly.

Accordingly, he washed and changed, then made his weary way downstairs once more to tell Felicia he had to go out and would eat his dinner cold on his return. Since no one else had taken the carriage, he did—two horses were faster than one, and he might manage a nap during the journey.

Remembering discretion at the hotel, he first asked for Sir John Morgan and only then inquired if Lady Morgan would see him. A few moments later, a comely young lady's maid with sparkling eyes appeared to take him up to her mistress.

The maid led him into a sitting room, where Cecily was pacing the floor and instantly dismissed the maid to the bedchamber beyond. She looked very pretty and worried, he thought with unexpected dispassion. How often had she looked like that during the short weeks of their courtship? Once, it had moved him to do anything to remove that frown, to make her contented again. Now, he doubted it meant very much at all except a means to an end.

"Oh, Cornelius, I am so unhappy," she declared, rushing to him with both hands held out. "Jack has been siding with his dreadful mother and berating me for immodest behavior!"

"Well, you are saying the same about him," Cornelius said reasonably. "And our flirtation at the ball was hardly discreet."

"Yes, but he says he is taking me home!"

"Is that not what you want? Or does he mean to abandon you there and bolt to the fleshpots of London?"

Her eyes widened. "He did not say. But I am having such an agreeable time here in Blackhaven—"

"Do you never talk to him, Cecily?" he interrupted.

"Not if he scolds me," she said sulkily.

She sat down on the sofa, patting the place beside here.

Cornelius remained standing. "What makes you think he is unfaithful? Does he not come home at night? Do you smell other women's perfume on his person? Does he receive letters he hides from you?"

"A wife knows," she insisted.

"A wife who talked to her husband might," he replied. "I have given you the opportunity. I have played my part and flirted until he notices. The point was not to initiate another quarrel but to bring you closer together. If you cannot even make that much effort, I'm afraid your marriage is doomed. If you truly wish to save it, you must *give* something. Here endeth the lesson."

It won him the faintest, saddest of smiles, although the surprised irritation lingered behind her eyes. "It's clear you have never been married. Are you abandoning me, Cornelius?"

"I am wishing you well."

A look of genuine desolation filled her eyes, and vanished as she laughed. "I suppose I always want my cake and to eat it too. I wonder what marriage to you would have been like?"

"Poor," Cornelius said. "And deadly dull. You would have been driven to flirt with Jack and then make a huge scandal by running away with him. He is a good man, Cecily."

"And you are not?"

"I would not be good for you."

For a moment, she searched his face, then smiled again and rose to her feet. Placing her hands on his shoulders, she reached up and kissed his cheek. He pecked hers in return and was about to step back when the door opened and Sir John Morgan walked in.

Cecily made matters worse by starting violently and staring at her husband in horror. "Jack!"

Cornelius wanted the world to open and swallow him, for Morgan looked like a man whose world was collapsing. At the same time, it was quite funny to be discovered so innocently parting and exactly the wrong construction made. If it had been a farce on the stage, Cornelius would have laughed. As it was, he offered his former employer a tentative smile of rueful amusement. Which acted as a red rag to a bull.

"Get out, you treacherous dog!" Morgan said savagely, striding forward with clenched fists.

"Sir, you quite misconstrue the situation," Cornelius assured him as Cecily fled weeping to the bedchamber beyond.

"The only thing I ever misconstrued was your apparent friendship."

"You may still count on my friendship, as you always could."

"Don't make me laugh. What would I want with such a worthless thing?"

"It may be worthless," Cornelius said, "but it stands. My meeting here with Lady Morgan is entirely innocent and, in fact, in your favor."

"Innocent!" Morgan exploded again. "You deny she cried off

the theatre with an imaginary migraine and summoned you while I was out?"

Cornelius hesitated. He could deny neither. "Lady Morgan asked for my help."

A harsh laugh broke from her husband. "Obviously! Name your damned friends."

Cornelius blinked. "You are calling me out?"

"I'll kill you."

"You don't want to fight me. I'm only a steward."

"Then what were you doing with your hands all over my wife?"

"Saying farewell as friends, which is all we have ever been to each other."

"Liar! But I suppose I can expect no better from you. You have no right to call yourself a gentleman."

"Then we had better not fight," Cornelius said evenly, through his tightening lips. "In any case, you know your wife is innocent."

"I know you are not!" Morgan drew back his fist.

So there was to be no elegant slap with a glove—which Sir John had dropped on the floor on his entrance. No doubt a good fistfight would be the best thing to relieve Morgan's anger so that he could see the truth presented to him.

But they were both strong, fit men. They would break up the room, bring hotel servants running from all over the building, gawped at by as many passing guests as could get there in time. And Cecily and the maid were in the next room. Speculation would be rife, scandal unavoidable, and Morgan was too angry and hurt to see that.

Cornelius sighed and set his hat on his head. He hoped Morgan would come to appreciate that it had, in fact, never left his hand since he arrived.

"You had better go through my brother Aubrey. And choose your own second with a care to his discretion. I believe one each should be sufficient in the circumstances. Good evening."

Somehow, he got out of the room, haunted by Sir John's bewildered, furiously pained expression.

What a damnably stupid mess. His second of the day. He should never have got out of bed.

TO ALICE'S RELIEF, by the morning of Helen's wedding, her sister seemed if not deliriously happy, then at least content with the situation. It was Alice whose nerves were in chaos, because she would see Cornelius.

The day before had been miserable. She had never imagined that twenty-four hours could stretch so appallingly to feel like weeks. But she had better get used to it. How had she allowed this feeling for Cornelius to get so out of hand? She had always been the sensible sister, her feet planted on the ground, her observation both acute and cynical. And yet with two words, he had reduced her to this.

She tried not to think of the years of loneliness ahead.

At least she would always have her music.

Not today, though. Today was for Helen. And if all Helen's sisters had their fingers metaphorically crossed to bring her luck, well, surely it would pay off. At least most of the castle guests had departed, including the Duke of Atherstone and his lugubrious chaplain.

Emotion almost overcame her in the church as Mr. Grant married Helen to Roderick Vale. She wondered if the gaggle of Vales on the opposite side of the aisle felt the same. She dared not look at Cornelius.

Mama had insisted on providing the wedding breakfast at the castle, and inevitably it was as magnificent as though she had spent months rather than days planning it. For Alice, most of it passed in a daze of worry over Helen's mechanical and yet somehow tragic smile, and her own misery over whatever it was she had lost with Cornelius. To make it worse, Lady Morgan, Mama's old crony, was present, though at least Sir John and Lady Morgan were not.

And then she found herself seated between Cornelius and Aubrey Vale for breakfast. Aubrey was a charmer. He was also an incredibly beautiful young man, though the shadows of too little sleep and too much brandy gave the impression of a fallen angel. Almost the complete opposite of Cornelius, he did not seem to be serious about anything, but at least he made her laugh, which relaxed her enough to talk in more than monosyllables and distracted her from the overwhelming presence of Cornelius on her other side.

Cornelius was turned attentively toward Serena as he laid down his knife and fork. His hands and forearm were all Alice could see of him. She loved his hands, their tender caresses…

As though he'd heard the improper thought, his hands dropped out of sight. While she smiled at Aubrey's nonsense, desolation swept over her.

Something warm and light as a butterfly wing brushed the side of her right hand in her lap. She wondered if she had imagined it, then she felt his fingers twist and curl loosely around hers.

Cornelius.

She clung to his hand, and he squeezed it in return before releasing her. The footman was about to remove his plate.

The incident was tiny, isolated, and yet it changed everything.

She smiled and meant it. Hope, intense and yet unspecific, surged once more. It meant that when Aubrey was in conversation with the lady on his other side, she could actually turn to Cornelius, although words eluded her.

He met her gaze, and it seemed that words were superfluous. She read the rueful apology in his eyes, and she smiled to give him hers.

He said, "Will you be at Felicia's charity card party tomorrow evening?"

"Is it Felicia's?" she asked in surprise. Her voice was mostly steady. "I thought Bernard had arranged it. Bernard Muir."

"Probably, but it is Felicia who is rounding up the Vales. And I believe the vicar's wife, Mrs. Grant, is playing hostess. So only Rod and Helen have an excuse for absence."

Before then, Helen would have had her wedding night. More than once, Alice had overheard her married sisters and Eleanor murmuring to Helen on the subject of tenderness and delights and trust. Until she had met Cornelius, Alice would not have believed a word of it. Her only experiences of an admittedly lesser intimacy with a man were slobbering kisses and violent, helpless suffocation, all of which she had found revolting. From her sisters' happiness with their husbands, she had known this was not a normal reaction, and so had assumed the fault to be her own.

Now, she felt a sneaking longing that it was not Helen and Roderick but Alice and Cornelius who would go home together to their own bed...

Her cheeks burned. Her whole body was in flames. She took a gulp of wine.

"Are you well?" Cornelius asked.

"Perfectly," she said hastily, and coughed delicately. "A mere tickle in my throat. Bernard has talked Mama into the card party since it is for charity—largely the hospital, I believe. I daresay we shall all play."

"Watch out for Felicia. She will win the clothes off your back."

At the opposite side of the table, the twins, on their best behavior, were clearly listening in, for they nodded proudly.

The company seemed jollier now, and Helen's marriage more hopeful, when Alice noted Roderick's gentleness and respect toward her. When the happy couple, apparently eager to get to their new home, set off from the castle, Alice waved from the steps, once more almost tearful because Helen had gone, moved on to her own life.

But it no longer seemed quite so sad. She would see Cornelius tomorrow.

LEAVING THE CASTLE, Cornelius found Aubrey sloping off to the King's Head.

"I'll come with you," Cornelius informed him, falling into step beside him over the bridge.

Aubrey's dramatic black eyebrows flew up. "Why?"

"I'm curious about your ladybirds."

"Can't you find your own?"

"I haven't been looking recently. Too busy."

"I will be too quite soon," Aubrey said cheerfully. "I'm going to help Rod with his newspaper."

"You are a mine of information," Cornelius replied. "Second only to the twins."

"We don't want a scandal sheet, but we have to appeal to the ladies, too. Some poetry, maybe." Aubrey frowned, twirling a rather dandified walking cane as they walked down the drive to the gates. The occupants of the passing Vale carriages waved at them. In response, Aubrey grinned and pushed his hat up with the knob of his cane. "Is this Daubin fellow any good?"

"Rubbish," Cornelius said. "He's lifted most of the verse in his book—which he published himself—from Byron and Sacheverill and Shelley, even Shakespeare, with a few grating changes."

"Damn it. Don't suppose *you* could write us something? You're always reading the stuff, so you must be able to churn out the odd verse."

Cornelius opened his mouth to refuse automatically. Alice's face swam before his eyes, wise, forgiving, generous… "I might."

"You wouldn't have to sign it if you're shy," Aubrey said. "We can just call you a local gentleman. And Lady Braithwaite says she will write to that Sacheverill fellow, who might be induced to send us something new."

Well, that should keep me busy... "I need to talk to you about something else entirely."

"To me?" Aubrey said in surprise. "What have *I* done?"

"You look guilty," Cornelius retorted. "Though in this case you're not. I am."

"Really?" Aubrey grinned with delight. "What have you done?"

"Nothing except try somewhat recklessly to help a friend, and now her husband has challenged me to a duel."

Aubrey stared at him. "A duel? *You?*"

Unreasonably annoyed, Cornelius scowled at him. "Am I such a poor creature? So staid and dull?"

"I don't see that it's staid and dull to avoid pointless death. I should know, I've faced it often enough."

"We've all faced it with you," Cornelius said awkwardly. "Even if not always in your presence."

"I know," Aubrey muttered, coloring. "I wasn't playing for sympathy. Whose pointless death are you aiming at, and on the strength of what trivial insult?"

"There was no insult, only misunderstanding. And I'd rather it never went as far as measuring twenty paces. The thing is, I named you as my second, so unless Morgan's realized his error, you're likely to receive a call from *his* second."

"Morgan? Sir John Morgan, whose steward you were for two years? I thought he liked you."

"He did. The trouble is, he has a wife."

"Cornelius," said his little brother, gazing at him with new respect.

"Don't be an idiot. I never touched the lady, and if I did, it would hardly be worthy of your esteem!"

"Depends on the lady in question. Don't turn stuffy on me now. Better save the rest until we have brandy in front of us, though. Not sure I'm strong enough without."

Having found a quiet table in the inn's taproom, and sat

down with pints of ale, Cornelius said, "So you will act for me?"

"As your second? Of course. Never been anyone's second before. Who will I deal with?"

"No idea who Morgan will choose. Do you know anything about the rules of dueling and your duties as second?"

"I read a book years ago." Aubrey, being a sickly child, had spent a lot of time reading. "There must be something in those local waters after all. Yours is far from the first recent duel in Blackhaven—I even heard the magistrate's son had called out Bernard Muir, who's the most amiable fellow you could meet."

"I've never drunk the wretched waters," Cornelius said impatiently.

"Maybe *that*'s your problem, then. Sure you want me as your second, though? Roderick, being a military man, has probably acted in lots. Might even have fought lots, for all I know."

"I don't think Roderick being around guns is a great idea just now. Even if he hadn't just got married. Besides, he and Julius would only tell me off."

"And you think I won't?"

"I never quite know what you will do, Aubrey, but I was fairly sure you wouldn't be appalled. On the other hand, I don't want to fight Morgan or anyone else, so be conciliatory. I never wronged him, but I am happy to apologize for looking the wrong way at his wife—whose name must not be publicly drawn into this."

"Heaven forfend. I doubt Alice Conway would approve of your fighting duels over other women."

Heat rose into Cornelius's face. "She has nothing to do with this."

"But what has she to do with you, most strait-laced of my brothers?"

"Nothing," Cornelius said ruefully. "What could I offer an earl's daughter?"

"Much the same as Roderick, with fewer nightmares and more appreciation of literature."

"Now that you're healthy," Cornelius said, "I am quite happy to thrash you."

"Best wait till you've thrashed Morgan. Oh, and if we have to go that far, we get to choose weapons, since he's the challenger. What will you choose? A farm implement?"

Cornelius aimed a halfhearted buffet at Aubrey's head, which his brother easily ducked.

Cornelius straightened in his seat. "Actually, that's not such a bad idea. Not the farm implements—they're damned dangerous—but why should we only consider pistols?"

"We can choose swords and first blood. Can't make it a killing affair." Aubrey frowned. "Can you even use a sword?"

"I can cut turnips with it."

Aubrey laughed. "Then let's hope Morgan's head is turnip shaped."

Chapter Sixteen

CECILY HAD BEEN rather thrilled by her husband's masterful anger and by his willingness to fight for her. Perhaps this was what should have happened two years ago. Cornelius and Jack should have fought over her then, and perhaps Jack would have realized how important she was and she would not now be in disgrace with him.

How laughable that Jack had finally snapped over a moment of pure innocence! When Cecily finally realized Cornelius had rumbled her. Up until that moment, she had been genuinely prepared for an *affaire du cœur* with him. In fact, it had quite excited her. But his eyes no longer looked at her with the tenderness of nostalgic love but with impatient tolerance. For that, she no doubt had the aristocratic Lady Alice to thank, whether the silly girl knew it or not.

Cecily loved a challenge, of course, and she might have been prepared to fight Alice for a night, at least, in Cornelius's excitingly unfamiliar arms. But Jack's fury put paid to that. Where she would once have defied him and gone her own way, she found it curiously arousing to obey his curtly issued orders. His cold, civil remarks to her in public or before his mother made her cast down her eyes and burn for him.

She always wanted what she could not have.

On the day Cornelius's brother married Lady Alice's sister,

Cecily returned to the hotel from a somewhat unsatisfactory shopping expedition. Crossing the foyer with her maid, she beheld two dazzling gentlemen just vanishing into one of the private parlors euphemistically known as coffee rooms.

She recognized the men at once—the taller one because he was the haughty and elusive Duke of Atherstone, the other being the romantically handsome poet D'Aubin from the castle garden party.

What an odd friendship. The duke was notoriously snobbish, and she was sure she had heard D'Aubin was merely the son of some wealthy tradesman who had tried to Frenchify his name to appear better born than he was. Sensing intrigue, Cecily thrust her parcel into the arms of her already-burdened maid.

"Take these up to my chamber," she said. "I have just seen an old friend, but I shall be up directly, if Sir John asks."

He kept close watch on her these days, rarely allowing her out of his sight for more than an hour, and even then, she was sure he paid her maid for information. Cecily walked toward the coffee room, pretending to be absorbed by a few newspapers on a nearby table.

Irritatingly, though she could hear the rumble of voices, she could not distinguish any words. There was a chair set close to the table, so Cecily drew it out—quietly so as not to alert any passing footman who might rush to help. She placed the chair against the wall, much closer to the door, seized a large news sheet at random, and sat down, spreading open the newspaper in front of her as though searching for something in particular. In fact, it hid that her head—particularly her ear—was leaning even closer to the coffee room door.

Now she could hear much better.

"...early on Monday morning," said the duke's thin, aristocratic voice. "You must order a post-chaise for six in the morning and have it ready and waiting by the castle gates. No one who matters at that hour will see it."

"Lady Alice will not be abroad at that hour," D'Aubin objected.

There came two short, genteel sniffs, as though the duke were taking snuff. "On Monday morning she will be."

"She has an assignation with Vale?" D'Aubin sounded alarmed. "I am no physical match for that lout."

"Vale will not trouble you. I happen to know he will be engaged elsewhere at that time. He may even be dead. It does not matter. He is not your main problem. Braithwaite is."

A chair scraped inside the room, making Cecily start and shake her newspaper. Hastily, she jumped to her feet and abandoned the mess of newsprint on the table before sailing toward the staircase.

"He may even be dead," Atherstone had said so callously.

He must have been talking about the duel between Cornelius and Jack. For the first time, the fight became real to her, not some romantic fantasy of knights dueling for her favor but a modern meeting with pistols that could easily kill, even from apparently minor injuries.

On top of that, though she didn't know why, Atherstone seemed to be aiding D'Aubin to abduct Lady Alice. Presumably to marry her, since Lord Braithwaite would never consider a match with a man of D'Aubin's birth. Cornelius, fighting the duel, would not be able to protect her.

Cecily did not care much for Lady Alice, largely because Cornelius so clearly did. But the girl had agreed to help her win back Jack's love. And rather to her own surprise, Cecily did not wish her to be harmed or forced into marriage with such a snake as D'Aubin clearly was. A stupid snake, in fact, seeing that he needed Atherstone to arrange his plots for him.

She found Jack in the sitting room.

"Who did you see?" he asked suspiciously, turning from the window.

Cecily sighed. "Old Mrs. Fanshawe. She takes the waters with your mother occasionally. Jack, are you going ahead with this silly duel?"

His eyes, never anything but veiled these days, shuttered completely. "That is not your concern."

"But it is! Even if you no longer care for me, I am your wife, and you cannot pretend I wouldn't be affected by this. I could be made a widow, or the wife of a convicted murderer. Have you thought of that?"

"I have thought of nothing else," he said with suppressed passion. "I shall do my best to be sure neither situation arises. But honor demands I do this."

She hung her head. "It is my fault. I should not have summoned Cornelius behind your back, but I've already told you I was only trying to win back your love. Even if I were not devoted to you, Cornelius is much too strait-laced to commit adultery."

"It is too late to go back," Jack said stubbornly, clearly still disbelieving her story.

She took a step nearer. "At least tell me who your seconds are. I have a right to know who will be on your side."

He closed his mouth, hesitating. "The Duke of Atherstone," he said.

ALICE WOKE THE following day, desperate for the evening card party when she would meet Cornelius again. All the turbulent emotions churning within made her restless.

When she suggested to Maria that they walk into Blackhaven to call on Helen in her new home, Maria was uncharacteristically downright in her refusal.

"Oh no, they need at least *one* day to themselves," she insisted. "They would really have been better going off on a wedding journey rather than being constantly interrupted by their families."

"You don't think she might *want* to be interrupted?" Alice asked anxiously.

"No, I don't."

"Then why *didn't* she go on a wedding journey?"

"Because Roderick would not ask Gervaise for the money, and he needs what he has—as well as his time—to establish his new businesses. Did you know he was starting up a Blackhaven newspaper?"

"Helen didn't say." Alice felt both defensive and hurt by the knowledge.

"She didn't tell me either," Maria said. "Michael got it from Roderick yesterday. Why don't we all go riding instead? Frances and Serena don't have long before they leave again for the south."

In the end, all the siblings—except Helen—and their spouses collected a picnic and rode out to the abbey ruins. Although the sky was gray as usual, at least it did not rain, and Alice found the excursion unexpectedly enjoyable. It was almost as if the clock had been turned back and some governess would leap out and tell them it was time to go home.

Except that everyone had more grownup memories of the place now. Frances and Serena remembered a painting contest with guests one spring, where Frances had engineered an assignation between Gillie Muir and Lord Wickenden.

"That was irresponsible," Gervaise remarked.

"Not at all," Frances argued. "Wickenden was always different with Gillie. Besides, she deserved some fun, and look what came of it. She is happily married, *and* tamed the Wicked Baron."

"That was the day you broke your leg," Serena told her brother, who winced and rubbed his healed bone.

"Helen painted some wonderful pictures of the abbey," Alice said wistfully. In fact, she had her suspicions that Helen had met Roderick here while doing so.

Serena nudged her. "She will be happy, Alice," she said gruffly. "You'll see. And she is only in Blackhaven. The rest of us are hundreds of miles away."

"I know." Alice accepted a glass of wine from Eleanor and sipped, listening to the music in her head and letting the chatter of her family wash over her like a wave of happiness. She was lucky, so lucky…

And there was Cornelius. He made her happy, too, in a way that was compellingly different. The strength of this feeling frightened her sometimes, but she could not bear to lose it.

Is it love? Do I love Cornelius?

That was overwhelming, too, though it made her smile and smile…

AS SHE STEPPED out of the carriage at the King's Head Inn, Alice's stomach churned with anticipation. *Cornelius…*

His family was definitely here, for there were the twins in the yard, Lawrence directing carriages and Leona accompanying the guests inside. Alice could have sworn the girl winked at her.

Mr. and Mrs. Grant were acting as hosts for the evening, but Alice barely heard their welcome or their instructions, for behind them Helen had caught sight of her family and rushed on them, laughing, so like the child Alice missed that a lump sprang to her throat.

Helen hurled herself into her sister's arms. "There you are! I'm so glad you've come—I have *loads* to tell you!"

The strain of the previous week seemed to have entirely vanished from Helen's demeanor. She looked more beautiful than ever before. She truly was so radiant that Alice laughed with joy as she hugged her sister.

"You are happy," Alice whispered.

"Unbelievably so," Helen whispered back.

There was no time for more, for the rest of the family were all but dragging Helen off. Roderick, watching from a distance, had a surprisingly tender smile on his otherwise hard face. And beside him was Cornelius.

Though Alice made no conscious decision, she found herself walking toward the brothers with her hand held out.

Roderick took it but bent and kissed her cheek. "I am permitted to kiss my sister-in-law."

"Am I?" Cornelius asked teasingly.

"Too far removed," Roderick said. "Go away, Cornel. Come and play whist with me, Lady Alice."

"Only if Cornelius and I can play, too," Helen said, taking her husband's hand and actually tugging him between the close-set gaming tables.

Cornelius laughed. "It's good to see him being led by the nose. I haven't seen him so happy."

"Nor I Helen," Alice replied. "I won't deny that I had my doubts."

"We all did. Can you play whist?"

"Badly."

"Me too. We are made for each other."

Alice laughed as she was meant to, but heat rose into her cheeks and she had difficulty breathing as they squeezed close together between the tables. At Helen and Roderick's table, Cornelius held her chair, and she felt the faintest caress on her nape. Excitement soared.

We are made for each other.

Whether or not he meant it, was it true?

Life with Cornelius versus life without him. There was no longer a choice there—they were related by marriage and were bound to meet. But he was not her brother. He was not even merely a friend. No other friend filled her with such emotion, such *hunger.* No one else deprived her of breath and made her pulse race.

More, she *knew* him, from instinct as well as from his beautiful poetry. She loved him for so many reasons, so many traits— his sensitivity and perception, his care of the Black Hill tenants, his feeling for the land, his compassion... Even his loyalty to Cecily was admirable.

"Play, Alice," Helen urged.

Alice blinked at the cards on the table and played one from her hand at random. Helen laughed. Cornelius fixed his gaze to her face, which deprived her of any remaining powers of thought.

"Sorry," she said to Roderick when they lost the game. "I seem to be woolgathering."

"Pay up," said Felicia Maitland cheerfully, appearing beside them with her notebook to record the winnings, a percentage of which was going to the town hospital.

"Perhaps you need some air," Cornelius said behind Alice. He was holding her chair again.

She rose quickly, her heart thundering, and when he took her shawl from the back of the chair and placed it around her shoulders, his fingers brushed her skin. Her hand trembled when she took his arm. She hoped he could not feel it.

There was a moment of dismay when she saw her mother's eagle-eyed observation from across the room, and then, unexpectedly, Eleanor joined them and Mama's attention relaxed.

"Ten minutes," Eleanor murmured. "Or she'll send Gervaise to find you."

As Eleanor vanished, Alice laughed nervously. "What a fuss about a short walk outside a busy inn."

"Not a fuss," Cornelius said, holding the front door for her. "Is young Lady Braithwaite not telling us that not all your family would be against us?"

"Why would any of them be?"

"Because you are the earl's sister," Cornelius said, threading her hand into the crook of his arm once more. "And I am merely steward of my brother's lands, with few prospects and no desire to be anything else."

"We are related by marriage."

"Is that why I have missed you?"

Her gaze flew up to meet his. "Have you?" she whispered.

"Every moment you aren't with me." With peculiar, controlled violence, he said, "Ever since we met, I have been telling myself you are annoying, a scold, an eternal critic, that we cannot talk without quarreling."

It was as if someone had thrown a stone at her heart. She

could not breathe for the pain.

"But we do talk," he said urgently. "Sometimes we quarrel—but what sort of friends, lovers, poets, musicians would we be if we could not disagree or accept criticism from each other? I've tried to tell myself that in kissing you, I am only trying to help you accept a husband when the right man comes along. But if that man ever comes, I will kill him, because I can't bear anyone else to touch you. Could you ever fall in love with me, Alice? Would you let me try to make you?"

Alice gasped for breath as she made sense of his words. They were walking around the inn, almost into the lights of the stable yard, so she drew back into the shadows of the building, tugging him with her.

"Why do you think I let you kiss me in the first place?" she demanded. Tears were spilling down her cheeks. "Why do you think *I* kiss *you*? I have loved you since before I even met you, only I was too stupid to recog—*Oh!*"

She broke off as her mouth was suddenly lost in his. With a sob, she fell back against the wall, and he came with her, his body as hard as his mouth. She threw her arms around his neck in blind passion, opening wide to him and to every wild, sensual feeling he inspired in her. She was so utterly overwhelmed, it was some time before she realized she was not remotely frightened.

But by then, his fingers had found the silly dampness on her cheeks, and he gentled his embrace and his kiss.

"I'm sorry," he whispered against her lips. "I love you so much—I never meant to make you cry."

She took back his mouth. "Love makes me cry," she murmured between kisses that deepened with every passing moment. He rested his hands on her hips, holding her to his as he moved against her with sweet, lazy sensuality. He kissed her eyelids, her cheeks, her throat, even nudging the neck of her dress to glide his mouth over the swell of her breasts. Her knees threatened to give way. Overcome by an impossible mix of delicious weakness and hunger, she would have given him anything. She *wanted* to give him everything, without being terribly sure what that entailed.

As his attention came back to her mouth, she adored the thundering of his heart against her. She moaned when he caressed her breast, flickering his thumb over her aching nipple, and arched into him. Wildly stroking his nape, she yearned to feel more of his skin, to have his body sliding naked over hers…

With a soft groan that was almost a laugh, he dragged his lips from hers, deliberately loosening his hold, though he did not release her.

He rested his forehead against hers.

"Alice, my Alice," he said huskily. "Are you my Alice?"

"If you are my Cornelius." And even if he was not.

"Cornelius, Simon, whatever… Does this mean you will consider marrying me? Without imagining I am after your dowry or your noble brother's favor?"

"Oh God, I want to cry again, or pound the pianoforte or something. Of course I don't imagine those things."

He raised his head, his excitingly warm, clouded eyes growing curious. "Why not? I am poorer than Atherstone or Glover or Daubin or any of your other suitors, I imagine."

"Because I know you." Until she said the words, she did not realize how true they were.

He kissed her once more, a soft, tender kiss this time, full of love, with only an echo of the wild desire that had so shaken her before. She was enchanted all over again.

Very reluctantly, she said, "We should go back before Gervaise comes and makes you marry me by Tuesday."

"I haven't compromised you yet by keeping you out all night."

She pressed her cheek to his, loving the feel of the faint stubble against her skin. "You can if you like. Shall we run away?"

"If you wish," he said at once. "But you might be more comfortable having the banns read and doing things at a more leisurely pace."

She sighed. "And I suppose you cannot abandon Black Hill at

a moment's notice."

"I like that it entered your head. Do you truly trust me so much?"

"I seem to. I'm not afraid of anything anymore. Not even Cecily."

"You need never be afraid of Cecily or anyone else. But speaking of her, there is something I—"

Over his shoulder, a movement in the dark made her gasp. "Someone is there!"

Chapter Seventeen

CORNELIUS SWUNG AROUND, shielding Alice with his body. "Who is it?" he demanded.

"Forgive me, I did not mean to intrude. You may count on my discretion."

The nervous, diffident voice seemed vaguely familiar to Alice. Where had she heard it before?

It sounded closer now, speaking more softly. "If you see Lady Alice, you might warn her not to approach waiting carriages early in the morning."

Cornelius started toward him, growling, "Are you threatening her ladyship?"

"No, no, sir, quite the opposite," the man said, clearly agitated, with an odd mixture of shame and servility.

Abruptly, Alice remembered his voice. "Mr. Jones! Atherstone's chaplain."

Even more alarmed, the man closed the distance between them, and since he had already clearly recognized Alice, she stepped out from behind Cornelius to stand beside him.

"I beg you to return the favor of discretion," Mr. Jones said earnestly. "His Grace is not of a forgiving nature."

Alice frowned. "Is the duke still in Blackhaven? I thought he had gone back to London."

"We are at the hotel," Mr. Jones babbled. "For how long, I do not know."

Cornelius was scowling over the first point. "Are you saying His Grace threatens Lady Alice?"

His gaze darting nervously around, Mr. Jones nodded. "I am to be the deliverer of a note you must not believe," he said to Alice. "On no account leave the castle early on Monday morning. Whatever you hear or read."

"What will she hear?" Cornelius demanded ominously.

"It doesn't matter," Mr. Jones insisted. "She must not leave. And I must go."

"Oh no." Cornelius's arm shot out and seized the chaplain. "I don't trust you further than I could throw you. What the devil are you up to?"

Mr. Jones closed his eyes with such obvious agony that Alice blurted, "You're frightened."

"And trembling," Cornelius said, his scowl more bewildered than angry now. "Come."

Alice followed as he marched the feebly resisting chaplain to the little bench in the empty inn garden and sat him down. Then he took a flask from his pocket, unstopped it, and thrust it into Mr. Jones's hand.

"Take a drink and tell us everything."

"What is it?" Mr. Jones asked, eyeing the flask with suspicion. "I do not do well with strong spirits."

"A sip will do you good," Cornelius insisted.

Mr. Jones took an unsteady sip from the flask and choked.

"You are afraid of the duke," Alice said gently, sitting down beside him.

Mr. Jones shuddered. "We should all be afraid of him."

"He certainly treats you with such appalling rudeness that one wonders why he keeps a chaplain with him," Alice said.

"A weak man of God may be a useful tool," Mr. Jones said bitterly.

"Is that what you are?" Cornelius asked. "Atherstone's tool?"

Mr. Jones nodded, eyes closed again in shame. "Don't ask me

what I have done. I cannot tell you. Just keep this poor child safe."

"I will," Cornelius assured him, "but why do you stay with such a man? Why do you do his bidding?"

"I am dependent upon him," Mr. Jones said. For a moment, he seemed about to spring up and bolt. Then he met Alice's gaze and added despairingly, "The welfare of my whole family is dependent upon him. He promised me one of the livings within his gift if I spent a year as his private chaplain to prove my worth. I did. What I saw…" He drew a shaking breath and another sip from the flask. "When I remonstrated with him, he told me I could leave his service and seek a living elsewhere.

"I had no other patron. He paid me well. I could care for my aging parents and send my young brothers to school, even a doctor for my sister's sick child… I am not proud, but I turned a blind eye. And then I became part of it, and he held my crime over my head to make me commit others. I cannot leave him because he is now my only possible employer. Who else would take on a priest who has taken part in false wedding ceremonies? Who has brought him…"

Mr. Jones buried his face in his hands. "I am debased and vile. I cannot even ask you to forgive me. All I have left is to occasionally foil his plots when he cannot find out I am to blame. So I warn you. And now I must go before I am seen with you."

He sprang to his feet and shoved the flask into Cornelius's hand. "Thank you. Thank you both for your kindness. God will bless you."

"Wait," Alice and Cornelius said at once, and he glanced back in alarm.

"You cannot go back to him," Alice said.

"I must, or my family starves."

"It seems to me," Cornelius said thoughtfully, "that this hold of Atherstone's over you works both ways. You know what he has done and could ruin him just as easily."

"Who cares what a duke has done?" Mr. Jones said wearily.

"A poor, sinning man of God is another matter entirely. Good-night."

Hand in hand, Alice and Cornelius watched his weary figure vanish into the darkness, his shoulders slumped in permanent defeat.

"He likes people to be afraid," Alice said. "Atherstone. We must find a way to help Mr. Jones."

"Yes," Cornelius agreed. "But you must also heed his warning."

"What is so special about Monday morning?" Alice asked.

"I'm sure we will find out."

"Together," Alice said, resting her head against his shoulder.

Cornelius's arm crept around her again.

Several minutes later, a hiss penetrated Alice's blissful haze.

"Psst! Time to come back!"

"Who is that?" Alice gasped, peering over Cornelius's arm.

"The twins, of course. And they are quite right!"

CORNELIUS'S HEART WAS bursting with joy because Alice loved him. The threat of Atherstone and the plight of his chaplain were very much secondary, as was his care for her reputation.

The twins' reminder was timely. "Quick!" they urged with glee. "Felicia and Bernard Muir are catching the cheat who stole from Maitland and made her poor!" Lawrence added.

For Cornelius, there was a fierce satisfaction in watching that play out, and in acting with his brothers to prevent the rat from leaving except under arrest. He was proud of Felicia and, seeing her with Muir again, hopeful for her happiness. It all added to the glow of his own.

Alice would marry him.

Somehow, he would build a home for her, but it would not be quick. Would she mind waiting? Or would she want to get used to the idea of being his wife? When should he speak to her brother? If Braithwaite withheld his permission, they would have to wait two years until she was of age, and even then she would be defying him.

The questions spun through his blissful delirium, even the next morning when he found himself in church, gazing at her in the Braithwaites' front pew.

He was briefly distracted by the emergence of Felicia—who had not come home with the rest of the Vales last night—from the vestry, closely followed by Muir and the vicar. The reason for this unconventional entrance became clear when the vicar called the banns not only for Julius and Antonia, and Lucy and Eddleston, but also for Felicia and Muir.

Grinning, Cornelius thumped the blushing Muir on the back. He hadn't seen Felicia look so happy since they were children.

Everything, surely, was coming right for them all in Blackhaven.

"There'll be none of us left soon," Aubrey muttered.

"Jealous?"

"Christ knows," Aubrey said savagely, taking Cornelius by some surprise.

What was going on with his rakish little brother?

Outside the church, while everyone embraced Felicia and shook hands with Muir, Cornelius moved toward Alice, who edged back from her own family to speak to him. Her smile was adorably shy and warm.

"I'm so pleased for Bernard and Mrs. Maitland," she said breathlessly. "We have known him forever, and he has always been such a good friend. One of the kindest people I know."

"He seems to be just what Felicia needs. What about you?" he asked, low. "Do you still want to marry me?"

"Yes," she said at once, and blushed enchantingly. "If you still want to marry me."

"More than anything, ever," he said intensely. He wished they were not surrounded by most of the town. He was desperate to kiss her. He contented himself with offering his arm, which she took, and they walked around the little churchyard looking for tiny patches of privacy.

"Will your brother consent?" he asked.

"He will in the end, when he sees that you love me. Of us all, only Frances really made a good marriage in the eyes of the world. But underneath Gervaise's stern exterior beats the heart of a romantic. He married for love, too."

When he sees that you love me... Her open trust in him made his heart ache with pride.

"Where shall we live?" he asked, to prevent himself simply taking her in his arms before everyone. "If you do not care for the cottage I showed you—"

"Oh, but I do!" she interrupted with such force that several people turned to glance at her. Blushing, she turned aside. "I love it. It would be perfect for us. I could see us there as clearly as I see you now. That is what confused me. I could not grasp what I felt for you, let alone what you felt for me."

"Then we *could* live there?" he said eagerly. "I'll speak to Julius, though I'm sure he will be happy about it. I can work on it in spare moments, and over the winter. Perhaps we can be married in the spring."

"Spring?" she repeated in dismay. "So far away."

It was his turn to blush. "I am not a wealthy man. I never will be."

Her fingers tightened on his arm for an instant. "I know, and I don't care. We *could* still be married sooner. I could live with you at Black Hill House, if you like. Then I could help prepare the cottage, supervise tradesmen, and so on while you are about your other duties."

Cornelius was momentarily speechless. All he could do was cover her gloved hand with his own where it lay on his arm.

"When would be a good time to call on your brother? Shall I speak to him now?"

She smiled and shook her head. "Go and celebrate your sister's betrothal. Bernard's family is great fun—you will like them, especially Gillie and Lord Wickenden. Why don't you come tomorrow afternoon? I will make sure to be in the castle."

"A good plan," he said mechanically, distracted by the sight of Aubrey on the other side of the churchyard railings, in conversation with none other than the Duke of Atherstone. Behind them, looking servile and miserable, lurked Mr. Jones. "Stick close to your family," he murmured, walking in their direction. "And don't leave the castle until we speak again."

She raised her eyebrows.

"Remember Jones's warning," he said urgently. He glanced around him, then lowered his head. "And remember I love you. Only you."

Abandoning her at Lady Tamar's side, he tipped his hat and strode toward the church gates.

Aubrey walked toward him. There was no sign now of either Atherstone or his chaplain.

"We have a problem," Aubrey said. "Morgan's second is the Duke of Atherstone. He claims Morgan will accept no apologies, though he is allowing swords as weapons. Won't budge on time, though."

Cornelius glanced at him. "Don't tell me. Tomorrow at dawn?"

Aubrey blinked. "Tomorrow at dawn."

IT WAS AN eventful day. As well as welcoming Muir to dinner as Felicia's betrothed, the Vales also welcomed a new half-brother, Alan Bryant, another of their rakish father's by-blows who had been respectably brought up by a wealthy family in Scotland.

Although young, quietly spoken, and clearly expecting a barbed welcome, Alan did not appear to be overwhelmed by the Vales en masse, even at their informal table, where everyone called to everyone else, wherever they sat. Muir and Felicia seemed to already regard him as a friend. And when Delilah, also illegitimate, greeted him with a cheerful "You too?" he actually laughed.

Of course, he was "twinned," as Lawrence and Leona endeavored to learn all they could of his parentage. For once, they got nothing out of their victim, and Cornelius regarded him with new respect.

But the main focus of dinner was Felicia and Muir and their upcoming nuptials. It scared Cornelius how much he would miss them all, how much he would let his family down, if something went wrong at tomorrow's duel. What if he died? Who would tend the land for Julius? His siblings' new happiness would be spoiled. And Alice…

"Spill the beans, Muir," Aubrey said. "Who won your duel this morning?"

"I fought no duel," Muir said. "We discovered there was no quarrel. This beef is delicious—my compliments to your cook."

Felicia smiled secretively into her wine, but the subject was dropped. A moment later, Betsy the maid entered and came up to Cornelius.

"There's a Mr. Harmondsworth arrived to see you, sir," she murmured. "I told him you were dining and put him in the office."

"The office?" he repeated, startled. "What's wrong with the drawing room?"

Betsy blushed a fiery red. "He says he's your man of business up from London. I thought the office was the right place for him."

"You're probably right," Cornelius said kindly, taking the card she belatedly proffered.

"What's going on?" Julius asked.

"I'm not sure yet," Cornelius admitted. "I wrote to Harmondsworth with a question, but I didn't expect him to answer in person. Perhaps I'd better go and see him. If you'll excuse me for a few minutes?"

He found Mr. Harmondsworth in the office, his coat over the back of a chair, going through papers he had taken out of his document case.

"Mr. Harmondsworth." Cornelius offered his hand. "I'm Cornelius Vale, my brother's steward. I hope it isn't only my letter that has dragged you all the way up here."

Harmondsworth shook his hand. "Well, it is, largely, but I regard the matter very seriously. I have never sold any land for Sir Julius or Sir George, and when I called on your man in Black-haven, I discovered that neither had he. Whatever documents you have seen must be forged."

Cornelius's brows flew up. Opening a drawer, he took out the sale agreement. "It looks like my father's signature and yours."

Harmondsworth tipped his spectacles farther down his nose and peered. "It's not even a good copy. That is not my hand or my ink. What is more, I would have used a higher-quality paper. It looks very much to me as though this Daubin and Sir George's old steward have conspired to steal from you because they didn't expect you to come back, and then forged this evidence to cover themselves. I suggest we put the fear of God and the law into everyone involved and get your stolen land back."

Cornelius smiled at him. "Come and have dinner. Then we can sort everything out and plan accordingly."

TO CECILY'S SURPRISED delight, her husband made love to her that night. Whether he forgave her or finally believed in her inno-cence, he did not say, but as she lay awake afterward, it came to her that he might have been saying goodbye.

Surely Cornelius would never kill Jack in this silly duel?

In any case, there was little she could do. In such matters of honor, women could never influence men.

But she could help another woman.

She had almost gone up to Alice at church to warn her, but Cornelius had been there, so attentive that her heart had been hardened. But Alice was so young, and how awful to be forced into marriage with such a cheating, ill-bred little weasel as Darcy Daubin. Or D'Aubin, whatever he called himself. Ridiculous man.

Besides, old Lady Morgan might be less critical if Cecily saved her friend the dowager countess's daughter from rape and ruin.

She drifted off to sleep and woke as Jack slipped out of her bed. It was still dark, and he was going off to fight his duel.

Don't. Please don't go.

She could never stop him. But she could impress him by saving Alice.

Accordingly, as soon as Jack left the room, she lit the lamp and dressed. Bizarrely, she almost ran into her husband and the Duke of Atherstone on the landing, and only just managed to hide herself behind a pillar in time. Jack's coat actually brushed against her, but he didn't notice. His face was white by the light of the lantern he carried.

When they were past, she slipped back to the staff stairs and fled down to the hotel's back entrance. No one was yet about in the dark stable yard, and she hurried outside. Even though no one would be able to see her, she drew the thick veil of her hat down over her face and flitted along the street and up the hill to the castle, a stark silhouette against the just-lightening sky.

By the time she reached the castle gates, she was panting in a most unladylike fashion. There was no sign of a carriage, and nothing had passed her in either direction, so she must be on time.

She had already decided that if she went right up to the castle, she might miss Lady Alice altogether—there were so many doors that she had no idea which Alice would use, and she might well lurk at the wrong one or lose her by sending messages via servants. No one seemed to be stirring yet, in any case. It was ridiculously early.

Concealing herself behind a tree to wait, she leaned against it to rest.

Where was Jack? She wondered if he was afraid.

Chapter Eighteen

SINCE THE TIDE was far enough out, Cornelius and Aubrey rode along the beach from Black Hill to Braithwaite Cove, which was the traditional meeting place for duelists.

Neither of them spoke. Up until now, Aubrey had not appeared to take the matter remotely seriously, as though it were a huge joke that his staid brother should indulge in such a dashing pastime as dueling. But now he was frowning and casting Cornelius worried glances.

At last, as the cove was in sight, lanterns swinging in the distance, Aubrey said abruptly, "You're really going to do this, then?"

"If I have to. I don't particularly want to make an idiot of myself dancing around the sand waving a sword at a man I respect, but needs must."

"Who are you?" Aubrey demanded. "And what have you done with my brother Cornelius? I suppose you are, secretly, an expert swordsman, just pretending to be a steward of the land?"

"No, I'm an expert steward of the land pretending to be a swordsman. Watch Atherstone. If he's involved, he is up to something. I just don't see what he achieves by this."

"Being rid of a rival for Lady Alice's affections?" Aubrey said innocently.

"Then why did he agree so easily to swords and first blood?

This is unlikely to kill either of us except by accident."

Morgan and Atherstone stood on the beach, stony-faced. Above them, on the road, stood a carriage. The castle glowered down at them in the slowly lightening sky. Inside, Alice would be asleep. Cornelius wondered how she would look, her hair strewn across the pillow, tumbled about her beautiful face, untroubled in slumber… God, he longed to make love to her.

He blinked himself back to reality and dismounted. Aubrey untied the long case from his saddle and, with a last scowl at Cornelius, went forward to meet the duke. As they opened the case, Dr. Lampton slid down the path from the road and stalked angrily toward them.

"I have deserving patients to see. How long is this idiocy going to hold me up?"

Atherstone gazed down his haughty nose at the doctor, who didn't look remotely impressed.

"I see you plan to stab each other rather than blow each other's brains out. If you had any. I suppose I should be grateful."

Cornelius, who had been ignoring Morgan as he should, cast him an involuntary glance at the doctor's words. Just for an instant, there was a shared amusement between them, then Morgan looked away.

Atherstone was making a great fuss about inspecting the rapiers, comparing their lengths and whooshing them audibly through the air.

"Where the devil did you find them?" he asked Aubrey.

"In the attic. They were my grandfather's. He was a most dashing blade, by all accounts."

"You'll forgive me if I say they give your principal something of an advantage over mine?"

"I doubt it. If we ever played with them, it was as children. But if you have another pair with you, we will happily consider them."

Atherstone returned to examining the weapons, testing their points.

He's wasting time, Cornelius thought uneasily. *Why is he wasting time?*

The silence stretched, broken only by the rush of the sea and the plaintive cries of seagulls. Cornelius breathed in, observing the sand and the rocks as though he had never seen them before, breathing in the salty tang of the sea. In the distance, he could hear the clip-clop of horses. Then that stopped too.

Atherstone swiped the swords through the air once more. Morgan was scowling at him, clearly as impatient as everyone else. It was about to rain.

Above, the rumbling of wheels and horses' hooves was borne on the wind.

Atherstone set the swords back in their box. "Let us begin."

"MY LADY," WHISPERED a voice, rousing Alice from her troubled sleep. "My lady!"

"What?" Alice blinked into the light of a candle, grasped in the hands of her maid. The pale light of dawn penetrated the window, for in summer she preferred to sleep with the shutters and the curtains open. "What's the time?"

"Early." Her maid Fenton's eyes were shining with pleasure. "A note was delivered for you, my lady. Urgently. A gentleman bade Letty the kitchen maid see that you got it at once. A matter of life and death, so he said."

Alice sat up, taking the folded letter from her maid. Fenton lit the lamp, waiting with great excitement.

A gentleman is injured and needs your help urgently. Speed and silence are of the essence. He awaits you beyond the gates. Please hurry before it is too late.

So this was it. The summons beyond the castle walls that Mr. Jones had warned her about. She was expecting it and didn't believe a word of it. And yet her heart leapt with fear, just in case it was true.

To Fenton's clear disappointment, she re-folded the letter, keeping it in her hold as she thrust back the covers and jumped out of bed. She didn't know what she expected to see from her window, which looked out onto the sea, nor toward either of the roads that led to the castle gates.

And yet she was rewarded by the sight of a long, thin figure clambering over the rocks just beneath the castle in the direction of the path down to the beach. Serena had held a waltzing party down there once and danced most romantically with Tamar— until Mama and Gervaise had come home unexpectedly.

Alice smiled at the memory. Gervaise had eventually come around to Serena marrying the feckless, penniless marquis. She wondered how long it would take him to appreciate a hardwork-ing steward.

Mr. Jones, if it was indeed him, paused just beside the path, crouching down and peering toward the beach. Poor Mr. Jones, forced into obeying the letter of Atherstone's instructions and fighting his rear-guard action against the spirit. What was he waiting for now?

Alice lifted the window sash and leaned out to see the beach properly. In the dull almost-daylight, figures were moving on the sand while others stood to the side. Something gleamed between the shifting, almost dancing men below. Swords?

Suddenly, she couldn't breathe.

"Remember I love you," he had said yesterday outside the church. *"Only you."*

Even at the time it had sounded oddly like a farewell, like something she should remember if ever…

Dear God, was he fighting a duel over her? Over someone else?

She spun around. "Clothes, Fenton!" she cried. "Now!"

THE CARRIAGE THAT arrived at the castle gates did not appear to be in a hurry. The horses merely walked. The coachman, his hat pulled down over his eyes, halted them silently with a tug of the reins. He did not turn them. Obviously he did not mean to drive back to the town but to carry on along the road across country beyond the Solway Firth, where he could more easily cross into Scotland.

Oh yes, Lady Alice would have been in deep trouble.

From her hiding place behind the tree, Cecily saw the curtain at the coach window twitch. She looked toward the castle, but although a fellow had come out of the lodge five minutes ago to unlock the gates, no one was now in sight. No sign of Lady Alice, either.

Cecily sighed. She would have quite liked Alice to know who it was that saved her, but the important thing was to do so, and that little rat Daubin deserved to be scolded to within an inch of his life. Cecily, living on her nerves for the last several days, was just the lady to do it.

Straightening her hat and her veil, she stepped delicately around the tree and onto the road, marching fearlessly up to the carriage, quite ready to verbally blister its occupant.

The door opened, and Darcy Daubin stepped down, resplendent in pale blue coat and a yellow striped waistcoat. His cravat was of a paler yellow, and there was lace at his cuffs. He was dazzling in a laughable kind of way, but Cecily was not deterred.

"Quick," he said urgently. "He needs you."

Cecily gasped and froze, blood ringing in her ears. Somehow, it was Jack in the carriage! Injured in the silly duel! How could Cornelius have done such a thing?

She almost charged the carriage, snatching Daubin's hand and leaping inside.

She had barely registered that the inside was empty before Daubin jumped up behind her and slammed the door. As the carriage lurched into motion, she fell onto the bench, and Daubin landed beside her.

"Lady Alice," he purred. "What an extraordinary pleasure."

ON THE BEACH, Cornelius and Morgan saluted each other with their swords and sprang into defensive posture, swords crossing but not touching. Neither were expert fencers. No doubt Morgan had learned the basics at school, as had Cornelius.

"Since we can finally speak to each other," Cornelius said, "I did not insult her, nor touch her except with innocent friendship."

Morgan's blade lashed out, but Cornelius held firm.

"Then why are you here?" Morgan demanded between his teeth. He lunged.

Cornelius parried. "Because you made it impossible not to be."

Morgan drove forward, and their blades clashed together several times. "Even now you are proclaiming innocence? Why? So that I don't banish her? So that you can get at her again another day?"

"I don't want *at her* at all," Cornelius snapped, breaking away and circling. "And more to the point, she doesn't want me. That was clear enough two years ago, when, yes, if I'd had a choice, I might just have fought you for her hand. I would have done anything for her, even hurt you, whom I regarded as my friend as well as my employer."

Morgan lunged low, and Cornelius crashed his blade downward into the other blade, twisting in an unskilled effort to disarm his opponent. He leapt backward when it didn't work, but at least he wasn't punctured.

"I know you wanted her then," Morgan panted. "I even felt sorry for you."

"To be honest, I felt pretty sorry for myself."

"So you thought you would try again? With less honorable

intentions?" Furiously, Morgan drove him back further.

"I have no intentions whatsoever toward your wife. My heart is with someone else entirely."

"Liar!" yelled Morgan, lunging once more. Cornelius only just managed to shove up his sword in time. "I saw you at the ball, teasing and laughing, gazing at her like a great, lovesick puppy!"

"Well, that should have told you something," Cornelius retorted. "Have I ever worn my heart on my sleeve? Be honest with yourself, Morgan. Were you not taking her for granted, leaving her with your—forgive me—dragon of a mother while you pursued your own interests? Cecily needs devotion, attention, and she wasn't getting it from you. She thought you had a mistress, and so she asked me to flirt with her to make you jealous. Apparently it succeeded beyond her wildest dreams."

For the first time, it was Cornelius driving Morgan back, though only because of a rock behind him that he had almost stumbled on, and the surging approach of the tide at his back. Cornelius could have pinked him several times over, but he contented himself with the schoolboy clash of blade on blade without much real purpose.

"You're lying," Morgan snarled.

"Why would I? Lady Alice was in on the plot, too, as were my youngest brother and sister. Cecily loves you, you dolt. Though you don't deserve it. See?"

Dropping his sword to point downward, Cornelius brought up his left arm at the same time. Morgan, lunging furiously, could not draw back in time, and drove the point of his sword into Cornelius's arm.

Blood ran out immediately, and Aubrey shouted, "Blood! Put down your swords! Honor is satisfied."

For a moment, Morgan looked furious enough to run Cornelius straight through. But his face was white and the sword dropped from his nerveless fingers. "Was that supposed to impress me?"

"Yes, a bit. You drew blood. I let you, but not because I am guilty. Can we stop this now and go and get drunk? Or even just have breakfast?"

Morgan's breath caught. He stared at Cornelius an instant longer, and then he laughed. "Damn it, Vale!"

Aubrey, relieved, was picking up the dropped swords.

Dr. Lampton stalked toward them. "Sit," he commanded Cornelius, who eased his hip against the nearest rock and watched the doctor open his case, take out a sponge, and wipe off the blood a little too vigorously before tying on a short bandage. "Don't do it again. And if you do, don't call me. Good morning."

"Thank you, doctor," Cornelius called after him.

Lampton swung his bag by way of response but didn't look back.

"Breakfast?" Morgan said.

"Breakfast," Cornelius agreed.

"Shall we repair to the hotel?" Atherstone suggested. "I, for one, intend to go back to sleep. May I offer you gentlemen a seat in my carriage?"

"Thank you, but we have the horses," Aubrey replied.

Cornelius could not trust himself to speak. If the sword had still been in his hand, he might well have lashed out at Atherstone, for what he had done to Alice. To preserve her good name, he could not, but he certainly would not eat with the swine.

Morgan thanked the duke civilly for his service, while Cornelius shrugged back into his coat. He and Aubrey collected their horses and led them across the sand toward the town, while the duke sauntered up the path that led to the road and his carriage. It struck Cornelius that His Grace moved like a very fit man and would have been a much more dangerous opponent than Morgan.

THE CARRIAGE RATTLED along the road from the castle, moving so fast that it lurched from side to side. For the first few minutes of her journey, Cecily was fully occupied in hanging on to the strap beside her so that she wasn't thrown onto the floor or hurled against either the window or her companion.

Once they were around the bend and, no doubt, far enough away for carriage and horses not to be recognized by any watchers from the castle, the driver slowed his horses enough to allow the passengers some dignity.

Through her veil, Cecily regarded the dazzling Daubin.

"Pray tell," she said frostily, "where you imagine you are taking me?"

Daubin smiled, his expression fond rather than threatening. "To your wedding, my lady. Rejoice."

"You really are a fool, are you not?" she said, and his carefully groomed eyebrows flew up.

"There is no need to be offensive," he said.

"On the contrary, there is every need. Do you imagine you can just abduct a lady without repercussions? I could see you hang for this! At this moment, I might even enjoy it. Either way, you are ruined, Mr. Daubin, and will be received nowhere." With that, she drew herself up from the seat with the aid of the strap and knocked sharply on the roof.

Daubin laughed and sat back against the squabs as though about to enjoy a stage performance.

"Alas, that will do you no good. Unless *I* command them, they will not stop before the Scottish border."

"Then command them," Cecily snapped, uneasy at last, for she did not want to give Jack more reason to doubt her.

Daubin ignored that. "As for charges of abduction—please, my dear. Before the coachman and any other lurking witnesses, you walked willingly, even eagerly, into my carriage."

"Because you lied to me!"

"I did," Daubin said complacently. "Be assured it is the last lie I shall tell you. I will be a most devoted and attentive husband,

and I dare to prophesy you will be a delightfully adoring wife."

"Under no circumstance will you and I ever become husband and wife."

She spoke with such certainty, such contempt, that the smile still lurking on Daubin's lips froze, and he stared at her, seeming to notice for the first time that she was veiled. At long last, suspicion sparked in his fast-blinking eyes.

Cecily tilted her chin and, under his horrified gaze, unhurriedly lifted her veil.

"Lady Morgan," she drawled. "You see your problem, sir? Also, my husband will kill you. He is quite experienced by now in dueling." She leaned forward. "Now, turn the carriage around and take me back to Blackhaven, you nasty, stupid little toad."

He stared at her, his mouth opening and closing like a landed fish's. Cecily felt somewhat triumphant, even powerful—until an ugly look began to spread over his face and his cold, cold eyes, and she realized that she was actually alone with a strong, angry man. She could expect no help from the coachman, either.

Then, from nowhere, a much larger equipage swept past, easily overtaking Daubin's already-speeding carriage. The passing carriage was splendid, with a crest on the side, and drawn by four beautifully matched horses. Its coachman's attention was clearly engaged with his team and the road ahead, but the two passengers were staring straight across at Cecily.

She waved wildly, battered her hands on the glass, shouting, "Help, help!" Not that they would hear her, but surely they would read her lips and her desperation…

Daubin began to laugh, a high-pitched, not remotely fearful sound. The larger carriage had already swept by before, with sudden crashing fright, she realized who it was she had seen.

The Duke of Atherstone.

Dear God, there would be no help from him either…

Worse, their own carriage slowed, then halted so abruptly that she was thrown back against the squabs, while the horses screamed in protest. Men's voices outside the carriage told her that the duke had, against all the odds, caused the halt.

Come to gloat, no doubt…

Quick as a flash, Cecily yanked the veil back down over her face, just in time before the carriage door opened and the duke stood there in all his understated aristocratic hauteur.

"Your Grace," said Daubin, sounding aggrieved, as though it was someone else's fault he had abducted the wrong woman. Cecily could not imagine why the duke would care.

"Perhaps I may be of assistance, ma'am?" the duke inquired. "You seem uncomfortable in your present surroundings."

She nodded mutely, trembling with genuine fear. If she could just persuade him to take her to the next inn… After all, whatever His Grace's grudge, it was clearly against Lady Alice, not her.

The duke kicked down the carriage steps and held out his hand. "Come," he said, and lashed Daubin with his mocking gaze. "As for you, you contemptible scoundrel, I shall deal with you later."

"What?" Daubin said blankly.

Cecily placed her shaking hand in the duke's and stepped down onto the road. With great courtesy, he conducted her along the few yards of road to his own splendid carriage.

He paused to speak to his coachman. "Stop at the inn while we decide how best to help her ladyship."

The coachman touched his whip to his hat, and the duke handed Cecily up into the carriage, where another, miserable-looking man awaited, his back to the horses. His eyes were both alarmed and curiously…thwarted.

As she sat down, Daubin ran into the road, spluttering, "My lord duke, I do not understand! What…"

"Jones," Atherstone said in a bored voice, and obligingly the other gentleman rapped on the roof with the hilt of his cane. The carriage moved forward, causing Daubin to leap out of the way. His beautiful boots and immaculate pantaloons were splashed with mud.

"What a commoner the man is," His Grace said with distaste.

"How fortunate that I was able to rescue you from such a scoundrel." He touched her hand, very lightly, leaning forward, his expression one of concern. How could this be the man who had encouraged Daubin to elope with Lady Alice? "You have been in a most unfortunate situation, and we must decide between us what it is best to do next."

"Sir, I am most grateful for your timely intervention," Cecily said nervously. "May I further count on your help to return to Blackhaven?"

The duke narrowed his eyes at once, gazing into her veil.

There was a certain distraction in his voice as he said, "If you decide that is the best way forward."

Without warning, he swept the veil back over her hat. She made an involuntary grab for it, but was too late. Defiantly, she dropped her hand into her lap and stared at him.

"Who the devil are you?" he demanded. "And where is Lady Alice?"

Chapter Nineteen

A LICE, HER GOWN half fastened and her hair pinned anyhow, had hidden those deficiencies under the hooded cloak Fenton threw to her as she ran from the bedchamber and hurtled along passages and downstairs to the door closest to the beach path.

Peering over the edge of the cliff, she could no longer see anyone, least of all duelers. Terrified that she was too late, she started down the path, then paused as she heard footsteps. Her knees gave way, and she crouched down as two men emerged from further down the path.

"Hurry," the Duke of Atherstone's voice snapped. "We haven't got all day."

He strode on—fortunately up the other fork toward the road rather than to the castle.

Behind him came his chaplain, Mr. Jones, who did catch sight of her. His eyes widened in horror, then he stumbled after the duke. "Coming, Your Grace…"

Alice stayed where she was, her heart thundering. Dear God, she'd almost run straight into the man she needed to avoid at all costs, the man who meant her harm… Would Mr. Jones tell him she was there, in order to save himself and his family?

Below her on the beach, Cornelius could lie hurt or dying. Surely he had not been fighting a duel with Atherstone? Although what else made sense?

She could wait no longer. With a smothered sob, she slid and stumbled down the path, which was at least quicker than taking the carved steps from further around the castle. At any moment, she expected to hear Atherstone's hateful voice or, worse, feel his powerful, heavy hand on her shoulder.

But before she had reached the beach, she heard the sound of a carriage and several horses trotting off away from Blackhaven. Taking a flying leap, she landed on the sand.

The beach was empty.

Whoever else had been here had vanished, as though into thin air…

But of course they had not! Jumping to her feet, she ran closer to the sea and peered in both directions along the beach. Toward Black Hill, the beach was empty and the tide too close to the rocky coast to encourage walkers.

In the other direction, toward Blackhaven, she could make out several figures, men and horses. Was Cornelius among them? Was he hurt?

As she ran after them, she wondered lots of other things. What on earth had possessed him to fight with the duke? Was Atherstone still in such a hurry because he meant to catch her at the castle gates? Would Mr. Jones get the blame when Alice did not turn up there?

God, what a vile man…

Running along soft sand was hard work. She had to slow to a panting walk, but at least she was catching up. She could finally make out that none of the men in front was carrying anyone else, and no one was riding on either of the horses.

However, closer to town there were inevitably more people around—fishwives and fishermen, the odd rider taking an early morning gallop on the beach, a couple of ladies with pet dogs on leashes. She could not shout after the men without appearing like a fishwife herself. She had to remind herself she would be easily recognized. Hastily, she drew up her hood over her half-tumbling hair, and held the cloak more closely around her. Light rain was spattering on the sand, adding to the mist over the sea.

Relieved to see her quarries leading their horses up the path from the town beach, she hurried after them, but, walking toward the high street, they vanished from her view. Where was Cornelius going? To Dr. Lampton? To the hospital? Or was the doctor with him?

With despair, she realized she had never even got close enough to assure herself that one of the men *was* Cornelius.

She ploughed on toward the high street, hoping for a glimpse. Instead, she was forced to stop as a disreputable-looking young girl stood right in front of her, bending to peer under the hood of her cloak.

"It *is* you," said Leona Vale happily, then to her nearby brother, "It *is* Lady A—"

"Sh-sh," Alice said. "I'm looking for your brother—have you seen him?"

"Which one?" Leona asked, as though playing for time.

"Cornelius. *Did* you see him? Is he hurt?"

Leona looked so startled that she wished she had not frightened the girl, who was now clutching her brother's hand.

"He's not hurt," Lawrence said scornfully. "Anyone could see that. We hid from him, since we're not supposed to be interfering anymore."

"Are you interfering with Cornelius?" Alice asked, frowning.

"Oh no," Leona said. "But we had to hide behind a cart when he came by with Aubrey and Sir John Morgan. They went into the hotel together."

"Sir John?" she repeated, startled. "Are you sure?"

"Quite sure."

Alice swallowed. "Was Lady Morgan with them?"

"No," said Leona. "They looked like men who wanted to have brandy for breakfast. Or at least *with* breakfast. At any rate, not to behave as ladies might wish." She exchanged a glance with her brother, and they both nodded. "We've changed our minds.

We'll come to the hotel with you."

If Alice wondered about being allowed into the hotel in her present garb and accompanied by two apparently urchin children, she quickly saw that the opposite was true. She did not even need to reveal her identity to the doorman, who grinned at the twins and simply opened the door for all of them.

"We're looking for my brother," Lawrence said amiably to the first footman who glanced at them. "I believe he came in with Sir John Morgan."

It was the hotel's policy to give out no information whatsoever about their guests, as Alice, Helen, and Maria had discovered in their mischievous childhood. But the footman merely smiled tolerantly and pointed to the back of the foyer and the coffee room door.

Please let him be there. Let him be well and unhurt, please God… She raised her hand to knock, but before she could, Lawrence's knuckles thudded against the door and he opened it immediately, bowing exaggeratedly to Alice and his sister.

Alice stumbled in.

Three men, all in casual morning clothes and seated at the table, gawped and sprang to their feet. One of them was Cornelius, looking so bronzed and hale and hearty that she sobbed out, "Oh, Cornelius!"

Rushing at him, she flung her arms around his neck, clutching him as though she'd never let him go. His arms closed around her, firm and secure, and she cried harder.

"Alice, oh, Alice," he whispered in distress, sitting down again with her on his knee. "What has happened to upset you?" He glanced from her shuddering body to the twins, who had at least closed the door.

"She was worried about you," Lawrence said. "Don't know why, so we came along to help her find out."

Alice, appalled by her own weakness, wiped her wet face on Cornelius's shoulder and raised her head. He handed her a handkerchief, and she blew her nose before offering it back.

Helpfully, Lawrence took it and stashed it in Cornelius's pocket.

"What are you up to, twins?" Aubrey demanded.

"What are *you* up to?" Leona retorted, picking up the brandy decanter. "It's only just seven in the morning!"

"It's medicinal," Aubrey said with dignity, then, more hastily as Alice turned on him in obvious fear, "Shock, you know. No serious injury."

Alice broke in. "Why were you on the beach at Braithwaite Cove?"

The men avoided looking at each other and shifted in their seats.

Alice grasped Cornelius by the shoulders. "Did you fight a duel with the Duke of Atherstone?"

"Of course not, and you were meant to stay in the castle out of his way," Cornelius exclaimed. "Dear God, what if he had caught you just as he meant to?"

"He ran right past me," Alice said impatiently, "and drove off in a coach, I think. He was in a terrible hurry."

"But what on Earth possessed you to leave the castle when you knew—"

She tried to shake him by the shoulders. "Because I saw people on the beach, and I was sure they were dueling. And I suddenly realized you were saying goodbye to me at church yesterday, just in case…" She hit her closed fist against his chest, raging, "How *could* you, Cornelius? What if you had *died*…?"

He looked harassed. Aubrey obligingly filled up his glass.

Cornelius didn't notice it. Shoving one hand through his hair—the other was holding Alice, most deliciously—he said reluctantly, "I wasn't fighting Atherstone. I was fighting Sir John."

She blinked across the table at Sir John Morgan.

"My fault," he said apologetically. "I got jealous—foolishly jealous—and challenged him. I see now why he has no interest in my wife."

Alice, blushing, closed her mouth and licked her lips, though she did not vacate Cornelius's lap.

"And now you're all friends," she said indignantly, although she wasn't quite sure what exactly she was indignant about. "Was Atherstone with you?"

"He was my second," Sir John said.

But Cornelius was staring at Alice. "More to the point, why was he in such a hurry?"

"To catch me at the castle gates," Alice replied, fishing inside her gown for the note she had received that morning. "Playing on my fears for you. It worked, too, only I went the wrong way and he didn't catch me."

"Then why," Cornelius said slowly, "did he drive off so quickly in the carriage? Why did he not wait around for you, closer to the castle gate? Was Jones at the gate instead?"

"No, Jones seemed to be waiting for Atherstone on the cliff path. He saw me but said nothing."

Cornelius scowled. "Something is going on here we don't understand."

"Shall we go and find out?" Lawrence offered.

"No," Cornelius snapped. "You stay away from Atherstone. For Leona's sake if no other. The man is a—"

A knock sounded at the door, and Alice, belatedly recognizing the impropriety of her perch on Cornelius's knee, hastily jumped to her feet.

Two footmen came in bearing trays of ham, sausages, eggs, mushrooms, and buttered toast, and pots of steaming coffee.

Sir John rose to his feet once more. "I'll just go and see if my wife is awake."

"Bring her to join us, if you like," Cornelius said distractedly.

As the footmen retreated again, his gaze shifted to Alice, disconcertingly warm, almost as if she were back in his arms. She flushed with pleasure.

"Were you truly so anxious for me?" he asked.

She wanted to deny it in her crossest voice but found herself nodding instead. "Who else would I be worried about?" she managed with a flash of spirit. "Atherstone?"

He threaded his fingers through hers and raised their joined hands to his lips, kissing her knuckles. The twins, helping themselves to toast and pieces of ham, watched with interest.

Alice cleared her throat. "Let me pour you coffee."

"Only if you sit and break your fast with us."

Her stomach rumbled in a most unladylike fashion, so she sat down, demurely poured two cups of coffee—the twins wrinkled their noses when offered—and helped herself to a piece of toast.

Cornelius sat beside her, close enough to feel the heat of his thigh almost touching hers. What a rather lovely day this was turning into after its awful start...

Sir John almost burst into the room, throwing a hastily scribbled note on the table.

"Cecily overheard Atherstone talking to some other villain and has gone to warn Lady Alice!"

It took a moment for the implications of that to sink in. Alice swallowed her toast. Cornelius laid down his fork.

It was Lawrence who put their thoughts into words. "That is why Atherstone drove off so quickly. He might have thought he had Lady Alice, but in fact he had Lady Morgan."

Cornelius took a large cup of coffee while he stood up. "Then we had better go after them."

"Where?" Sir John said, actually tearing at his hair. "We don't even know which way they went from the castle!"

"Toward Carlisle," Alice said, thinking back to the hoofbeats and the rumbling wheels she had heard from the beach. "And the Scottish border. I am not of age. He could not marry me in England without Gervaise's permission. And he does not like to lose."

"Cecily has thwarted him," Sir John said in a strangled voice. "I must get to her!"

"I'll come with you," Cornelius said, shoving him toward the table. "Eat something, quickly. Even if it's only a mouthful."

"I'll come, too," Alice said, jumping to her feet.

"You will not!" Cornelius cried.

"Don't be selfish!" Alice replied. "Cecily might need another woman with her."

"We'll come too," Leona said. "We're very useful."

Cornelius, who had been glaring at Alice, suddenly muttered, "You're right, Alice. You come. And twins, you are indeed very useful. In this case, I want you to take a message to the Earl of Braithwaite at the castle. Tell him Alice is safe with us and where we are going."

"The Scottish border," Lawrence said.

"Hopefully we won't need to go so far! I'll go and hire a carriage."

"WHO THE DEVIL are you? And where is Lady Alice?"

The duke's question hung between them.

Cecily had never been so frightened in her life. Out of the frying pan… But she was not no one.

She lifted her chin. "I am Lady Morgan."

Atherstone blinked. Unexpectedly, he laughed.

"My husband will be most grateful to you for rescuing me from that awful man," she added in a rush.

"Will he?" Atherstone's eyes were like ice. His upper lip had a nasty, angry curl to it. It twitched.

Cecily rushed on, "So, if you could see your way to be of further service, we would both be in your debt. Perhaps you would either return me to Blackhaven or let me down at the first inn so that I might hire a conveyance?"

"Why would I do that?" the duke said, looking her up and down in a manner that was hardly respectful.

Cecily needed him too badly to scold. "Because it is vital that I get back to Blackhaven as soon as possible. I am very afraid that my husband was involved in a duel this morning, and I do not know if he even survived."

She was sure Cornelius would not have killed him—not deliberately, at any rate—but there was no point in telling the duke that. She needed all the sympathy she could extract.

"He did survive," said the other man, who had remained silent up until now. "They both did."

Atherstone cast him a glance of pure venom that almost threw Cecily. What in the world was going on here? Not entirely acting, Cecily gave a little sob of relief and resorted to dabbing the corner of her eye with a tiny wisp of embroidery and lace.

"And now you have quite upset my plans," the duke told her. "I do hope that was not deliberate?"

Cecily jumped with fright. She had indeed gone to the castle gates to upset the duke by warning Lady Alice. Daubin's appearance had thrown her, as had her fear for Jack. She hung desperately to the truth.

"That vile man lied to me!" she said tearfully. "He made me think Jack was wounded in the carriage, and then he drove off before I could even see no one else was there! He thought I was someone else."

Atherstone sat back. "Perhaps you are a friend of Lady Alice?"

Cecily widened her eyes at him. "You imagine we formed a conspiracy to play a trick on you and Mr. Daubin? How dare Your Grace? I am a respectably married lady!"

"So you are. Which has its compensations."

Again, those contemptuous eyes raked her from head to toe.

"Perhaps we should stop at the inn, as Your Grace first planned," the other man said nervously.

"What an excellent idea. For once." The mixture of coldness and lust in his gaze was terrifying. "We must decide what compensation is due me for my inconvenience."

If they had not been traveling so fast, Cecily might have seriously considered throwing herself out of the carriage and taking her chances with the road and any traffic coming the other way. She even started forward once, more from instinct than conscious thought, and instantly, belying his lethargic posture, the duke seized her arm in a grip that hurt.

"You would not do anything truly foolish, would you?" he said softly.

Cecily, who still harbored hopes of persuading him to help, forbore from retorting.

To her dismay, they turned off the main road and along a track to a half-hidden inn. If anyone was following, or looking for her, they would never find her here!

But she was being silly. She was not some foolish chit of no account that the duke could assault and abandon. She was the wife of Sir John Morgan, and though she had been somewhat tempted of late, she really did not want to be anything or anyone else. Tears pricked at her eyes as the carriage halted at the rather dilapidated house, but she blinked them away, determined to show no fear.

Perhaps there would be someone kind in the inn—the inn-keeper's wife, even—who would help her?

No doubt to prevent her bolting, Atherstone helped her down from the carriage and clamped her hand to his arm as they walked into the inn.

A slovenly woman greeted him like an old friend before he interrupted, "A private parlor, if you please."

"Right away, sir. Come right in."

"Breakfast," the duke commanded as he walked past her into the parlor, all but pushing Cecily in front of him.

Since the main room was deserted, there seemed little point in making a fuss about the parlor. What could happen while breakfast was being served and consumed? And at least the other man, the generally silent Mr. Jones, was with them, looking miserable.

But then, Atherstone had turned silent, too. While he ate his way through the not terribly appetizing breakfast, he watched Cecily like a cat who had found a mouse to play with.

She barely nibbled at a slice of toast, despite not having eaten that morning.

The duke laid down his knife and fork. "Go away, Jones."

Without a word, Jones rose and bowed to her. Despite the rather terrifying sympathy in his expression, he turned his back and walked out of the room.

"Well," the duke said, pushing his chair back from the table. "What compensation do you offer me for my inconvenience?"

"My gratitude. And my husband's."

"That will hardly teach you not to interfere in my affairs. How did you come to be at the castle gates to fool the inestimable Daubin?"

"I wished to stop my husband's duel. Someone told me such affairs were normally conducted near the castle."

"You are a terrible liar." The duke threw his napkin on the table. "I think your ladyship listens at doors, like the meanest serving wench."

Cecily blushed furiously, not least because that was exactly what she had done. "Your Grace is unkind to a lady alone, fearing for her husband's life."

"Then let me set your mind at rest. Your husband was last seen scuttling toward Blackhaven with two of the Vale brothers, with the stated aim of getting drunk."

She doubted she hid her despair at that news either. No one would save her.

"Did you think to curry favor with the Earl of Braithwaite's family?" the duke murmured. "You have really rather done them a disservice, you know. Lady Alice could be a duchess by now. You, on the other hand, will be merely yet another faithless, adulterous wife. Will Morgan beat you?"

She jumped to her feet in agitation, and saw the disturbing flare of lust in his eyes once more.

"On second thought," the duke added, "perhaps I don't care. I believe we will compensate each other for our wasted time."

Oh, dear heaven, now what do I do? "I must go to the cloakroom," she said, inspired, bolting for the door.

Inevitably he was before her, catching her hand before he

opened the door himself and bellowed, "Landlady!" He smiled frostily. "I would hate you to get lost."

Her main purpose was in fact to waste time, although she desperately needed someone on her side.

"Where is Mr. Jones?" she asked the woman as soon as they were out of earshot.

She cackled. "Praying, like as not."

Cecily stared at her. "He is a *clergyman?*"

"Chaplain." He shrugged. "Could be defrocked, for all I know! There you are. I'll wait. And I wouldn't be too long if I were you. He'll only come in after you."

Cecily let out an exclamation of outrage, though it sounded more like a moan of fear. Atherstone was a duke. He was afraid of no one. How could she make him so?

She could try making herself as unattractive as possible, but she had the feeling this would make no difference to Atherstone. She doubted he would even recognize her tomorrow. All he wanted was to assuage his anger, take out on someone else the failure of his appalling plan.

She wished she had never even thought of warning Alice against the plot.

Emerging from the cloakroom, she found the landlady still waiting for her. She veered across the room toward the front door of the inn.

"Fresh air," she said vaguely. But again, the duke materialized before her, and in no time, she was bundled back into the parlor, the door firmly closed.

Clearly prepared to waste no more time, the duke immediately took her in his arms, forced her body hard against him, and slammed his mouth down on hers.

Cecily's shocked senses went numb. Her ears rang.

And then suddenly, the door of the room flew open.

Chapter Twenty

THE CARRIAGE AND pair hired at the Blackhaven Hotel, carrying Alice, Cornelius, Aubrey, and Morgan, would not have halted so early in the pursuit had Alice not suddenly glimpsed a familiar figure striding furiously along the road in the same direction.

"It's Darcy Daubin," she exclaimed, turning to peer out of the back window. "He's waving at us. Quick, get the jarvey to halt…"

"For that creature?" Cornelius said contemptuously.

"Yes! Cornelius, *what is he doing there?*"

Cornelius rapped on the ceiling, and Morgan, angry at the delay, glared from him to Alice.

Alice ignored him, watching Daubin run along the road toward him. His once-shiny boots and beautiful, light pantaloons were splashed with mud, and he was sweating with exertion by the time he stood gasping at the door, which Cornelius pushed open.

Daubin almost stopped breathing. His gaze flew from Cornelius to Alice and the other occupants of the carriage. When he saw Morgan, he let out a moan.

Cornelius reached down, grasped Daubin by the front of his coat, and hauled him into the carriage, depositing him on the floor among their legs and slamming the door.

"I never touched her!" Daubin screamed.

In rage, Morgan drew back his fist, but Aubrey caught his arm.

"Don't be an idiot," he advised. "We need to know what he does."

"It was a mistake! A genuine mistake," Daubin gabbled. "I mistook her identity and took the wrong lady!"

"From where?" Cornelius asked so softly that Alice barely heard him.

"From just outside the castle gates," Daubin muttered.

Cornelius's lip curled, his face so filled with icy contempt that, for the first time ever, Alice was afraid of him. "You were doing Atherstone's dirty work."

"I was not!" Daubin cried. "It is my greatest, fondest wish to call Lady Alice my wife. His Grace was helping me…" He let out a wail. "Or I thought he was! But he stopped the carriage and took her from me! He thought Lady Morgan was Lady Alice! She was veiled, which was how I mistook her in the first place."

Sir John rapped furiously on the ceiling, and the carriage set off again.

"*Then*," Daubin cried in outrage, "my dashed coachman refused to follow the duke. He said it was more than his life was worth to disobey His Grace, and he was going back to Blackhaven. He left me standing in the road like a fool! And I have been a fool," he added hastily, under the glare of both Cornelius and Sir John. "I was so angry, I was determined to confront His Grace about betraying me—"

"His Grace betraying *you*?" Cornelius said. "Not of your own behavior in trying to abduct one lady and instead endangering another? You really are a vile little worm, aren't you? I should throw you out the damned carriage!"

Alice caught his arm. "No, no, not yet. Sir, where will the duke take her? To Scotland?"

"He has no need to go to Scotland. He has a tame clergyman in tow. And a special license which he pretended was for me, but it is bound to have his name on it…" He cringed before the cold fury in Cornelius's face and the sudden start of Sir John. "He instructed his coachman to drive to the nearest inn. You might catch up with him there! After all, there is no point in his trying to marry Lady Morgan."

"There was no point in his trying to marry me, either," Alice said testily. "I am only nineteen, and he does not have my brother's permission."

"But he would get it," Cornelius said. "After the event, Braithwaite would not challenge the marriage because you were alone with him—or would have been. Look how he forced Helen to marry—"

"He doesn't have the earl's sister," Sir John interrupted. "He has my wife, and he is not going to be happy."

"No, he isn't," Cornelius agreed grimly. "We'd better look for them at the first posting inn…"

"Wait," Alice said. "He wouldn't have taken me anywhere I could be helped until I had spent enough time in his company to be truly compromised. Gervaise could have found out somehow and come after me. He would have hidden us away somewhere."

At the back of her mind, she was amazed at herself for thinking so logically. She might shudder at the thought of being in Atherstone's power—and she *did* shudder on poor Cecily's account—but she was not afraid. Because she was with Cornelius.

"He definitely said *the inn*," Daubin said sulkily. "I heard him."

"Misleading us all?" Aubrey suggested.

"Or…" Cornelius frowned as though in remembrance. "The *Goat and Shoe Inn!*"

"I've never heard of it," Alice said, but Cornelius had already leaned out the window, yelling instructions to the coachman.

"You wouldn't," he said to her. "It's hardly the sort of house frequented by gentlemen, let alone ladies. But I surveyed as much of the country around Blackhaven as I could when I first came here. I found the Goat by accident, and I'm sure it subsists more on smugglers' bribes than hospitality."

"Would Atherstone really stop at such a place?" Aubrey asked.

"He might well if he wished no one to find him. Atherstone plays to win."

The carriage lurched off the road and along a track that was barely wide enough for it. Alice could easily imagine loaded horses and donkeys carrying barrels of wine and brandy along here on a dark night.

Ten minutes later, they only just saw the sign of the Goat, half hidden among overhanging trees. Barging past the furious slattern who tried to halt them at the door, Morgan went roaring up the stairs.

"Don't let him commit murder," Cornelius called over his shoulder to Aubrey. Alice had already seen the door off the empty common room and marched resolutely toward it.

Cornelius caught her hand and squeezed it before brushing past her and throwing open the door.

WITHOUT ANY FURTHER warning, Atherstone was yanked off Cecily and thrown across the room.

Cecily whispered, "Cornelius," between numb lips as she stared at the large, imposing man who suddenly filled the room with his presence. She did not remember him like that. He had changed and grown over the last two years, and even in her present circumstances, the sight of him thrilled her most oddly. Yet it also clarified that she had made the right choice, because she could never have controlled Cornelius Vale.

Oh, Cornelius… Tears started in her eyes. "Have you killed Jack?"

"Of course he has not killed Jack," Lady Alice—*Lady Alice?*—said scornfully as she brushed past Cornelius into the room. "He is searching upstairs and will be here directly."

By then Atherstone had risen to his feet, apparently unperturbed, and was brushing down his coat.

"Lady Alice," he drawled. "What a pleasure. Did you bring her to make a swap, Vale? Or am I to be left with both queens on the board?"

Cornelius did not deign to answer. Instead, he spoke to Cecily. "Come."

"Remain where you are," Atherstone warned her. "You know what a dangerous pastime it has become for you to rush to any man who calls. She has already been with Daubin and me. And the landlord, for all I know." He reached out casually to stop her, but Cornelius took one step forward, and the duke paused—perhaps from sheer surprise, perhaps because, like Cecily, he had suddenly realized that something in the man merited respect, or at least careful handling.

"All that good breeding," Cornelius marveled. "The ancient name and great title, and yet there you stand, not even a gentleman but an odious little commoner."

Cecily doubted anyone had ever spoken to His Grace like that in his life. Dull redness suffused his cheeks. His eyes lit with a strangely stunned fury.

From upstairs came a shriek and the sound of a young man's laughter. Cornelius's lips twitched with amusement, but his gaze did not leave the duke.

A clatter of footsteps sounded, and then Cecily's husband all but fell into the room.

Jack stood before her, glaring at the duke, breathing like a bull, all but pawing the ground. "You black-hearted, treacherous scoundrel!"

The duke recovered his urbanity. "My dear Morgan," he said, "if you cannot control your own wife's fancies…"

Jack's fists clenched even tighter. In an effort to head off trouble—Atherstone was still a powerful nobleman—Cecily cast herself into her husband's arms. "Oh, thank God, thank God! I didn't even know if you were alive or dead!"

"And yet," purred Atherstone, "here you are with me. Shall we tell your dear husband how willingly you walked into my carriage? Or will we let my chaplain break the news?"

It was sheer malice on Atherstone's part, lashing out to make someone suffer because he had failed to catch his prize Lady Alice, who stood now at the side of the unexpectedly splendid Cornelius Vale. She looked proud and astonishingly beautiful, her eyes sparkling with indignation.

"I came to warn you," Cecily blurted.

Alice flashed her a smile. "I know. But His Grace used Mr. Daubin to do his dirty work—I imagine so that no one could ever point an accusing finger at him, and also so that he could play the hero and rescue me. He had already paved the way by trying to pretend to me he was not nearly as black-hearted as he is. It was very kind and brave of you."

"It was," Cornelius agreed, and Cecily almost preened, only Jack was holding her too tightly, and that was loveliest of all.

Until, over Jack's shoulder, a slight movement in the gloomy doorway caught her eye.

"Cornelius!" she screamed, but it was too late.

The arm of Atherstone's villainous coachman had snaked around Alice's neck, yanking her away from Cornelius. A gleaming knife was held to her throat.

IT HAPPENED SO suddenly that Alice had no idea who held her, or what the cold, sharp thing prickling at her skin was. Uncomprehending, she gazed at Cornelius, who was suddenly white, his eyes desperate.

The duke laughed. "Well done, Johnson. Take Lady Alice and Jones to the carriage. I will join you directly." He smiled mockingly around the stunned company. "I believe no one will disagree."

Alice, furious that victory had been so abruptly snatched away, forgot to be afraid. She wanted to scream. Instead, she elbowed her captor so sharply in the ribs that he grunted. Of course he would not kill her! His master intended to marry her!

She stamped on his foot and kicked her heel back into his shin, and then there was a mighty crash, an instant of stillness, and then Johnson's arm loosened as he slid to the floor.

Cornelius snatched her out of the way of his falling body, unable to speak as he hugged her to him.

Aubrey, left holding only the handle of the heavy earthenware water jug he had broken over the coachman's head, looked pleased with himself.

"Always there at the right moment," he said. "I should be promoted to head of the family. Do we want to go now? Or bury His Grace first?"

To his credit—maybe—the duke did not look remotely afraid. In fact, his voice was almost bored as he strolled toward the window. "Quite the turning wheel of fortune," he sneered, gazing through the grubby glass. "Though it appears more of a farce. You weary me, and may..." He paused and then began to laugh softly. "How priceless. I believe I have won after all."

"Why?" Morgan growled. "Have you brought in another coach-load of thugs?"

"Far from it, my dear fellow. Merely an earl, and I didn't bring him."

"Vale sent for Braithwaite," Morgan told his wife.

Alice knew she should leave Cornelius's arms, but it felt so sweet to be held like this. Perhaps just one more moment...

"How very thoughtful of you, Vale," Atherstone continued. "You have just won me the game... Braithwaite, most timely. My lady, I am so sorry to greet you in such squalid surroundings."

Gervaise and Eleanor had indeed swept into the room. At the sight of so many people, they both stopped dead.

"Unhand my sister, sir!" Gervaise snapped, glaring at Cornelius, whose arms had already loosened. Alice's tightened for a moment, then she took his hand instead, and his fingers closed around hers, reassuring and wonderful.

At his haughtiest, Gervaise was all but looking down his nose. "I would not have believed this from a member of your family."

"What, that we have just rescued Lady Morgan from a wicked abductor?" Aubrey said innocently. "I have to say, Lady Alice is brave as a lion."

Gervaise blinked, disconcerted. "What?" He pulled himself together while Eleanor's perceptive, anxious gaze swept over Alice. Gervaise took a deep breath. "We are here because of some garbled story from your twin siblings, who were very anxious for us not to believe Alice had been abducted by Cornelius Vale."

"Which, of course, is exactly what you did think!" Alice said furiously. In her agitation, she almost pulled free of Cornelius's hand, then changed her mind and clung all the harder. "*No one* abducted me."

"Sadly, she is trying to protect her seducer," the duke said. "Shall I take him outside and thrash him?"

"Try," Aubrey said with taunting amusement.

"What has happened?" Gervaise demanded.

Alice tumbled into speech at the same time as Atherstone. Maddeningly, Gervaise held up his hand to silence his sister, who glared at him with outrage.

"I was warned by my chaplain," Atherstone said smoothly, "of Vale's designs upon Lady Alice. Seeing how well his brother had done in similar circumstances with Lady Helen—"

"The circumstances are not remotely similar!" Alice exploded. "And what do *you* know of the matter anyway?"

Atherstone shrugged elegantly. "People talk. I infer, I confess. At any rate, warned by my Mr. Jones, as I have said, I pursued the pair here. I found them by luck, though I cannot swear I was in time. I found them, I am afraid, in here, quite…disarrayed. Of course, I called my man to deal with him—that's him at your feet," he added. "The other Vale hit him to aid his brother."

Everyone gazed at him.

"Take a bow," Cornelius muttered, "you contemptible—"

Alice tugged his hand to silence him. "If that is the tale everyone believes, then I had better marry Cornelius," she said blithely.

"Oh, well countered, Alice," Eleanor murmured.

"No brother," Atherstone said witheringly, "would by choice marry his sister to such a man. Braithwaite, you are already aware of my honest desire to marry Lady Alice. I would still make her my duchess, if you would allow it. In fact, the matter may be dealt with in minutes. In the hope of her, I obtained a special license some weeks ago."

Again, everyone stared at the duke.

"Counter that," Aubrey murmured to his brother. "Please."

"He doesn't need to," Alice said in a suddenly cold voice. "I will not marry the Duke of Atherstone, and neither he nor you, Gervaise, will force me into it. I am not Helen, and I am not influenced by threats of ruin to my family. No one here will breathe a word of this. Even Atherstone, since, without the bridal prize, he just appears a fool and loses your respect and alliance."

"Alice, wait in the carriage," Gervaise commanded.

"I will, if Cornelius escorts me," Alice said, refusing to be dismissed like a naughty schoolroom miss. "And so that there is no misunderstanding, know that the only man I shall ever marry is Cornelius Vale."

"You'll notice he has not offered!" Gervaise snapped.

"He cannot get a word in," Alice retorted. "And if he no longer wishes to marry me, then I will marry no one. Ever."

Instantly, Cornelius dragged her hand to his mouth. "Of course I want to marry you," he said hoarsely. "I will wait for you as long as I have to."

"My lord," said Eleanor, who never called her husband that, "I believe this is one of those occasions when you must listen to the family you know, not the strangers you do not."

Gervaise's distracted gaze met hers, then shifted to Alice. "Why him?" he barked.

"I don't know," Alice whispered. "I love him. It's as if I loved him even before I met him, and now that I have, it only grows deeper and sweeter, like music that swells and swells and never stops..."

Cornelius, smiling in wonder, touched her cheek.

Aubrey whistled.

The duke said, "I believe I am going to be sick."

"Best clear off, then," Gervaise said. "For the ladies' sake. For my own, I never cared to be in the same room as a man who tells me such barefaced lies."

Alice beamed at him. "Gervaise, you are the best of brothers."

"A pity," the duke said, sauntering across the room, his face expressionless. "Do feel free to help yourselves. The breakfast, sadly, will be cold, but the brandy is very tolerable." He paused beside Alice, and Cornelius put his arm protectively about her. "It might just have been you," he said obscurely, and stepped over his groaning coachman. "Johnson," he snapped. "Jones!"

"Jones is with us," Cornelius said. "And his family will not be harmed."

There was the slightest of pauses, and then the smallest, curtest of nods. The duke strolled straight out of the inn, Johnson stumbling after him.

Chapter Twenty-One

S O MUCH HAD occurred that day already that when they arrived at Braithwaite Castle, Cornelius was surprised to find luncheon was still going on.

"I'm sorry I doubted you," the earl had said gruffly in the carriage. "You have always been honest with me and have done me several favors. I should have continued to trust you. I just care for my sisters so deeply, I cannot bear the thought of anyone taking advantage."

"I could have been more open with you," Cornelius allowed. "And to be frank, until very recently, I wasn't even sure where I stood with Alice."

Alice almost danced into the dining room, where she kissed her mother's cheek soundly and proclaimed, "I am going to be married!" She then dashed back to Cornelius and dragged him forward by the hand. "And here is my betrothed, Mr. Cornelius Vale!"

Cornelius bowed, feeling the heat rise to his face.

The dowager countess's beady eyes regarded him coldly. "Is that so?"

"It is," Braithwaite said, entering with more dignity. "Vale has made an offer, which both Alice and I have accepted."

"We shall see," the dowager said. She signaled to the footmen. "Join us for luncheon."

It was not exactly a comfortable meal for Cornelius, interrogated as he was by Alice's sisters and brothers-in-law. The dowager said nothing, but observed him constantly.

"Don't worry," the young countess murmured beside him. "Gervaise will talk her round. She already likes Roderick, and she has less reason to. For the rest, they only want Alice to be happy."

"I know." And he did. Were his own family not the same, in their less functional, much more secretive way?

"I suppose you have not had time to consider where you will live," Braithwaite said.

"There is a beautiful cottage at Black Hill," Alice said. "A large one, with views to die for, even better than Helen's!"

"It needs a great deal of work," Cornelius said apologetically. "But there is space for us at Black Hill House until it is ready."

The dowager countess laid down her fork with deliberation. "Then the wedding is to be another swift, hole-in-the-corner affair?"

"On the contrary," Cornelius said evenly. "If you and his lordship agree, Alice and I would like to have the banns read and be married in around a month."

"A good compromise between eagerness and good sense," Lady Torridon, the eldest sister, said gravely, although her eyes teased.

"Frances is all about good sense," Alice said sarcastically.

"Or at least eagerness," Lady Tamar said, then jumped as, presumably, her sister kicked her under the table. "Ouch!"

Braithwaite chose to ignore his sisters. "Do you need workmen for your cottage? I can loan you mine and summon anyone else necessary from Blackhaven."

Cornelius's heart leapt, although pride made him demur. "I could not impose."

"Call it a wedding present."

Alice was desperate to visit Helen in town, and no one, even the dowager, objected to Cornelius escorting her. Before they left, however, a note from Felicia reached him, inviting Alice to dinner that evening. And since Helen and Roderick were invited, too, that was also permitted.

Alice then dashed off to change into more suitable evening garb, while one of the Braithwaite carriages was summoned to convey them first to Roderick and Helen's house in Blackhaven, overlooking the sea.

Helen and Roderick were discovered in her studio upstairs. They made a rather delightful vignette. Roderick, more contented than Cornelius had seen him in years, lounged by the window in his shirt sleeves, reading a book spread against his crossed knee. Lady Helen, a paint-strewn smock over her gown, was busy composing a portrait of her husband.

At sight of her sister, Helen let out a squeak, threw down her brush, and rushed to her. "Alice! Is it true? Is it true? And are you coming to dinner at Black Hill, too? Oh dear, have I got paint on your gown?"

Laughing, Alice hugged her back. "Yes, yes, and who cares?"

Roderick stood lazily, putting his coat back on in honor of their visitors, and grinned as he held out his hand to Cornelius. His grip was hard. "I wish you as happy as me. You could not be more so."

In the company of Rod and Helen, Cornelius felt his tensions ease away. He, a mere gentleman steward, was accepted by the Braithwaites. The wonder of marriage to Alice awaited, with all its joys and sorrows, quarrels and reconciliations, excitement and comfort. He, who had thought he would be lonely all his life, had found her.

"It might just have been you," the vile Atherstone had said. Cornelius believed he understood him. But Cornelius had won her. She was his, as he was hers. An addition to his eccentric family who were surely about to scatter again. And yet they would always be his, too.

He had much food for thought.

Julius's Antonia, Lucy's Eddleston, and Felicia's Bernard were all discovered at Black Hill too, and many toasts were proposed and drunk to the newest happy couple.

"Tell all," Lucy commanded as they all sat down to dinner. "Where did you first meet?"

"At the assembly room ball, of course," Aubrey said. "It's where you all met your match."

Alice smiled and did not dispute it.

Cornelius picked up his wine glass. "Actually, we first met in a bookshop in London, where she learned my best-kept secret."

Alice met his gaze, uncertain but approving.

"What secret?" Felicia demanded.

"I'm afraid I write poetry as Simon Sacheverill."

He couldn't recall ever reducing his family to silence before.

"That makes sense," said Roderick, who had once made fun of him for reading poetry. "Good for you."

"Actually, it's damned good stuff," Julius said with unexpected force. Then he coughed. "Who'd have thought of you, you great lout?"

And everyone was grinning at Cornelius and slapping his back, even his sisters.

"Didn't you know?" the twins asked their siblings in clear surprise, and set everyone laughing again.

"I'm telling you because you're family," Cornelius said, "but I'm still entitled to privacy from the rest of the world if I want it."

"Course you are," Julius said.

Alice took his hand under the table and squeezed. "Of course you are," she agreed, and her eyes shone with pride in him.

"Actually, that reminds me," Julius said, his one eye gleaming with mischief. "With all the excitement, it slipped my mind, but Harmondsworth paid a call on Daubin Senior this morning. He wouldn't tell me exactly what transpired, but I gather he put the fear of the law into Daubin, threatening him with charges of theft and forgery and promising long prison sentences for each. The result is, Daubin's sheep have vanished from the hill, and we have a satisfyingly vast banker's draft by way of compensation for the land he 'borrowed' in previous seasons."

Cornelius grinned with delight and raised his glass. "To Harmondsworth!"

"And to you for spotting what Daubin was up to in the first place. I've suggested to Barton he might prefer to move nearer his daughter in Lancashire. He got backhanders for his part in it, and he told everyone the fields were let and sold with our knowledge, so his neighbors are going to be *very* displeased with him."

"Good riddance to the surly, lazy—"

"Also," Julius continued, "apparently young Daubin's volume of poetry is largely plagiarized. Harmondsworth told Daubin Senior that he was encouraging several poets, including Lord Bryon and Simon Sacheverill, to sue. It all makes much more sense now I know *you* are Sacheverill."

Cornelius flushed. "I gave Harmondsworth the ammunition, but I didn't tell him I was Sacheverill."

"Apparently he extracted Daubin's promise to remove all his son's volumes from circulation. He seemed to doubt that there were many of them."

"To poetry!" Aubrey cried, raising his glass in yet another toast, and Cornelius didn't know whether to laugh or cry. With difficulty, he opted for the former.

"Goodness," Leona said some time later, "you are all married or spoken for now. There are only two of you left!"

"Who's next?" Lawrence demanded, grinning.

"I am on the shelf," Delilah said firmly, and raised her glass to Aubrey. "Here's to you, little brother."

"Shab off," Aubrey said.

FOUR WEEKS LATER, Mr. and Mrs. Cornelius Vale stood outside their picturesque cottage and gazed out over the countryside to the sea. The carriage, which had brought them there from the wedding breakfast at the castle, was rumbling off again into the distance. Blackbirds were singing, hens chuntering away, as Alice slipped her hand into his.

"You are distant," she said softly. "Do you regret this?"

His fingers gripped hers. "Dear God, of course not! You have made this the happiest day of my life. And now that we are finally alone, I want very badly to make it the happiest day of yours."

"You already have!" She raised her face to his, and he kissed her, at first with the sweet gentleness she was used to, and then with growing hunger.

"These weeks have passed so quickly," he said. "We have been so busy with the house and with family, there has been so little time for us. You must know that I want you in every way known to man—and probably a few dreamed up only to me!—but if you want to wait, my love, we can do that too. There is no rush. We have the rest of our lives."

Alice closed her eyes with overwhelming relief. She had so feared he was having second thoughts and felt trapped by her.

"Is that all?" she said huskily, and kissed him with all the sensuality she had. "Come," she whispered. "Come."

Hand in hand they walked over the threshold and into their welcoming, deserted home. All work had been completed mere days before the wedding, and there would be no servants in the house until tomorrow. So, with no embarrassment, just growing, breathless excitement, she led Cornelius through the hall to the staircase and along the narrow passage to the big front bedchamber. No one could possibly see in the window, so she did not draw the curtains. Watery sunshine enhanced their view to the sea.

She eased his coat from his shoulders. Under his watchful gaze, she removed his sleeve buttons, increasingly aroused by his labored breath.

She laid the buttons on the dressing table and swallowed before she met his warm, slightly desperate gaze. "I want you to know that my fear of—of intimacy vanished some time ago. Probably when you first kissed me, in fact. I love you and I trust you, and... And oh God, Cornel, please will you kiss me, show me...?"

The rest was lost in his mouth as he ravished hers. Slowly, sweetly, he undressed her and caressed her trembling, naked body to pleasurable, burning need. He laid her on the bed and covered her with his hot, smooth body, whispering endearments and exclamations of delight. With hands and lips, and his whole body, he seemed to worship her until, achingly, she received him into hers and he brought her patiently and tenderly to joy. As she brought him.

"Well," he murmured teasingly some time later as she lay dozing in his arms. "No criticism, my love?"

She smiled, feeling feline and sated. "None," she whispered. "None at all."

Epilogue

Three years later.

THE DUCHESS OF Kelburn's ballroom, built onto the back of her London house, was packed with guests. Soon, they could not all fit in unless they sat down in the rows of chairs set out in blocks facing a beautiful pianoforte. Beneath the massive chandeliers, gentlemen in austere black and white evening clothes mingled with the gorgeous colors and sparkling jewels of the ladies.

The noise of guests' greetings and chatter was like a roar. Only occasionally could Alice distinguish individual words, and they were not always encouraging, let alone flattering.

"My dear, it will be an ordeal! The music is always dreadful at these charitable affairs…"

"Who is this Mrs. Vale? I have never heard of her. I do so hate amateur musicians who always murder my favorite pieces…"

"Why did Her Grace not invite Frederick Baird to play instead? I suppose he is too busy…"

Feeling very alone, and very exposed—she had not played in public for more than a year—Alice glanced up at the musicians' gallery, empty this evening apart from one serious, beloved man and a dementedly waving, very small child.

Alice could see the child's lips moving as he tugged at his

father's hand like a bell rope. She read his lips. "Look, look, it's Mama!"

Her heart swelled at the sight of them. The nerves that had always paralyzed her before public performances faded to manageable levels. Her son Louis—named for the great Ludwig van Beethoven—loved music, but might fall asleep. If he misbehaved or called out, Cornelius would whisk him away.

Fortified by her husband's smile, she made her way toward the duchess, who was clapping her hands to call her guests to order.

A lady whispered, "Goodness, she is very young, is she not? Like some debutante about to inflict her appalling and misnamed accomplishment on a cringing Society!"

Why do I put myself through this?

"This evening is all about educating the poor," the duchess pronounced. "The worthiest of causes, and surely the foundation of a great nation. To be here, you have all made great contributions already. From the bottom of my heart—and the hearts of the still-ignorant poor!—I thank you. I hope, if the music pleases you, you will be inspired to give even more.

"Now, I wish you introduce you to this talented lady who has so generously agreed to entertain us. Please welcome Lady Alice Vale."

There was a wave of enthusiastic applause—hopefully from those who had heard her play before—among the politer ripple of the majority.

Amidst the noise, someone said, *"Lady Alice?"*

"Lady Alice Conway, by birth. Lord Braithwaite's sister. Vale is her married name. She lives mostly in the north, I believe, near that spa town that is so wretchedly difficult to get to, though the waters…"

"God, she must be dreadful. I wish I had thought to plug my ears."

"No, no, I believe the duke's sister, Lady Arabella, recommended her. Besides, I danced with her in her first Season—lovely girl, so amusing. Quite the original..."

Rising from her curtsey, Alice tottered the few steps to the pianoforte, and the noise faded to silence. Seated, she spread her fingers over the keys. *Let them remember, let them play...*

They played.

IN THE GALLERY, Cornelius smiled and crouched down to let Louis lean against him. Together, now that Alice had relaxed and lost herself in playing, father and son let the music wash over them.

Life was good for Cornelius. He loved the land at Black Hill, which, after a couple of difficult years, was finally profitable again. The tenancies were all filled and doing well. Their people were happy. Cornelius knew he smiled more. Life with Alice was never dull and never lonely. Somehow, he managed to love her more with every passing day. And she, generous and passionate by nature, was utterly devoted to him and to their son.

Sometimes, he could not believe that such happiness would last. But while it did, he treasured it, as he treasured Alice and Louis.

Below, the attitude of the audience had subtly changed. They no longer listened from mere civility. Some looked pleasantly surprised. Others seemed enchanted. Others either smiled joyfully or wiped a tear with the changing moods of the music.

She played stunningly. The prickle of Cornelius's tears was due to pride in her. Before Louis was born, they had traveled as much as they could, to Edinburgh and London, to Paris, Vienna, and Rome, listening to many of the greatest musicians in the world. Undaunted, Alice had adored and learned, and this was the result.

Beyond the music, his head began to form words to the emotions surrounding his wife. Most of his poetry came back to Alice now, in one way or another. Another collection had just been published, to critical acclaim, and there was no denying the extra money was useful. As Sacheverill, he very occasionally contributed to Roderick and Aubrey's newspaper. More often, he wrote amusing verses for it, signed only as "a Blackhaven gentleman."

Louis had grown heavy against his legs and arms, but he was smiling as he dozed. It would be poetic, Cornelius thought, if Louis became a musician as gifted as his mother. He would take the world by storm, as Alice never would or could.

Each piece she played produced increasingly rapturous applause, until at the end, everyone surged to their feet, and the duchess looked ecstatic because the money would flow even faster into her charity coffers. And besides, she was enjoying a major social success.

All but bursting with pride, Cornelius carried a now completely unconscious Louis down the gallery steps. As always, Alice fled to the comfort of his arms, emotion pouring into her kiss.

They did not return to the ballroom, but took the carriage back to Maria's house, where they were staying for a week.

"Isn't it funny," Alice said dreamily, "how one's ambitions change? Once, it irked me so that I would never do more than play to a few aristocratic philistines. I was so desperate to escape, to play for the world, if only I could become good enough."

"Don't you think you are?" he asked.

She snuggled against him. "I was good tonight," she said happily. "But actually, no. I no longer want to devote my entire life to playing. There are so many other components in life. There always were—my family, fun and adventures, Blackhaven… But I think I needed you to show me that. I will always have the music, and I will never stop playing. I will always be proud and tearful when my music is published and played by a musician I admire. But it is you, Cornelius—you and Louis—who are my life."

He buried his lips in her hair to hide his emotion, although she would know. She always knew.

"As you are mine," he whispered.

About the Author

Mary Lancaster lives in Scotland with her husband, three mostly grown-up kids and a small, crazy dog.

Her first literary love was historical fiction, a genre which she relishes mixing up with romance and adventure in her own writing. Her most recent books are light, fun Regency romances written for Dragonblade Publishing: *The Imperial Season* series set at the Congress of Vienna; and the popular *Blackhaven Brides* series, which is set in a fashionable English spa town frequented by the great and the bad of Regency society.

Connect with Mary on-line – she loves to hear from readers:

Email Mary:
Mary@MaryLancaster.com

Website:
www.MaryLancaster.com

Newsletter sign-up:
http://eepurl.com/b4Xoif

Facebook:
facebook.com/mary.lancaster.1656

Facebook Author Page:
facebook.com/MaryLancasterNovelist

Twitter:
@MaryLancNovels

Amazon Author Page:
amazon.com/Mary-Lancaster/e/B00DJ5IACI

Bookbub:
bookbub.com/profile/mary-lancaster

www.ingramcontent.com/pod-product-compliance
Lightning Source LLC
Chambersburg PA
CBHW060440310726
48977CB00001B/271